Girl Having a Ball
By
Rhoda Baxter

Want a free book?

JOIN MY MAILING LIST and get a FREE copy of *Girl At Christmas* – a novella in this series. You also get *After All This Time*, an exclusive short story that you can't get anywhere else.

The link is at the end of this book.

Enjoy *Girl Having A Ball*.

To my family, always.

Chapter One

STEVIE HAD TO KNOCK twice before she heard footsteps approaching. Marsh opened the door, wearing an apron.

'Stevie!' He stepped aside to let her through. 'You're early.'

'I thought I'd come straight here from work. Is that okay?' It felt like ages since she'd last seen him. He seemed older. Peering at him she decided there was a smattering of grey appearing in his thick brown hair. It made him look a bit more like their father.

She thrust the bottle of wine at him. 'I got you this.'

'Thanks.' He took the bottle and gave her a curious look. 'How are you? Are you all right?'

She nodded, no longer sure how to greet her brother. They had once known everything about each other, but since he'd got married things were ... different. At first it had been okay. They had spoken regularly and Stevie visited often, even helping with the redecorating. But lately, Marsh seemed more and more distant. When she did manage to speak to him, he seemed distracted.

'Don't I get a hug?'

Stevie threw her arms around him and squeezed.

'Are you sure you're okay?' Marsh hugged her back. 'You look a little sad.'

She wanted to howl 'I miss you. I miss the flat. I miss being able to call you whenever I want. I miss you being all mine.' But instead, she said, 'I hate my crappy job. That's all.'

'No luck with any of the applications then.' He released her and ushered her towards the kitchen. 'Come through and tell us about it. I've got to check on the oven.'

The kitchen was part of the new extension and was lovely and airy. The summer sun poured in through skylights, giving everything a warm glow. Pans simmered on the Rayburn. At the far end, Jane was arranging a salad. She looked up when Stevie and Marsh entered. 'Hi Stevie.'

Jane's appearance made Stevie do a quick double take. Even though she was a little skinny, Jane had always been beautiful and healthy. Now she looked wan and tired. There were bluish shadows under her eyes and her cheekbones were more prominent. She was wearing a loose cotton shirt, which, Stevie was sure, hid more signs of lost weight.

'Oh my God. Are you okay?' The words were out before Stevie had time to censor them.

Jane cast a quick glance at Marsh. 'I'm fine,' she said. 'I've just been a little ... poorly of late.'

Stevie glanced at Marsh, who was busying himself at the oven. She knew him well enough to know when he was avoiding eye contact. Something was going on. If Jane was ill, that would explain why Marsh was so preoccupied, but then, why hadn't he mentioned it? She turned back to Jane. 'Is it something serious?' she asked, pulling out a chair and sitting down, just in case it was.

Jane looked surprised. 'No, nothing bad.' She laughed. 'Why? Do I really look that awful?'

There was nothing forced about Jane's laugh, which made Stevie relax a little. 'Oh no, you look fine. Just tired. And pale.'

Jane nodded. 'That sounds about right. I'm a little anaemic.' She tapped the side of the salad bowl. 'I think this is done. I'll just take it to the dining room.'

Once Jane had left, Stevie turned her attention to Marsh. 'What's going on?' she whispered. 'Is Jane okay? She really doesn't look well.'

Marsh's eyes darted to the doorway where Jane had disappeared. 'Don't worry. She'll be fine in a few weeks.' He looked as though he wanted to say more, but Jane returned.

'Stevie, why don't you tell us what's going on with you?' she said. 'Do you want a cup of tea? Or wine?'

'Wine please.'

'I'll get it,' said Marsh. 'You sit down.'

'Thank you my love.' Jane slipped into a chair. She turned her attention to Stevie. 'So, how's the job hunting?'

Stevie sighed. 'Lousy. It's horrible. There's no one hiring in the events management sector. They're not even offering work experience.'

'I can imagine,' said Jane. 'Most places are cutting back on entertaining at the moment, I guess. Our firm isn't having their usual summer client party thing this year, are they?' she said to Marsh.

'Nope,' he replied, apparently too busy with what he was doing to elaborate.

'Have you spoken to Louise?' asked Jane. 'She might need an assistant. You've worked for her before, haven't you?'

Stevie propped her elbows on the table and put her chin in her hands. 'Yeah. I've asked. She can't afford one.'

Marsh put a glass of wine in front of Stevie.

Stevie took a sip and felt the liquid warm her mouth. 'I'm so fed up, I'd do it for free, to be honest, just to get out of the shitty envelope opening job I'm in.'

Marsh handed a hot drink to Jane and dropped into a chair next to her. 'Is that a good idea? How are you doing for money?' He leaned forward, his forehead furrowed.

Stevie laughed. This was familiar territory. Until last year, Marsh had managed her trust fund. Just her rotten luck that the year that she'd finally turned twenty-one and gained control of her inheritance, the stock market should collapse, leaving her with much less money than she'd been expecting.

'I'm making enough to buy food and pay the council tax,' she said. 'But only just.'

Marsh frowned. 'Perhaps you should think about an alternative career. You know, something that pays a little better. You could—'

Stevie rolled her eyes. 'Marsh, we've been through this. I'm going to spend a year trying to get into the event management thing and then I'll have a rethink. You agreed that would be no worse than taking a gap year like all my friends did.'

'But—'

'Besides,' Jane cut in, 'it's nice to give your dreams a chance. You never know where it might take you.' She smiled. 'Life is so much more pleasant if you're doing something you love.'

Marsh smiled at his wife. He picked up her hand and laid a kiss on the back of it. There was such intimacy in the gesture that Stevie had to look away.

'I suppose you're right,' said Marsh. He turned to his sister. 'But only a year, right? You don't want to be drifting for ages and suddenly find you're thirty.'

'Oh Marsh, stop being such a fuddy duddy!' said Stevie. 'I'm not totally stupid.'

'I never said you were,' said Marsh, falling into the pattern of their regular argument. 'But you do—'

He was interrupted by someone rapping on the door. 'Oh no.' He jumped to his feet. 'That'll be Louise and Jim. Dinner's nowhere near ready.'

Jane started to stand, but Stevie beat her to it. 'I'll get it,' she said. She sped for the door, leaving Jane to calm Marsh down.

Dinner was fun. When Marsh had first become Stevie's guardian he had been just twenty-one and at university. For a short time, Stevie had moved into his student house, which he'd shared with some friends, including Jim and Louise. Louise had been particularly kind to Stevie and the two of them remained firm friends, even after Marsh used the money his parents left him to buy a flat where he and Stevie could live.

Louise had left working for a successful event organising company to set up on her own, just before the credit crunch hit. Stevie had worked for her one summer. Inevitably, the conversation turned to work.

'It's so unbelievably boring,' said Stevie. 'I'm folding paper all day. I can feel my brain dying by degrees.' She took a big sip of wine. 'To make things worse, there's this horrible man who's worked there since he was sixteen who keeps asking me out. When he finally got the message that I wasn't playing hard to get and really wasn't interested, he told everyone that I asked him out and he turned me down.'

Louise looked uncomfortable. 'I wish I could help you,' she said. 'I really do. But I really can't afford an assistant right now. All I can offer is a good reference.'

'Mind you,' said Jim. 'You're good enough that you've had to turn people down.' Tall, ginger-haired and jovial, Jim was a patent agent in the same firm as Marsh and Jane.

Stevie raised her eyebrows.

'It was a charity job in Oxford,' Louise explained, giving her husband an annoyed glance. 'It was too far away and not enough money.'

Stevie nodded. No sense in working for nothing. 'I'll keep looking until my year is up and then I'll take whatever boring job I can get.' She fixed her eyes on Louise. 'I've got a good chance of making it work, Lou, haven't I?'

Louise nodded. 'It's a very competitive environment at the moment. It's hard to make a name for yourself.'

There was a pause. Marsh frowned.

'Shall we have dessert?' Jane asked.

'I'll get it.' Marsh laid a hand on his wife's arm. 'You sit down.'

'Why don't you get another bottle of wine?' Jane nodded towards Jim's empty glass. She herself had been drinking fruit juice all evening. They disappeared into the kitchen together. Everyone else watched them leave.

As soon as they were out of earshot, Stevie leaned towards Louise. 'Do you think something's wrong with Jane? She looks awful.'

'She does,' said Louise. 'And, she was drinking fruit juice all evening ...'

'It's not anything serious, like cancer. I asked Marsh.'

Louise stared at her. 'Cancer?'

'It's not that. Marsh said ...' Stevie stopped. Louise was grinning at her. 'What?'

'There might be another explanation,' said Louise. 'She's looking ill, she's not drinking ...' She nodded expectantly at Stevie, prompting her to make a connection.

Before Stevie could answer, Jane and Marsh returned. Jane carrying a bottle of champagne and Marsh a large dish of crumble.

'We were just commenting,' said Louise, giving Stevie a meaningful glance, 'that Jane's looking a bit pale. Is everything okay?'

Marsh put the crumble down and went over to stand next to his wife. 'Actually,' he said. 'We've got something to tell you.'

Jane grinned. 'We're having a baby.'

Louise and Jim were on their feet at once, hugging and kissing the expectant parents. For a moment, Stevie was unable to move. Marsh was going to be a father. It had been hard enough when he'd found a wife. She already felt the space between them growing as he became more and more a husband, and less and less her brother. How much worse would it be with a child? Looking up, she saw Marsh watching her. She forced a smile and stood up. 'Congratulations.'

She gave him a hug. She struggled for something more to say, but couldn't think of anything. So she gave Jane a gentle hug and a kiss instead and returned to her seat.

'How far along are you?' asked Louise. She was a mother of three and expert on pregnancy.

'Twelve weeks,' said Jane. 'We had our scan yesterday.'

Twelve weeks. The words clanged into Stevie's heart. Three months. Marsh had known about this huge change in their lives for three whole months and not told her. There was once a time when she would have been the first to know about anything that went on in his life, just as he would of hers. Three whole months. No wonder he'd sounded like he was avoiding her. It was because he had been.

Stevie gulped down a mouthful of wine. She knew she would lose her brother to other people eventually. But she hadn't been prepared for it to happen so quickly or for the separation to feel so complete.

Eventually, they got round to eating the crumble, but Stevie didn't really taste it. Inside her, long buried feelings were clawing their way to the surface. She couldn't bring herself to look at Marsh. She focused on her wine glass instead, drinking far more than she should.

As everyone helped clear up, Stevie found Marsh taking her elbow and steering her into the living room.

'Stevie,' he said.

She forced her head up to meet his eyes. 'Marsh.'

'Are you okay?'

'Never better,' she said, flatly. 'My brother's going to be a daddy ...' She tried to beam at him, but her face wouldn't obey. She rubbed her forehead and sighed. 'Although, I'd have expected to know about it a little sooner.'

For a moment Marsh didn't say anything. 'I'm sorry. It's been really difficult. Jane's been so ill and she had a lot of bleeding and we weren't sure the pregnancy was going to hold.'

'And you thought it was better not to tell me? And what if something *had* gone wrong? Didn't you think I might want to know what was upsetting you? I know I'm not the world's most brilliant person, but I'm family. We used to tell each other everything, Marsh. Everything.'

Marsh gave her a small smile. 'Well, not everything.'

Somehow him trying to make a joke of it, made it worse. The anger that she had been trying to keep at bay boiled up. Stevie shook her arm free from his grip. 'Three months! And I had to find out the same time as Louise and Jim. Three. Months.'

'Stevie, we didn't tell anyone. You're the first people we told.'

'What about Jane's family? I bet you told her mother.'

His silence told her everything she needed to know.

'Congratulations, Marsh. I'm sure you'll make a great dad.' She turned and headed towards the hallway.

'Stevie, where are you going?'

'Home.'

He took hold of her arm and looked as if he was about to object, but changed his mind. 'Let me call you a taxi. You're too drunk to walk home alone.'

'I don't need a taxi.' She picked up her jacket. 'I can look after myself.' She tried to put her arm into a sleeve and missed.

Marsh shook his head. 'You're overreacting.' He held the jacket for her so that she could shrug it on.

Stevie spun round and nearly fell over. 'Am I? I don't think I am. You think about it. If it had been the other way around, how would you feel?'

'I said I was sorry, Stevie. It's ...'

Stevie stopped him with an upraised hand. 'Save it for someone who cares.' She opened the door and lurched out.

'Stevie.' He followed her out and took her arm. With his free hand he used his phone to order a taxi. 'Sit.'

Stevie sank onto the concrete steps. Marsh sat beside her. She turned her back to him.

'I'm not going to try and reason with you when you're in this sort of mood,' said Marsh, speaking to the back of her head. 'I'll come see you tomorrow, when you're sober.'

Stevie said nothing. They sat there in silence until the taxi arrived.

Stevie slit open another envelope with the letter opener. Her eyes scanned for the name of the client and she stapled and tossed the papers into the correct pile without engaging her brain. She'd been at work for four hours and had lost the will to live about three hours and fifty-five minutes ago. Her head hurt from the night before and her anger with Marsh was simmering away inside her. How could he keep something so important from her? Okay, Marsh loved his wife and wanted to spend time with her, but he would never keep secrets from Stevie. Not without prompting. At least, he wouldn't have before. The world was different now. She gutted another envelope and wrenched the letter out.

A movement at the edge of her vision made her jump. She turned to find Gloria, the line supervisor, standing just behind her shoulder. Gloria reached across, hooked the last letter with a red painted nail and checked that it was in the correct pile. It was. There was a slight tightening of the over-glossed lips.

Stevie pulled her earphones out. 'Can I help you?' she said, as sweetly as she could manage.

Gloria's eyes narrowed while she tried to figure out if Stevie was insulting her. 'Lunch break.'

'That's great. Thank you.' Stevie smiled an insincere smile and popped the finger protectors off. 'I appreciate the personal service.'

The line manager tapped her clipboard. 'One hour,' she said.

'Of course.'

In a bid to cheer herself up, Stevie splashed out cash she didn't have on sushi and a magazine. When she returned to the lunchroom there was already a group having their lunch, discussing *Dragon's Den*. Stevie sat at the other end of the table, where the Formica had chipped off in a large triangle, and turned her music up to drown out the conversation. She loved *Dragon's Den*. She and Marsh used to watch it together.

She squeezed the lemon over her sushi and gasped as the lemon juice stung a paper cut on her finger. That would teach her to take her thimble off in a fit of misguided rebellion.

She stuck the fingertip in her mouth to suck the lemon off. There was a collective snigger from the men at the other end of the room. She rolled her eyes. This job was beyond awful. If only she had something else to go to, she'd walk out of there in a minute.

Something chimed in the back of her mind. She tried to think back to the conversation before Marsh's announcement. There had been something else. Something Louise had said about a job in Oxford that she'd turned down. If she could just get one job, it would be a start. She picked up her phone and sent off an email.

She nodded to herself. That's what she could do. If she organised the event in Oxford for minimum pay, she could use it as experience. Maybe even meet some other people who might become clients. Okay, it wasn't as good as getting a job with an established company and moving up, but there was nothing wrong with freelance. She could start small and build herself up. Why had she not thought of this before? The very thought cheered her up. So much so, that she was almost smiling when she opened her magazine.

One of the boys from across the room came up to Stevie. 'Hey Steph?'

'Stevie.' She corrected him automatically, without bothering to lower her magazine. He was going to ask her out. Again.

'You doing anything Friday night?'

'Washing my hair.'

'Is that what you do every Friday night?'

'Yes.'

'Except last Friday night, right?'

She lowered the magazine a fraction and looked at him. Where was this going?

'Chris says you spent it banging each other's brains out.' He grinned, making his spots crowd together on his cheeks.

Stevie glanced over to see Chris smirking at her from across the room. She raised her magazine again.

Before anyone could come up with a retort, Gloria materialised. 'Your hour's up,' she said, stopping in front of Stevie.

Stevie glanced at her phone. She still had ten minutes to go. This was one of Gloria's power games. It was no longer funny.

'I've got ten minutes.'

Gloria leaned forward, her face close enough for Stevie to see the cracks in her foundation. 'Listen. I'm the manager around here. And I say that your time is up.'

'That's not——'

'I don't like your attitude, young lady. Now get back to work before I report you.' Stevie stared at the woman. It was unbelievable that such bullying went on. Gloria met her gaze.

'I could report *you* for bullying,' said Stevie.

'What bullying?' Gloria turned to the men who were watching with interest. 'Do you see any bullying lads?' The men all shook their heads and focused on their meals. Gloria turned back to Stevie, triumphant.

Stevie blinked. Gloria smiled and turned away.

Anger that had been bubbling inside her all day coalesced into a point. Stevie decided she'd had enough. She picked up a leaflet that had come with her magazine. It was white on the reverse side.

'Gloria?' she said. 'Can I borrow your pen a moment, please?'

Gloria half turned. 'Certainly not. Get back to work.'

Stevie sighed and fished a pen out of her pocket. She wrote I QUIT on the back of the flyer, and signed and dated it. She plonked the paper down on top of Gloria's precious clipboard and walked past her.

'You're supposed to give one day's written notice,' Gloria shouted after her.

Stevie didn't stop. What were they going to do? Sack her?

TOM PRESSED HIS FINGERTIPS to his temple. The migraine radiated from the side of his head, pain branching into his eye-sockets and jaw. He gritted his teeth and looked back at his computer screen. Nope. It was no use. He needed a break. That was one of the things the doctor had suggested. More frequent breaks from the screen. That and getting some rest. He rubbed his temples again and sighed. Maybe food would help. It was lunchtime, near enough.

He messaged Olivia.

He had known Olivia Gornall since primary school, when they'd got into an argument and he'd announced that if she wasn't a girl, he'd have thumped her. Og being the scrappy maniac that she was, had called him sexist and pushed him over. He'd grabbed her arm and they'd both ended up in the mud. They'd been best friends ever since.

When she'd got a job in the legal department of the same firm as him and he'd taken her to the pub to meet his colleagues, some of the more macho guys had found it hard to believe that he could be best friends with a girl he wasn't sleeping with. But one night of being out-drunk, out-cursed and generally out-bloked by Og, soon sorted out the doubters.

Tom:

Og. Lunch?

Oliva:

Meet you by the lifts in ten.

Ten minutes. He may as well take a look at that email from his mother that he'd been putting off.

From: Dr Evelyn Blackwood

To: Tom Blackwood

Hello Darling. Guess what, Dan's latest paper is going to be published in another journal. What a coup for his publication record. It will stand him in good stead with this new funding application he's involved in. I must open a bottle of wine when he's next around.

Will you be coming home this weekend? It's just that the lawn needs doing again.

Mum

Tom clenched his jaw so tightly that his teeth ground together. It was always about Dan. Bloody Dan. Not content with being older, Dan had to be cleverer and taller and best at everything. Tom might have made it onto his mother's radar if he'd been the one that settled down and started a family first, but bloody Dan managed to do that about two minutes after graduating from university too.

Remembering the doctor's comments about mindfulness and breathing, which he had scoffed at at the time, Tom took a deep breath and let it out before replying asking his mother to pass on his congratulations to his big brother. Then he locked his computer, grabbed a jacket and strode out to meet Og.

She looked up from her phone. 'Pub?' she said, by way of greeting.

'Perfect.' Tom pressed the button to call the lift.

The pub was already fairly busy. Tom grabbed a table and Olivia went over to the bar to order. She always got served faster than he did. Tom dropped his jacket over the back of his chair and rolled his shoulders, trying to relieve some tension. The pain above his eyes was soothed a little by the dimmer lighting inside the pub. He rubbed a knuckle over his brow, trying to ease the pain.

Og returned with two coffees and a flag for their food order. Tom noticed the two guys at the table next to them turn to check out Og. That happened a lot around her. Tall, with short spiky hair and long legs, Olivia tended to attract the sort of men who were only after one thing. One of the guys spotted Tom and looked away. He got that a lot too –

people thinking that there was something going on between him and Og. Not a chance.

At one point in their teens, when Og had stopped being one of the boys and turned into a girl, there had been a few months of awkwardness that had ended in a snog, which freaked them both out so much that they decided never to go there again. After that, their relationship had never wavered from the platonic.

Og slid into the seat opposite him. 'So, what's going on?'

'Where do you want to start,' said Tom. 'Mum just emailed me to tell me that golden boy is getting something published in another journal.'

Og raised an eyebrow over her coffee cup. 'So what?'

'What do you mean, so what? I tell Mum about the Doha job and I get "that's nice dear". Dan gets his name in a magazine and she's telling everyone.'

Og gave a theatrical sigh and put down her cup. 'We've been through this. Evelyn's an academic, so she understands what Dan does. The business world ... not so much. Don't take it to heart.' She grinned. 'How is Dangerous Dan these days?'

'He's off gathering beetles or something again.' Tom waved a hand dismissively. 'They've left poor Alice with Mum again. Why did they have her if they're just going to ignore the poor kid?' He rubbed a knuckle into his forehead again.

'Headache?' said Og. 'Did you have your doctor's appointment? What did they say?' She poked his shoulder. 'Is it old age catching up with you?'

'I'm only six months older than you. Cheeky cow.' He smiled and immediately felt a little better. 'The doc says the headaches are probably caused by stress. Apparently, if I take it easy, the headaches and insomnia will go away. He even offered to sign me off for a month. But I can't do that, so he's given me some sleeping pills so that at least I can sleep a couple of nights.

'Wait, wait. Why, exactly, can't you take some time off? Sounds like you need it.'

'Don't be stupid. I can't take time off now. I've got two weeks to wrap up this project. And then I have to prepare my pitch for the Doha job. Dhidre is going for it too.'

Og pulled a face. 'Oh, you've got to do a good job then. You can't be beaten by a woman who wears white stilettos.'

Tom stared at her. What kind of a criticism was that?

'What?' said Og. 'I can speak girl.'

'O... kay.'

A waiter brought the food. A burger and chips for Tom and a pasta dish for Og. For a few minutes their conversation stopped as they both concentrated on eating.

Og tore off a piece of garlic bread. 'What happened with that other job you applied for?'

Tom groaned. 'Lambert Kassel. I've got a second interview on Friday.'

Og looked impressed.

'I'd much rather get the Doha job,' he said. 'More money. More kudos.'

'Yeah, but you said you'd enjoy the LK job more. Money and kudos isn't everything, you know.'

Tom put his cutlery down with exaggerated care and stared at her. 'Who are you and what have you done with Og?'

She pointed her fork at him. 'Shut up and eat your food.'

Tom grinned. 'Anyway,' he said. 'How are things with you? How are your brothers?'

BY THE TIME STEVIE reached her building, the feeling of elation had started to wear off. Leaving the job was all well and good, but that meant she had to find something else to do to pay the bills. She scowled as she jabbed the button on the lift. Life as an independent adult was turning out to be more difficult than she'd expected. First Marsh got married, then the recession ate her trust fund, she couldn't find a job that didn't suck and her brother was keeping secrets from her. What else could go wrong?

She walked down her corridor, sorting through her keys for the right one. She put the key in the lock. It didn't turn. She tried it again. Then, she carefully turned the door knob. The door opened. Stevie stopped and stared at it for a moment. She was sure she'd locked it when she left. Cautiously, her finger on her phone ready to dial 999, she pushed the door open.

'Oh good, you're home.'

'Marsh? What the hell are you doing in my flat?' She went in and slammed the door shut behind her.

'You weren't here, so I let myself in.' He produced the spare keys from his pocket. 'Just like I told you, in my message.'

There had been several messages from him. She had deleted them without reading them. She had to get those keys off him. If she wasn't allowed to know about his wife's pregnancy, he shouldn't be allowed to have a spare key to her flat.

'What do you want?' She threw her bag into the corner.

'I wanted to apologise.' He took a step towards her.

Stevie held up a hand. 'I'm not really interested, Marsh.' She'd had enough of the whole day. She was feeling angry, tired and starting to panic slightly. All she wanted right now was to sit in front of the telly and eat ice cream.

'Look. I know I hurt—'

'I said I'm not interested.' She put her hand on the door to open it. 'I'm not having the best of days, so can you kindly get out of my flat?'

Marsh stared at her. 'What's wrong?' he said. 'Other than our little argument, I mean.'

How did he do that? How could he tell that anything had happened?

'Nothing.'

Marsh's eyes narrowed. 'Is it something to do with work?'

She hesitated. Only for a fraction of a second, but it was long enough for her brother to jump to conclusions.

'What's happened?' He studied her. When she didn't reply, he said, 'Oh no. You've been sacked. Haven't you?'

'No. I haven't been sacked.' She looked away. 'I quit. Actually.'

'Stevie!'

'I'll get another job. I can look after myself.'

Marsh didn't look convinced. 'Clearly, you can't. This is the third job this month.'

'This is the third job this month.' Stevie mimicked him. 'Stop treating me like a child.'

'Stop acting like one then.'

That was what he always said. She had never found a suitable retort to that. Stevie wrenched the door open. 'You have no right to come in here and tell me how to live my life. You're not my guardian anymore. And after the way you've treated me, I don't even want to call you my brother anymore. Now get out of my flat.'

For a moment Marshall looked like he'd been stung. Then anger flared in his eyes. 'Fine.' He picked up his coat and briefcase. 'Don't come to me when you need help.'

'And give me back my spare key.'

He threw it onto the kitchen counter as he walked out. The door slammed. Stevie stood still and listened to the sound of his footsteps receding. It was only when she was sure he'd gone that she let herself burst into tears.

Chapter Two

From: Tom Blackwood

To: Louise Edwards

Hi Lou

My mother tells me that you've found someone who might be mad enough to take on organising her event. Just wanted to say thank you.

I assume this person is happy to do it on the cheap. Are they any good?

From: Louise Edwards

To: Tom Blackwood

Stevie is just starting out, so she'll take a smaller fee. She doesn't have much solo experience, but she has done work for me in the past and I can vouch for her being a bright, flexible and honest person.

Lou

TOM FROWNED. HE NOTICED that she hadn't answered his question. On the one hand, his mother was getting desperate. On the other hand, there was something about Louise's evasiveness that made him uneasy... and why did the name 'Stevie' ring a bell? He fired off another email to Lou asking for more details.

From: Louise Edwards

To: Tom Blackwood

Really, not much else to tell you. Except, you might remember her. She's Marshall's sister.

Tom stared at the email. 'Shit.'

He remembered her alright and, more to the point, he remembered Marshall. The last thing he wanted was to come back into contact with Marshall or any of his family.

Tom scowled at the screen. Louise had already been in touch with his mother. All he could do was hope that Stevie would be too expensive or do something to put his mother off. The headache that he'd been ignoring all afternoon surged up with a vengeance.

No. It was too risky. He pulled out a couple of painkillers and swallowed them with his tepid coffee. There was nothing for it. He would have to go down to Oxford and handle it himself.

IT WAS THE SORT OF dream where she knew she was asleep, but she couldn't wake herself up. Stevie walked into the hall of the house she had grown up in. Looking down, she could see her pale legs appearing from under the grey school skirt. The house was exactly as she remembered. The nice portrait photo of her and Marsh had pride of place in the hall. A photo taken outside Marsh's student house was tucked next to the frame. There were shoes collected under the coat rack. Post on the bottom step.

The photo was taken the last time they'd all been together. They'd gone to see Marsh at uni and were standing outside his student house. Less than a year later, her parents were dead.

Stevie looked up at the stairs, a feeling of dread starting to rise in her chest. She didn't want to go up, but her feet moved of their own accord. Her heart beat faster. Her hands felt clammy. She tried to stop, but her feet kept going.

As she got near the top, her sense of panic increased until she was breathing in shallow gasps. 'It's a dream,' she said, and tried to pinch herself. Her feet took her onward. Onward. Into her parents' bedroom. Onward. To the foot of their bed. And there they were. Lying peacefully side-by-side in their best clothes. Each with a lily held in white-gloved hands.

Tears slid down Stevie's face and she knew she was crying for real. They were her parents, but not her parents. The thing that animated them, that made them more than just their bodies, was gone. She tried to study their faces and found them curiously formless. She knew they had eyes, noses, mouths in the right places, but she couldn't remember the detail of any of them. Each year, it became harder and harder to recall. Rarely, when she was least expecting it, something would trigger a memory so strong that it would knock her off her feet – a waft of aftershave, the clink of a wedding ring against a china cup, the smell of lapsang souchong – and then, just as quickly, they'd be gone.

Slowly, she backed away from the figures on the bed, half wishing, half dreading that they would sit up. Once she reached the door, she was able to run. She turned and fled to Marsh's room. Marsh. The only one she had left. He was lying on his back, white gloved fingers interlaced on his chest. Stevie reached forward, her hands shaking. Fingers outstretched, she reached towards his cheek. His skin was drained of colour. She stared at his chest, there was no sign of him breathing. Her fingertips were millimetres away from his face. Trembling, she leaned closer.

She woke up with her arms held out in front of her. Her face was hot and wet from crying. To be awake was a relief, but the realisation that her parents really were dead was always savage. She curled up into a ball and reached, as she always did, for her phone. It was turned off. Stevie frowned. She never turned her phone off. As she turned it back on and let the glow light up the hollow she'd made under the duvet, she remembered. She was avoiding Marsh's phone calls. As the phone came to life, she saw that there was another missed call from him.

Her hands were still shaking as she dialled in his number. Her memory was faster than the address book. Her thumb hovered over the dial button and she thought of him, in bed with his warm pregnant wife. He wouldn't drag himself out of bed to come and comfort her now.

She stared at the phone, debating. Finally, she hit cancel. She was alone now. All alone. She would have to learn to live with it. She threw the phone to the bottom of the bed, curled up tighter and started to cry all over again.

The next morning, Stevie woke up with a headache. She took two paracetamol and finally looked at her messages. There were four voicemail messages and three texts from Marsh, all of which she deleted without opening. There was also a message from Dr Evelyn Blackwood, suggesting she came up on Saturday to meet her.

Stevie stared thoughtfully at the message. Louise had made it clear that there wasn't much money involved in the venture. However, it was a break. And a break was just what she needed, in every sense of the word. Oxford would be quite fun to explore. It would almost be a holiday.

Louise had also mentioned that Dr Blackwood's son was a certain Tom Blackwood who had lived in the same shared house as Lou, Jim and Marsh. Stevie cringed. She'd had a terrible crush on Tom when she was thirteen. But that was a long time ago ... and she would be working for his mum, not him. She probably wouldn't even see him.

She drew her shoulders back and sat up straighter. If she was to be all alone in the world, she might as well make a go of looking after herself. After all, she'd looked after her stressed out brother while he was doing his qualifying exams and managed to take her own GCSEs at the same time. If she could look after two of them, surely she could manage on her own. This project of Dr Blackwood's could give her just the opportunity she needed. It also meant that she'd be spending a lot of time away from London, which made it even less likely that Marsh would catch her. That would show him.

Feeling defiant, she walked over to her pin-board and took down the picture of her family outside Marsh's student house. She looked like a child in it. She replaced it, face down. Still, that didn't seem to be enough of a gesture. Searching her room, she saw a postcard of Harrison Ford as Indiana Jones.

'You'll do,' she said and pinned him up so that he covered the back of the photo. 'Now then,' she said to the postcard. 'You are about to see the transformation of poor needy little Stevie into Stevie the strong woman.' She threw her arms out and lifted her chin. 'Ta daa.'

Chapter Three

THE HOUSE WAS IN A quiet road in North Oxford. Walking along the sun-dappled pavement, Stevie felt as though she'd stepped into another world. The houses were all set well back from the road and stood, elegant and aloof, in detached grandeur. Every house had at least three floors and high pointy roofs with chimneys. She smiled to herself. It was impossible to feel harried in such tranquil surroundings.

What an ideal place for an event venue. Most of the houses appeared to be used as offices by different departments of the university. Louise had mentioned that Dr Blackwood was planning on running the house as a B&B. She imagined Oxford attracted visitors all year round and business would never be slow.

Dr Blackwood's house had a gabled white porch and high gothic windows. Stevie half expected there to be some sort of interesting door knocker and was disappointed to see a plain one, with a laminated notice saying 'please ring the bell' and pointing to an electronic doorbell. She rang and waited for what seemed like ages. Wondering whether there was no one in, she rang the bell again and crouched to peer through the ornate copper keyhole. Through the hole she could see a sunlit hall with red and yellow tiles on the floor.

A shadow moved as someone walked towards the door. She quickly straightened up.

The door, which was twice as wide as a normal door, swung open to reveal a teenage girl in skinny jeans and a Triphoppers tour T-shirt.

'Yes?'

'I'm Stevie Winfield. I'm looking for Dr Evelyn Blackwood.'

The girl frowned for a moment, and then her expression cleared. 'Oh, you're the party organiser. Come on in.' She opened the door wider and let Stevie past. 'I'm Alice. I'm Evelyn's granddaughter.'

Stevie gawped at the hall. It was enormous. To one side a big, carpeted staircase wound past long windows through which the sun poured in. The walls were a warm shade of primrose and the whole effect was like stepping into a light filled cocoon.

'We only finished painting it last week,' said Alice. 'Do you like it?'

'It's amazing.'

'Why don't you wait in the library?' Alice led Stevie into a room off the hall. 'I'll go tell Gran you're here.'

The library turned out to be just that. The walls were lined with books, their multi-coloured spines as decorative as any wallpaper. Light slanted in through more tall windows, casting the room in patches of bright and dark. A number of mismatched comfy chairs were arranged around a fireplace. Stevie sank into one of them.

This place was incredible. It was like a stately home, only real people lived here. In her mind's eye she saw people in evening dress milling around the room. Lighting could be a problem. She looked up to the ceiling and saw a chandelier. 'Oh wow.'

Any precious books would have to be removed, of course. She leaned forward to look at the colourful spines and discovered that, rather than the learned tomes she was expecting, they were mostly modern hardbacks. She was sitting, it seemed, next to the eighties' bonkbuster section.

Stevie went to the window and looked out. The garden descended via steep steps into a sunken lawn. An old-fashioned wooden gazebo gleamed white in the summer sun. 'Oh my,' she said. She tried to see further along to the other end of the garden, but her view was blocked by the deep columns of the windows.

Someone opened the library door, making Stevie jump. She turned round and saw Alice, half in, half out.

'Gran says she'll be along in a minute. Do you want a cup of tea?'

'Oh, yes please.'

'Do you want to come with me to the kitchen? I can give you a mini tour of the house on the way. You can leave your stuff here, if you like. It'll be perfectly safe. There's only you, me and Gran here at the moment.'

'I'll just get my notebook.' Stevie grabbed what she needed and followed Alice out.

'This is the hallway,' said Alice as they passed through it again. She stopped at the first door. 'This is the front room.' She opened the door to a room that was almost as big as Stevie's one bedroom flat. 'We don't use it for much at the moment, but we've ordered a TV and we're hoping the B&B guests will be able to use it.'

Alice ushered Stevie out and down the corridor before she could absorb the particulars of the room.

'We've got a small bar here.' She pointed to a large hatch with a rolling blind. There was a note with 'wet varnish' written on it propped against the wall next to it. 'I know it's traditional to have the bar in the same room as the lounge, but Gran couldn't bring herself to put one in the front room. So we're getting that hatch thing sorted out instead.' There were no bottles in evidence.

'I take it your Gran has a licence to serve alcohol?' Stevie poised her pen to make a note.

'Uh-huh.' Alice shrugged.

Stevie added a question mark to the end of her note, not convinced the teenager actually knew the answer.

Alice led her into the biggest kitchen Stevie had ever seen. 'This is the kitchen. But we tend to use it as our dining room too.'

A huge stove dominated one end of the kitchen. White cupboards lined the other walls. In the middle of the room was an old-fashioned farmhouse table with wooden chairs tucked in under it. It took Stevie a full minute to stop gawping and start making notes. While Alice put the kettle on, she walked around and found a stack of certificates in clip frames. Alcohol, catering, fire safety. Most of the certification appeared to have been taken care of.

'The previous planner lady checked those things out anyway,' said Alice.

'Why did she leave the project?'

Alice pulled a face. 'Lady Beryl.'

'Lady Beryl?' Stevie tried to sound casual, but alarm bells were starting to ring. If this woman had caused someone to leave the project already, things didn't bode well.

'Yeah. She's one of the trustees of the charity group. She can be ... difficult sometimes. Sally – that's the other planner – had a bit of a dispute with her.' Alice handed Stevie her tea. 'Don't worry. I'm sure it won't happen to you. Gran's had a word with Lady Beryl. She's promised to behave.'

'Ri-ight.' Stevie frowned. Party planners were a resilient bunch. This Lady Beryl was likely to continue to be a problem. Still, she told herself, she needed this job, no matter how hard it was. She filed the information to consider later. 'This house is incredible.'

'Isn't it?' said Alice proudly. 'It was in a terrible state when Gran and Gramps bought it. We all worked on it to get it renovated. It took years, but it looks good now, doesn't it?'

'Yes, it's beautiful.'

'Dad and Uncle Tom think Gran should sell it and make a fortune, but Gran says she's sticking to the plan.' Alice glanced down at her tea. 'I think she feels she owes it to Gramps.'

Ah. An emotional connection. Stevie made a quick note to follow up. 'What happened?'

'To Gramps?' Alice shrugged as though she didn't care, but her eyes misted over. 'He had a heart attack. One minute he's painting the window frames. The next minute ... pfft.' She waved a hand to indicate that he was horizontal. 'Gran called an ambulance but he didn't make it.'

'I'm sorry.' Stevie knew from experience that there was nothing she could say to make things any better, but it didn't stop her wishing there was.

Alice shrugged again. 'It happens.' She looked away. 'He was old. At least it was quick.'

Stevie nodded and, not knowing what else to say, took a sip of tea. Before the silence could get awkward, someone stamped up the outside steps and entered the kitchen from the back door.

A small woman with short grey hair entered, brushing cobwebs off her shoulders. 'Hello.' She strode up to Stevie and shook her hand. 'I'm Evelyn Blackwood. You must be Stephanie.'

'Stevie. Please, call me Stevie.' She winced at the woman's enthusiastic grip.

'Then you must call me Evelyn. Has Alice shown you the house yet? I see she's given you tea. That's fantastic. I was up in the roof void, I'm afraid. Hence the cobwebs. It needs cleaning out. Damned useful storage space though,' said Evelyn without pausing for breath. 'Nice of you to agree to take this job.'

'I haven't taken it yet,' Stevie said quickly, before Evelyn spoke again. 'I have quite a number of questions to ask—'

'Quite right too. Come. Let's show you round the rest of the house first. Come, come.' She shooed Stevie, who had to abandon her tea, out the kitchen and back into the main house. Alice grinned and waved goodbye.

Evelyn took Stevie through a bewildering maze of corridors and stairways, showing her the parts of the house that were to be the B&B and the parts that were to be rented out as venues to local groups. As they walked, Stevie did her best to interrupt Evelyn to ask the questions on her list.

'All that's really left to organise is the food, the entertainment and where to put people,' said Evelyn. She opened the door to an old-fashioned wooden conservatory.

'So, basically, the whole party,' said Stevie. Sunlight filled the glass-walled room, raising the temperature several degrees higher than inside the house.

'Goodness. Best get those windows open.' Evelyn dragged a chair over to the window.

'Here, let me.' Being taller, Stevie could reach the latch by stretching.

'Thank you.' Evelyn moved on to the next window.

'Another question,' said Stevie, over her shoulder. 'Would I be working for the charity? Or for you?'

'Ah.' Evelyn wobbled a little on her chair and paused to steady herself. 'Good question. We didn't think about that with Sally because she was doing it for free. I think you'd be working for the charity really.' She carefully descended. 'I did mention we can't pay very much, didn't I?'

'We can discuss that in a minute,' said Stevie smoothly. 'Tell me more about the charity.'

'Oh yes.' Evelyn brushed a stray wisp of hair off her face. 'We ladies are a group that gets together to do fundraising. We're mostly retired academics or academics' wives, like Beryl. Anyway, this year, we chose a charity in Sri Lanka. It's called Project PEDS. Ghastly name. It was set up by a group of American doctors and it's raising money to buy equipment for a new children's hospital in Sri Lanka. The old one got swept away by the tsunami.'

Evelyn paused before going on to the next window and shook her head. 'Terrible business that. All those people who lost everything. It makes one so glad to have what we have.' She looked up towards the house, visible through the glass roof of the conservatory. 'Anyway, where was I? Oh yes, Priya, one of our ladies, is from Sri Lanka and suggested we adopt it this year. We're hoping to raise enough money to buy equipment for an operating room.'

Stevie felt at a loss for what to say. 'It ... sounds like a very good cause.'

'Oh it is,' said Evelyn. 'Priya showed us some photos of people from the village. You know, survivors. There were these babies. Oh, they were so beautiful. It breaks your heart.'

Stevie nodded. The cause did sound like a good one. For some reason, it had brought a lump to her throat. Perhaps it was the mention of babies. Or being grateful for what you had. At least it wasn't an orphanage. She probably would have burst into tears if it had been. She forced herself to concentrate on her notebook.

'You mentioned food. Do you have a caterer lined up?'

Evelyn looked surprised at the change of subject. 'I think Sally was talking to one, but when she left in a huff, she didn't tell us who it was.'

'No caterer.' Stevie wrote 'aaargh!' in her notebook, but kept her expression neutral. 'Any leads on entertainment?'

'No.'

Stevie added another exclamation mark to her notes. 'And you mentioned where to put people. How many people can this place take?'

'About a hundred and twenty,' said Evelyn. 'But that's only if we include the garden.'

Stevie looked at the garden. It was gloriously sunny. 'The weather should hold for the next four weeks.'

'It's not that. The garden—' Evelyn's phone beeped. 'Excuse me.'

She answered it. 'Beryl, can I call you back? Yes, under a minute. Bye.' She hung up and pulled a face. 'That was Lady Beryl.' She paused. 'Lady Grayingham really, but that's a bit of a mouthful.' She fluttered her hands, as though waving the irrelevance away. 'Blooming nuisance, that woman is, but she's a generous donor and chairwoman of the charity group, so we must be nice. Hang on, I'll get Alice to come and show you the garden.'

She pulled her phone out again. 'This house is so big, we keep losing each other in it. So Tom bought us all these iPhone things to keep in touch. It's made the world of difference. She sent a text. There, Alice should be along in a minute. I'll just go and phone Beryl back.' She disappeared back into the house.

After finding a seat, Stevie looked at her notes and did a quick calculation of how much the ball was likely to raise from ticket sales. She tapped her pen against her notebook. She only had a rough idea of the budget, but she could see that the event wasn't likely to raise much money for the charity, let alone enough to pay for an event planner. She wondered if she should just walk away. It wasn't going to make her any money. And it was a huge job for her to undertake without help.

She sighed. Maybe opening envelopes for minimum wage wasn't so bad. It was pretty mindless, but at least it wasn't stressful. If she could find another job without a supervisor with despotic tendencies, she might be happy.

There was a noise just outside the window. Stevie turned round to see a sparrow hopping along the wisteria stem. She smiled. Sitting there, in the sunshine, with a big challenge to occupy her, she suddenly felt happier than she had been in months. If she got this job, the extra work would mean that she had less time to think about Marsh and Jane and the sprog they were having. The thought of her brother made the smile drop from her face.

Despite the open windows, it was still hot in the conservatory. Stevie noticed that the door to the garden was also open. She cast a glance at the door to the house. There was no sign of Alice.

The wisteria that covered the side of the conservatory had put out runners that were visible through the grille work on the wrought iron steps, making Stevie feel like she was descending into somewhere primal where nature had taken over.

At the bottom was a riot of flower bushes. Some attempt had been made to cut them back to make a path that ran the perimeter of the sunken lawn, but the plants threw higgledy-piggledy arms into the path.

She tried to get her bearings. Peering through the plants, she located the white gazebo she'd seen from the library. She set off in the direction that she thought the library would be. With the foliage towering either side, she felt as though she were exploring a particularly colourful jungle. When she came level with the front of the house, she saw the front porch. As she watched, a man bounded up the steps and rang the bell. He leaned against a pillar to wait for someone to open the door.

Stevie instinctively drew back so he couldn't see her. From where she was, she could see him perfectly. He was tall, with dark curls verging on needing to be cut. His handsome face was set in concentration. There were deep frown lines on his forehead. He was tapping his mobile phone impatiently against his thigh.

The door opened and Stevie heard Evelyn's voice saying 'Darling! How lovely to see you.'

The man smiled. The frown eased briefly, making him look not merely handsome, but drop dead gorgeous. He went in and disappeared from her view.

She stood still, staring at the spot he'd vacated. There was something familiar about him. She wondered how she could have met him. You'd have thought she'd remember meeting a man like that. He was definitely the best looking specimen she'd seen in ages.

'Stevie?' Alice clanged down the metal steps from the conservatory.

'Yes.' Stevie returned from down the path.

'Hello,' said Alice. 'Sorry I took so long. I was on the phone. How did you get on with the tour?'

Stevie dragged her thoughts back from the man. 'It was good, thanks. The rooms look great.'

Alice's phone beeped, and she looked at it. 'Gran says she and Uncle Tom are in the library and you should come up.'

Uncle Tom? Stevie turned as though looking back at the garden. Tom Blackwood. That must have been the man she'd seen a few minutes ago.

No wonder she hadn't recognised him. The Tom Blackwood she remembered had been pale and stubbly, with long hair in a ponytail. Clearly the last nine years had changed him for the better.

She turned back to Alice and smiled. 'I guess we'd best go see them, then.'

Chapter Four

THEY'D NEARLY REACHED the entrance hall when Alice's phone rang again. 'The library's just over there.' She pointed. 'Can you find your own way? Is that okay?'

Stevie watched Alice scurry off, already chatting. The people in this house seemed to live on their phones. She thought of her own phone, safely turned off in her pocket. Perhaps she was just as bad when she wasn't trying to avoid Marsh.

Come to think of it, she had spent a lot of time on the phone when she was a teenager. The main reason her phone wasn't constantly ringing nowadays was because most of her friends were trekking around the Far East on their gap years. Feeling a little lonely and unloved, she walked slowly across the hallway. The door to the library was ajar.

'But Mum, she has no experience whatsoever.' A man's voice, from inside the library.

Stevie stopped.

'I know Louise suggested her,' he continued. 'But she implied that she's too young and flighty.'

What? Stevie blinked. Lou wouldn't say that about her? Surely not? She'd worked for Lou before and there had never been any problem. Well, apart from that one time she organised the flowers for the wrong day.

'She's just a kid, after all. She's barely older than Alice.'

Why did people insist on treating her like she was ten years old? First Marsh, then Louise, now this guy who hadn't seen her in nine years. How dare they? All doubts about whether she wanted to take the job vanished. She was going to take this sorry excuse for a party and turn it into a brilliant event. And she would do it without Louise's help. That would show them.

'Hmm,' said Evelyn. 'Beryl says we should try and press her to do it for free, like Sally did.'

There was a pause. Then, 'Okay, I suppose that's a good idea. If she's willing to take it on at such short notice, she can't have much else on. So, maybe she'll be desperate enough to do it on the promise that people would recommend her.'

'Well, we can't afford to pay much, anyway,' said Evelyn. A spoon tinkled against a cup. 'Here you go darling. Have a biscuit as well. I'm glad you're here. I'm so rubbish at negotiating with people.'

'Glad to help, mother. Glad to help.'

Stevie's lips pressed together. Just a girl? Desperate? Who did he think he was? He may have grown up and become handsome, but he was still a prat.

If Evelyn had asked her to do the project for free in return for recommendations from her friends, Stevie would have considered it. After all, Evelyn's friends sounded like exactly the sort of people who would have daughters to marry off and retirement parties to arrange. But now, having heard Tom's cold analysis of how to take advantage of her inexperience, she decided she would drive as hard a bargain as she possibly could. She might not take it all at the end, but they didn't need to know that. Lifting her chin up, she rapped on the door and walked in.

Tom was standing by the window, with his back to her. Evelyn was pouring more tea. 'Ah Stevie. This is my son Tom. Tom, this is Stevie.'

Tom turned round, taking a bite from his biscuit. His eyes widened. For a moment he looked stunned. Then he coughed violently and thumped himself in the chest.

Stevie took a step back, alarmed.

Evelyn reached up and gave Tom a sound smack between the shoulder blades. He gulped and carried on coughing, although there was less urgency to it now.

'I'll be fine in a minute,' Tom wheezed, in between coughs. 'You carry on.'

Evelyn gave him an exasperated look and turned to Stevie. 'Anyway, what do you think? Will you take it on?'

'It's certainly a challenging project. There's a lot that still hasn't been taken care of.' She gave Evelyn her most business-like smile. 'And you haven't said how much you were willing to pay.'

'Well ...' Evelyn glanced at Tom, who was still bright red in the face with the effort of trying not to cough. 'We were rather hoping that you'd do it for free.'

'For free?' She let her voice betray nothing more than mild curiosity.

'Well, Sally, the previous organiser, was doing it for the charity. For free. I mean, the charity committee are pretty influential and wealthy women and some of the guests are likely to be in need of party planners soon. You're sure to get a whole load of recommendations off the back of this one project – assuming you do a good job, of course. Which I'm sure you will.'

'Right,' said Stevie. 'I see.' She paused, as though to think it over. 'I'm sorry Dr Blackwood. We seem to have both wasted our time this afternoon. It was nice meeting you.' She turned to leave.

'Wait!' said Evelyn. 'How ... How much did you have in mind?'

Stevie named her sum.

'We can't ...'

'That's preposterous,' said Tom, having recovered his voice. 'You have no experience to speak of. No client recommendations. From what I can tell, you don't even have a proper business to back you up. That sort of sum is daylight robbery.'

'And we can't afford that,' said Evelyn.

Stevie ignored Tom and concentrated on Evelyn. 'I know you can't,' she said. 'I only have a rough idea of your budget, but from what I can see, you'll be lucky to break even. That's if you sell at least a hundred tickets. I'm guessing you've sold a load to friends and family and you've got about two thirds of the tickets left to sell. Am I right?'

Evelyn didn't say anything, but a slight twitch gave her away.

'I have an alternative suggestion. I will do the project for the cost of my expenses and forty per cent of any profit you make.'

'Forty per cent! Don't be ridiculous,' Tom said.

'Is it ridiculous?' said Stevie. 'You have no caterer, no marketing, no plans for publicity and no idea how you're going to fit everyone in the house. The garden looks like the wilds of Borneo and you have this Lady Beryl woman who is so difficult that even a friend can't stand working with her. You have four weeks to get all of this sorted out and you can't afford anyone but me. You can barely even afford me.' She took a deep breath. She didn't want to say this, but there was a principle at stake. 'Take it or leave it.'

Tom gave a short 'Ha!'

Evelyn raised her hand and silenced him. 'Ten per cent.'

'Mum ...'

'Twenty-five,' said Stevie. Twenty-five percent of not very much was still not very much. It was lucky she wasn't doing this for the money.

Evelyn hesitated.

Stevie seized her opportunity. 'Great. That's settled then.' She strode to Evelyn and shook her hand. 'I'll head off now and make some calls. I'll be in touch tomorrow with some ideas.' She gave Tom a sweet smile. 'Nice to see you again, Tom.' With that, she turned around and walked out.

As she closed the door behind her, she heard Evelyn say 'I like her.'

From: Olivia Gornall

To: Tom Blackwood

So, how did it go negotiating the poor girl out of a job?

From: Tom Blackwood

To: Olivia Gornall

Not so good. I seem to have lost my touch some-what.

She got Mum to agree to give her twenty-five per cent of the profits. Mind you, sounds like there isn't going to be much of a profit from this ball anyway. So I guess it's not such a bad deal after all.

From: Olivia Gornall

To: Tom Blackwood

This girl got the better of the famous Tom Black-wood negotiating skills? And she took a job that you didn't want her to get?

Oh, I need details. Tell me everything. And no glossing over the embarrassing bits. I've held your ponytail out of the toilet while you were throwing up. You owe me.

From: Tom Blackwood

To: Olivia Gornall

I wish you'd stop going on about that. That was over ten years ago. I wish you'd just let me get sick in my hair. I could have just washed it and saved myself years of grief.

From: Olivia Gornall

To: Tom Blackwood

Yeah, yeah. Now TELL ME!

From: Tom Blackwood

To: Olivia Gornall

Since you insist.

Mum gives me a cup of tea and a biscuit. I'm standing there, psyching myself up for battle. Stevie comes in. I turn round, expecting to see a skinny, flat-chested thirteen-year-old with acne and braces. Instead I find myself looking at a gorgeous woman with chestnut brown hair and an amazing figure. In the past few years she's filled out perfectly and in all the right places.

Anyway, she was so stunning, I caught my breath. Unfortunately, I also caught my biscuit. By the time Mum had thumped me and I'd coughed the bloody thing up, I'd lost my edge.

She walked all over us.

There you have it. The details.

Foiled by a custard cream.

From Olivia Gornall

To: Tom Blackwood

LOL! So much for the legendary Blackwood skill and charm. Shame you didn't get to wow your mother with your razor sharp negotiating skills.

I take it you're not as dead set against the girl as you were this morning then.

From: Tom Blackwood

To: Olivia Gornall

Well, she HAS effectively agreed to do the gig for the cost of expenses. From what I've seen and heard, this ball isn't going to make any profit. Twenty-five per cent of bugger all is bugger all.

Typical. The one chance I get to show off in front of Mum, I go and choke on a biscuit. I give up. I'm just going to have to live with being the lesser son.

Anyway, I'm planning to avoid going to Mum's until after the ball. I don't want to run into Stevie again. Even if she is rather nice to look at.

Chapter Five

From: Vienna Jansen-Verlag

To: Tom Blackwood

Tom Darling, how are you?

It's been the longest time since I last saw you. I'm going to be popping up to Oxford several times in the next three weeks. My client is based up there and prefers for me to come to them. Do you still go and see your mum some Sundays? I could pop up early for my Monday meeting and you could show me round your charming mansion. I haven't seen it since your parents started doing it up, I'd love to see what they've made of it.

I haven't seen your mother since the funeral. How is she?

Also, I've got a corporate schmooze coming up on the 23rd of next month. Black tie. Can you do it? Please say you will. I need a body to accompany me and I can't think of a body I'd rather be attached to than yours!

Vienna

X X

TOM SCROLLED THROUGH his calendar. Twenty-third. He could do that. He hadn't seen Vienna in months. In fact, not since he'd taken her to the works Christmas event. He smiled. A black tie do with Vienna would probably be the best thing to take his mind off work. Even though she and he had been a disaster as a couple, there was no one quite like Vienna when it came to having a good time.

From: Tom Blackwood

To: Vienna Jansen-Verlag

Vienna

Of course you should go up and see the house. I'm sure Mum will be delighted to see you too. The house looks fabulous. Mum's done a great job finishing off what she and Dad started.

Just give me a bell on the Saturday beforehand, so that I can make sure I'm there to meet you.

Re the company party. Of course. I owe you for the last time.

Gotta go. Work to do.

From: Vienna Jansen-Verlag

To: Tom Blackwood

Fantastic that you can come to the event. We can go back to mine afterwards for post party drinks. ;-)

Looking forward to it.

Vienna

X X

STEVIE SPENT THE NEXT few days furiously brainstorming and making phone calls. She went up to Oxford midweek to meet Evelyn's friends in the charity group. They turned out to be a group of three, all sitting in the library, having tea and biscuits. Stevie accepted a cup of tea and smiled attentively as Evelyn introduced her to the two others.

Both ladies were middle aged and exuded a sort of confidence that came from knowing their strengths. Priya, the lady who was championing that year's charity, was a soft-spoken Sri Lankan. She had brought a folder containing information on the charity, which she showed Stevie. She had lost friends and relatives to the tsunami and her passion for the cause was contagious. By the time she'd finished, Stevie wanted to help the poor children as much as she could.

Lady Beryl, whom Stevie had imagined to be a large woman, was actually a small, chubby lady with elegantly cut silver hair and perfect posture. Her voice, however, was pure Lady Bracknell. Stevie expected her to say '*A handbag*?' at any moment.

'There's usually more of us,' said Evelyn. 'But Jean's ill with bronchitis, Greta is on one of her consulting jaunts and Hilda and June have gone to Australia for a wedding.'

'So.' Lady Beryl's lips stretched into the shape of a smile, but her gaze was pure steel. 'What plans have you got for us then Stephanie?'

'Please, call me Stevie.' She opened her notebook. 'To be honest, what I have is a long list of questions.'

Everyone was watching her with interest, apart from Lady Beryl, who was eyeing her sceptically.

'First of all, the tickets. How many have you actually sold?'

The women exchanged a few glances. 'Not as many as we'd like,' said Evelyn. 'About forty.'

'Okay. That's not great. I'm assuming you've approached all your nearest friends and relatives?'

All three ladies nodded.

'So we need to promote this to the wider public. Fine. Now, I gather you haven't done any advertising as yet, is that right?'

More nods.

'Okay, we'll start by taking out an ad in the local paper. I'll phone up and check prices.' Stevie wrote this down. 'Does anyone know anyone famous?'

There was some silence as the ladies thought about it.

'Why is this relevant?' said Lady Beryl.

'Because, if we can get some famous people backing the cause, we're more likely to get people interested. Especially, if we can persuade the famous person to come to the ball. People will come along hoping to see them.'

Lady Beryl digested this. 'Sounds awfully ... tawdry.'

Stevie smiled. 'You're right, of course. But needs must. It is a good cause and a little bit of the common touch would be worth it if we can raise more money.'

'I suppose.'

'I know a novelist,' said Priya, suddenly. 'Used to be a student of mine. Shame she went into the novelist business really. She had the potential to be a brilliant historian.'

'Is she famous?'

The lady named someone Stevie had never heard of. 'Why don't you see if she'd like to come?' said Stevie. 'And maybe she could talk about it on her website.'

A few more suggestions were thrown in and various people tasked with acting on them.

'Next,' said Stevie, bracing herself. 'Catering.'

'We've *got* to have a good caterer,' said Lady Beryl. 'We're not doing a main meal, just canapés and *amuse-bouche*. They've got to be excellent or else it looks awful.'

'I see,' said Stevie. 'But there's a small problem.'

'Which is?' Lady Beryl's eyebrows arched.

'We can't afford one. Also, all the ones recommended by my contacts are busy and can't fit us in at such short notice.' She didn't have any contacts. She'd phoned everyone local she found on Google.

'Surely you're not suggesting we do without nibbles,' said Lady Beryl. 'Don't be ridiculous, girl. People will be drinking and they have to have something to soak up the alcohol. Or else there'll be absolute mayhem.' She fixed Stevie with a stern glare. 'Don't you know anything?'

Stevie forced herself not to react to the criticism. 'What I'm suggesting, Lady Beryl, is that we cater for the occasion ourselves.'

There was a murmur of concern.

'Sounds risky,' said Priya. 'Don't you need all sorts of health and safety certificates before you do that? In case you poison someone.'

'Exactly.' Lady Beryl snorted. 'Stupid idea.'

Stevie glanced at Evelyn. They had discussed this before-hand.

Evelyn smiled, a little triumphantly. 'Actually,' she said. 'We do have an accredited kitchen right here in the house.'

Everyone turned to look at her.

'But there's only you who has any certification,' said Lady Beryl. 'You can't make canapés for a hundred and twenty people all on your own.'

'Only one of us needs to be accredited,' said Evelyn. 'And I am, so we could, legally, cater for the ball ourselves.'

'Making canapés for a hundred and twenty,' said Priya thoughtfully. 'Just us. Sounds like fun. Let's do it.'

'But ...' Lady Beryl sputtered.

'A vote?' suggested Evelyn. 'All those in favour?'

Two hands went up. Lady's Beryl's stayed firmly in her lap.

'Well,' said Lady Beryl. 'Fine. I just hope we can come up with an acceptable menu with the so called budget.'

'Actually.' Stevie pulled out a wad of paper. 'I've got some suggestions, with approximate costings.' She handed them round.

There was silence as everyone read the proposed menu.

'It's a bit ... predictable,' said Priya, after a moment.

'Is this really all the money we can spend?' Evelyn said. 'Seriously?'

'I'm afraid so.' Stevie scanned the list. She had done her best, looking up recipes and prices on the internet. She had been expecting some resistance, but not this level of disappointment. She bit her lip, then, remembering she had to look professional, took a small sip of tea in an attempt to seem nonchalant.

'This will never do,' said Lady Beryl, frowning. 'You haven't even got angels on horseback.'

Stevie stared. She had no idea what the woman was talking about. Evelyn leaned forward. 'Scallops. It's a sort of canapé,' she whispered. Aloud she said, 'We can't afford scallops, Beryl. You can see that.'

'But we can't serve ... this. This is the sort of thing the students would serve.' She injected a huge amount of contempt into the word students.

Priya laughed. 'No, they'd serve crisps and nuts.'

'Graduate students then,' Lady Beryl snapped.

'Perhaps, I could help,' Priya said.

Everyone turned to her. 'Since it's a Sri Lankan charity ... How about Sri Lankan nibbles?'

Stevie perked up. 'Is it likely to be expensive?'

'Not particularly,' said Priya. 'I have enough recipes and expertise. I can show you how.'

'No offence, Priya,' Lady Beryl said in a voice that suggested she was going to cause it anyway. 'But isn't Sri Lankan food palate-searingly hot?'

Priya smiled. 'Not if you don't put any chilli in it.'

Lady Beryl looked thoughtful. 'I must admit,' she said slowly. 'It does have a certain ... *je ne sais quoi* to have Sri Lankan food at a ball for a Sri Lankan charity.'

'Excellent,' said Evelyn. 'That's settled then.' She beamed. 'I'm liking the sound of this already.'

'Okay. I'll sort out a menu. We might have to go to London to buy some ingredients,' said Priya.

'That's not a problem. I live in London.' Stevie scribbled notes. 'Shall we discuss prices and things?'

From: Krantz Solutions

To: Tom Blackwood; Dhidre Smith

Dear Tom and Dhidre

I have arranged for a projection meeting with Pickering for Tuesday the 10th. I should inform you that Matthias will be attending the meeting in person.

Regards

Marjorie Verita, PA to Matthias Groenberger.

From: Krantz Solutions HR

To: Tom Blackwood

Dear Thomas

Thank you for your interest in the position of Regional Manager, Doha office. We are pleased to invite you to a formal interview at 14.00 on Wednesday the 11th of July, please come prepared to give a thirty

minute presentation on your ideas of how to set up and maintain the Doha office and how you would expand our footprint in the Middle East area.

Regards

Gillian Smythe

Human Resources

TOM STARED AT THE TWO emails. Two presentations in two days. His heart accelerated. Pain burst above his eyes, forcing him to screw them shut. He put a hand to his head and stood up, slowly. Out of the corner of his eye, he noted someone looking up away from their screen. He moved the hand from his forehead so that he could pretend he was merely pushing back his hair. Moving as casually as possible, while feeling his head was in a vice, he walked out of the office floor and made straight for the stairwell.

Once out of sight, he leaned against the wall and rubbed his forehead furiously to ease the pain. He pulled out the two packets of painkillers that he had in his jacket pocket. Which sort had he taken earlier? The doctor said he could alternate paracetamol and ibuprofen if he needed to. He popped two pills from one of the packets and swallowed them dry.

Two presentations. He had barely enough time to prepare for one, let alone two. Even though the insomnia gave him more hours to work in, his ability to work was draining away, making him slower and slower. It was becoming difficult to hide. Og was right. He needed to do something about it. But what? He couldn't ease up on his work, when he was hoping to get the job in Doha.

Tom groaned. Pulling out his phone, he messaged Og.

Tom: Two presentations in two days. F***

Almost immediately, his phone rang. He answered. 'Og.'

'Where are you?' she whispered. This was code for 'who can hear you'. It didn't do to show weakness on the office floor sometimes. Especially if you were a bloke who wanted to advance. It was all about having the balls to carry a deal through. Competence was pretty much a secondary consideration.

'Fire escape,' he said. 'My floor.'

'Be right there.'

He closed his eyes and waited. A few minutes later, heels clicked on concrete and Og turned up.

She gave him a long, hard look. 'You look like crap,' she said. 'You shouldn't be at work.'

'I've taken some more painkillers. I'll be fine once they kick in.'

She came and leaned against the wall next to him. 'Seriously Tom, you don't look well.'

'I'm fine.' He rubbed his hands over his face. 'It's just that I've got phase two of the Pickering project and the Doha interview panel a day after each other. One of the VPs is going to be there for the Pickering one.'

Og pulled in her cheeks. 'You're got stuff prepared for them both, right? You said so.'

Tom sighed. 'Yes, but it's nowhere near ready. I'm still busy trouble-shooting the handover on part one of the project and I won't have everything until the day, pretty much. And I've got to keep all my slides and conclusions updated as we go. I haven't got enough time to cover it all as it is. Now I have to do a second presentation. I don't know where I'm going to find time to do that. Not to mention the fact that I've promised to do stuff for Mum.' His voice tightened with panic. 'And my head feels like it's splitting in two, which isn't bloody helping.'

There was moment of silence. Then Og put a hand on his arm. 'Tom. Don't hate me ... but are you sure you want this promotion? You're making yourself ill.'

He turned to look at her. As teenagers, when his family were all but ignoring him and her life was falling apart, they had been there for each other. They had seen each other at their ugliest and weakest and still managed to be friends. If Og was worried, he should listen. Except he didn't want to. He needed to do something to get ahead in his career.

'I want this promotion,' he said, talking through his teeth.

'If this is about your mother—'

'No. It's about me.' He pushed himself away from the wall. 'Besides, I can't let bloody Dhidre win.'

'That's a fair point,' Og conceded. 'But after the interviews. Take some time off, will you Tom?'

'Yeah,' he said. He would. If he ever found the time when there wasn't something urgent that needed doing. He took a deep breath and forced himself to focus. The pain in his head was receding now. Time to get back to work before someone wondered where he'd gone. Or worse, Og got into trouble. 'We'd best get back ... Thanks, Og. You know.'

She grinned at him. 'Yeah well, you owe me.'

Chapter Six

WITH PRIYA WORKING on the catering, Stevie turned her attention to the rest of her list. Top priority was advertising. She and Alice designed an advert to go in the local papers and information sheets. A slightly larger version was turned into flyers, which they personally delivered to carefully selected bars, pubs and restaurants around the city. By the end of the day, both Stevie and Alice were exhausted.

'Do you think it'll bring in enough people?' said Alice, as they sat in the front room, each stretched out on a sofa. Evelyn had poured them glasses of cold apple juice and told them to go and relax after their endeavours.

'I don't know.' That was an understatement. Stevie doubted they'd sell nearly as many tickets as they'd need to. She needed to think of another way to shift more tickets. She stared out of the sunlit window and let her mind wander. 'If only there was a way to make it the event to be seen at.'

Alice picked up a magazine and flicked through it. 'Hmmm. Apparently Coldplay were at the St John's college ball this summer. I would have liked to have gone to that.'

Stevie glanced across at her. 'How did you know? About Coldplay, I mean?'

'There was a buzz about it on the Facebook group.' Alice didn't even look up from her magazine. Clearly a 'buzz on Facebook' was a commonplace occurrence.

Stevie sat up, an idea coalescing in her head. 'Which Facebook group?'

'There's a Facebook group attached to the Triphoppers website,' said Alice. 'Someone on there was going to the ball.' She smiled. 'Actually, once she mentioned it, a couple of other people wanted to go as well. I couldn't afford it, of course. Besides, Mum and Dad would *never* have let me stay out all night like that.'

Stevie knew a lot about Triphoppers. They had burst onto the scene a few years back when they appeared on a TV talent show. They had been in the charts ever since. But more than that, Stevie's sister-in-law, Jane, was Ashby, the lead singer's, ex-girlfriend. Even though she and Ashby were no longer on speaking terms, Jane still kept in touch with the other band members. Especially the drummer, Pete. Stevie had met Pete at Jane and Marsh's wedding. She remembered him as being kind and down to earth, not at all like a pop star. She'd talked to him at length and even told him about her aspirations of becoming an event organiser.

'This buzz,' said Stevie, carefully, her mind still thinking through the possibilities. 'How does it start?'

Alice shrugged. 'Dunno. I guess someone posts a message about it. You know, like "I'm really excited about going to see Coldplay" or something and people get talking about it.'

'Could you mention this ball on there?'

Alice pulled a face. 'Well, it's not really the sort of thing people are into ... you know. Charity balls. I mean, it's not as if someone famous was coming or anything.'

'What if ...' Stevie closed her eyes, an idea becoming more solid as she spoke. 'What if I could persuade someone famous to come? Say, someone from Triphoppers.'

Alice sat up, eyes shining. 'Do you *know* someone from Triphoppers. It's not Ashby is it? Do you know Ashby?' She dropped her magazine. 'He's *so* gorgeous. He's just ... incredible.'

'No,' said Stevie quickly. 'I don't know Ashby. I'm just thinking there might be a way to get someone from the band to come.'

'Really?' said Alice. 'That would be so cool! How are you going to do that?'

'I'm not sure yet.' Stevie frowned and pinched the bridge of her nose. 'I'm working on it.'

Of course, getting in touch with Pete would mean contacting Jane. Which would mean trying to act normal around Marsh. She wasn't sure she was up to that just yet.

It was Sunday and Stevie was at the house in Oxford again. She was standing in Evelyn's office, watching her rummaging around amongst the piles of paper on her desk.

Despite her increasing familiarity with the house, this was the first time Stevie had been in the office. It was a little room holding a desk, a phone/fax, a computer and several precarious looking stacks of paper. The room had once had a fireplace and still had a mantelpiece that now sheepishly framed the computer. On it were several photographs. The biggest was of a man, greying at the temples. He was shading his eyes and laughing into the sun. Stevie stepped closer to study it. He must have been Evelyn's husband. Next to it was a smaller photo of Evelyn, her late husband and her two sons. The resemblance between Tom and his father was unmistakable.

'That's my Frank,' said Evelyn, coming to stand next to her. The normal sparkle in her eyes dimmed a little. A small sigh escaped her.

Stevie recognised it. She felt something similar whenever she looked at the photo of herself, Marsh and her parents. 'You must miss him.'

'Every day.' She sighed again. 'This house ...' She waved a hand to indicate the rooms and corridors. 'It was his dream to rescue it and turn it into a place where people lived and moved again. He said it had seen too much to be allowed to live in its own echoes.' She walked slowly back to her desk. 'The boys think I should sell up and move to a small flat and maybe write text books, but ... I don't know. Working on the house, I can almost imagine he's still here, you know. Working on a different room. Sometimes I feel I can almost hear him. I can't listen to *Any Questions* anymore. I keep thinking I'll hear him explode and shout at the radio.' She smiled. 'He did that. Every time. He used to get so cross.' She stopped and looked out of the window, blinking.

Stevie felt tears threaten. 'I ... know what it's like.'

Evelyn turned blue eyes towards her. 'You do?' She gave Stevie a glance up and down. A glance that said 'What can someone as young as you know about loss?'

'My parents died when I was thirteen.' She'd said it so many times before that it no longer stung. What stung were the times when she forgot it and expected them to be waiting for her when she got home. Or when she opened her birthday cards and felt the lack of the one that was no longer there. 'I still miss them. Even after all these years.'

Evelyn looked away. 'I'm sorry.'

'Don't be.'

There was a moment of silence. Evelyn sniffed. 'Oh dear me.' She brushed a tear away with her palm. 'Excuse me a second. If the doorbell rings, will you answer it? It'll be Tom. He usually comes to visit on a Sunday.' With that, she scuttled out of the door.

Stevie stared after her. She hadn't meant to upset Evelyn. On the other hand, she knew it hadn't been her fault. Evelyn clearly missed her husband. She turned back to the mantelpiece and the photo of Tom. He hadn't made a very good impression on her the last time they met. He'd come across as arrogant and opinionated and he clearly didn't like her. On the other hand, he came to see his mother regularly and mowed the lawn for her. A man who did that couldn't be all bad, could he?

The doorbell rang. Should she answer the door? What if it wasn't Tom? It could be anyone. The bell rang again. She peered hopefully down the corridor. No sign of Evelyn.

The bell rang a third time, a little longer than before. The person outside was clearly getting impatient. Hesitantly Stevie trudged to the front, opened the door a crack and peered out.

It was Tom. Dressed in jeans and a rugby shirt, he looked casual and, frankly, gorgeous. 'About time,' he said. 'I was starting to get ...' He peered into the gap between the door and the frame. 'Oh,' he said. 'It's you.'

Stevie opened the door and let him in. 'Nice to see you too, Tom.'

'Where's my mother? And Alice?'

'Busy and out, respectively.' Stevie caught a whiff of aftershave as he brushed past. Despite her dislike of Tom, she couldn't resist a quick glance at his behind as he strode past. Nice.

'Uh-huh.' He paused in the hallway, as though trying to decide what to do.

Stevie frowned. She didn't particularly want to be friends with Tom, even without his attitude, he was distractingly attractive and she knew that sort of thing only interfered with a good working relationship, but if she was to get this ball to turn some sort of a profit, she was going to need his help.

'Tom, wait a moment.' She joined him. Her shadow fell across him as she got in the way of the light coming from the windows above the staircase. 'I know you don't like me. I'm not sure why.' She paused to see if he would reply to the implied question.

His eyes came up to her face briefly, then looked away. 'It's complicated.'

What kind of an answer was that? Stevie shrugged. 'Fine. I know you think I'm too young and inexperienced to do this job, but your mum hired me. You know as well as I do that I'm being paid well below the going rate, so I'm not trying to rip her off.' She took a step closer to him. He took a small step back. He was still glaring at the floor.

'But, if I'm going to be helping with this ball, it would be really nice if we could at least be civil to each other.'

Finally, he looked up. The corners of his mouth twitched. He thought she was funny? What a patronising git! Stevie swallowed her anger and offered him a hand. 'So, friends?'

'Okay.' Tom shook her hand. His grip was firm and warm.

Evelyn came hurrying down the stairs. 'Hello darling!'

'Hello Mother.' He kissed her on the cheek.

'Come and have a cuppa. We're just going to discuss things about the ball.'

Tom pulled a face, then glanced at Stevie and said, 'Okay. Fine. Anything to help.' He followed them meekly into the library.

The main thing Stevie needed from Tom, was help with the garden. She told him so.

He stared at her, frowning. 'The garden?'

'Yes. It's in desperate need of attention. The flower bushes need trimming, the herb garden needs sorting out. It's the sort of thing that would only take a few days to do, but it makes sense to sort out who's going to do it.' She looked expectantly at him.

'Me? I'm sorry Stevie, but I work. I can come and do bits for you on a Sunday, but that's as far as my commitment goes.'

'What about Saturdays?' She hadn't meant to ask that question out loud. She had been wondering what he did with himself outside of work, and the words just came out.

'I work on Saturdays.' He gave her a withering glare.

'What? Through choice?' Stevie couldn't believe anyone would do that.

Tom shrugged. 'What can I say? Married to my job.'

Stevie recovered her composure. Professional. She had to be professional. 'I'm sure we can manage with just Sundays. We can all pitch in.'

Tom didn't look pleased at the suggestion, but he sighed and agreed, in very bad grace, Stevie thought.

'Brilliant.' She gave him her most radiant smile, it usually mellowed people. He looked away.

Grumpy bugger.

From: Olivia Gornall

To: Tom Blackwood

Tom. Do you fancy a game of squash this eve? Stress relief. How'd it go showing the house to the lovely Vienna?

O

From: Tom Blackwood

To: Olivia Gornall

Vienna hasn't been yet. I'm planning on using her as an excuse to escape before mum ropes me in for more jobs. You know what it's like. There's no arguing with her.

I'm busy trying to stay out of the party planner's way. She keeps giving me things to do too.

From: Olivia Gornall

To: Tom Blackwood

Sounds like a right battleaxe.

From: Tom Blackwood

To: Olivia Gornall

That's the trouble, she's not a battleaxe. She's only twenty-two and very attractive. Trouble is, she doesn't seem to realise this. Today, she gave me a lecture on how it would be easier to get through the project if I was civil to her. She was standing in the light, wearing a thin cotton shirt and, with the sun shining behind her, I could see right through it. It was all I could do not to look.

Of course, she thought I was just being rude and avoiding eye contact.

From: Olivia Gornall

To: Tom Blackwood

So, ask her out then.

Of course, you'd have to let the lovely Vienna down gently.

From: Tom Blackwood

To: Olivia Gornall

I keep telling you. Vienna and I aren't an item. We just have a friendly arrangement, that's all. Friends with benefits, if you like.

I can't ask Stevie out. There's a bit of history there from a long time ago.

Gotta go. Vienna's here.

STEVIE AND ALICE WERE walking around the garden, making a list of jobs that needed to be done. It had once been beautiful, but had been left to itself for too long. The only things that had been cared for were the lawn and the gazebo, although closer inspection revealed that the benches inside the wooden structure were in need of attention. Stevie's planner's mind was whirring away, listing all the things that had to be done. Beyond the lawn was what would have been a rose garden and around the corner, the remains of a herb garden. Stevie stopped and breathed in the smell of rosemary and thyme. It was salvageable. It just needed work.

She was scribbling notes when there was a peal of feminine laughter. Both she and Alice looked up to where Tom was standing on the veranda outside the conservatory, talking to a woman with sleek blonde hair.

'Who's that?' Stevie whispered.

'That's Vienna. She's Uncle Tom's booty call.'

'His what?'

'Booty call. You know, dial-a-shag. They used to go out. Now they just meet up every so often for a shag.'

Stevie stared at Alice in disbelief. 'Really?' She looked back. Tom and the woman were coming down the metal steps into the garden. Vienna was wearing tight black jeans, a figure hugging white T-shirt and stilettos. Her hair was a perfect curtain of palest blonde. Her make-up was immaculate. Everything about her screamed 'city girl'.

As she watched, one of Vienna's heels got caught in the grillwork. Tom knelt down and gently freed it. Vienna laid a hand on his shoulder. The gesture was somehow intimate. Tom took her hand and helped her down the last couple of steps.

Yes. They're definitely sleeping together. For some reason, that irritated her.

'She's half Scandinavian,' Alice whispered.

That would explain the hair. She didn't even need to bleach it for it to look like that. Cow. Stevie lowered her head and focused at her clipboard. She was here to do a job. Not ogle the boss's son. 'We'd best carry on with the list.'

'Oh Tom, the house is simply da-arling!' Vienna's voice drifted across the lawn. 'And this garden, it's so charmingly wild. I love it. It's so ... atmospheric.'

'Charmingly wild,' Alice muttered. 'Why doesn't she just say "overgrown"? Silly bitch.'

Stevie eyed the tumbling petunias and bleeding heart flowers. 'Charmingly wild ... Do you think we could get away with that?'

'What? Calling things by stupid euphemisms?'

Stevie laughed. 'No, I meant having a part of the garden that looked a little wild. The lawn is pretty well kept. We can tidy the herb garden and the rose beds. But we could leave the path with the flowers on as it is, like we've done it on purpose.'

Alice looked across the lawn at the riot of blossoms. 'So there'd be lots of flowers for people to see.'

'The plants are so tall over there, you can barely see the house.' She pointed to the tangled mass of flowering shrubs at the opposite end from the gazebo. 'We could move the bench there and they could pretend they've wandered into a whole different world.' Alice's eyes sparkled. 'That sounds brilliant, Stevie.' She looked at her with frank admiration. Stevie suddenly felt awkward. Alice was only about fourteen and was clearly starting to see her as some sort of role model. Flattering though that was, Stevie didn't feel like a grown up. The idea that someone might consider her to be worth emulating was laughable.

'Stevie. Alice.' Tom was walking across the lawn, with Vienna tottering along behind him. 'Have you got any tickets for the ball? Vienna wants to buy one.'

'Alice? Your little niece, Alice?' said Vienna. 'Oh my goodness, you've grown. You were just a little girl when I last saw you.'

Alice gave Vienna a poisonous glare. 'People get older.' She looked Vienna up and down.

'Sad but true.' She smiled at Stevie and extended a hand. 'And you must be one of Alice's little friends. I'm Vienna.'

Stevie drew a sharp breath, too taken aback to shake the offered hand.

'This is Stevie. The new event organiser,' said Tom. 'We're hoping she will rescue the whole project and turn it round.'

Vienna gave Stevie an appraising look. 'Gosh. Sorry. You have such lovely young skin.' She flicked her hair back over her shoulder. 'So you'll be the girl with the tickets, then?' She gave Stevie a winning smile. Clearly, she'd reassessed Stevie as an adult and decided that she was no threat. 'I've got an early meeting the next day, so I won't be able to stay the whole night.' She looked meaningfully up at Tom. 'But I'd love to support such a good cause.'

'Of course. I always carry a ticket book with me, as it happens.' She whipped a booklet out of her shoulder bag. 'Just the one ticket? Or will you be bringing a friend?'

'No, just the one.' Vienna grinned, showing perfect teeth. 'My usual date will be here already.' She put her hand on Tom's arm.

Tom's smile looked a little uncomfortable.

Later that day, Priya came round with a list of ingredients that she needed for the Sri Lankan snacks. 'They're all available from a place in Cricklewood, in London,' she said. 'I can make the order by phone and make sure they have everything ready, but I'll need someone to pick it up.'

Stevie was gazing out of the window. Vienna had left and Tom was mowing the lawn. It was a hot afternoon, so his rugby top lay crumpled on the steps. His iPod was clipped to his waist and looked almost luminous white against his tan. She watched his muscled back as he pushed the mower up and down. He had a very nice back. Why was it that all the nice-looking men in the world were either taken or grumpy buggers. Or, in Tom's case, both.

Stevie sighed. Still, there was nothing wrong with admiring him from afar, was there.

'Stevie?'

Stevie jumped. 'Sorry Priya,' she said, turning round. 'I was thinking about the garden. What was that?'

Priya repeated what she'd said and handed her the list. Stevie scanned through. There was quite a lot of stuff. It looked like it would be heavy. She wouldn't possibly be able to carry all that back from London on the bus. She said so.

'Oh dear,' said Priya. 'What can we do?'

'I could hire a car,' Stevie suggested.

'Tom's got a car,' said Evelyn. 'He can pick it up. And give you a lift too, next Sunday. You can save on bus fare.'

While the idea made sense, that would mean that Stevie and Tom would be stuck in the same car for a long time. Somehow, Stevie didn't think he'd go for that. 'Shouldn't we ask him if he minds?'

'Oh yes. Hang on.' Evelyn struggled with the sash window and got it open. She leaned her thin torso far out of it.

Stevie had sudden visions of the sash window crashing down and chopping Evelyn in half. She hastily put a hand on the window, ready to catch it if it slipped.

'Tom,' Evelyn hollered. 'Oi, Tom!' She waved her arms to get his attention.

Tom paused, removed his earphones and stopped the mower. 'Yes?'

'Come here a minute, we've got to ask you something.'

He nodded. Much to Stevie's disappointment, he re-trieved his T-shirt. She caught a glimpse of an impressively toned stomach as he pulled it over his head, and then he was covered up.

'What's up?' Tom sauntered into the library a minute later, bringing the smell of freshly cut grass with him. 'Oh, hi Priya.'

'We need someone to pick this stuff up from a place in Cricklewood.' Evelyn took the list off Stevie and pushed it into Tom's hand. 'Priya will get them to have the whole order ready. All you'd have to do is pick it up.'

Tom frowned as he scanned the list. 'Okay.'

'Oh, and you can give Stevie a lift in. It's pointless her spending all that money on the bus when you're coming here anyway.'

'I can get to the shop early and check that the order is all there,' suggested Stevie quickly.

'In fact,' said Evelyn. 'Why don't you give Stevie a lift home tonight? There's no point her sitting on a bus when you're going the same way.'

'Oh, no,' Stevie protested. Spending hours trapped in a car with a handsome man who thought she was a brainless child was fine when there was a good reason, like her needing a car to get the stuff to Oxford. To do it with no good reason was just madness. 'It would be out of your way.'

'You don't know where Tom lives. How can you know it's out of his way,' Evelyn pointed out. 'Besides, you can tell Tom all about the plans you have for the garden and advertising and things. He might be able to add some helpful sug-gestions.'

Yeah, right. Tom Blackwood, offer her helpful sugges-tions. Like that was going to happen.

Tom looked like he was going to argue, then looked at his mother and sighed. 'Fine. Where do you live?'

With Evelyn standing over her, Stevie had no choice but to tell him.

He sighed again. 'That's not out of my way,' he said with no trace of enthusiasm in his voice. 'I'll give you a lift.'

'No really, you don't need me intruding on your down time,' said Stevie, trying to give him an out. 'I'll be fine on the bus. I've got a weekly ticket anyway.'

Tom glanced at her. She thought she caught a glimmer of something in his eyes. Relief, probably. 'Are you sure?'

'Absolutely.'

Tom turned to Evelyn. 'If you don't mind, Mum, I'm go-ing to head off as soon as I've finished the lawn. I've got a pretty important interview tomorrow and I need to prepare.'

'If you don't know what you're going to say by now, you won't learn it overnight,' said Evelyn. 'But you should get some rest, so that you're nice and sharp tomorrow.'

Tom practically ran out.

Stevie couldn't help but feel slightly offended. He hadn't even bothered to pretend that he'd like to give her a lift. She shook her head and turned her thoughts back to the tasks at hand. The less time she spent thinking about Tom Black-wood the better.

Chapter Seven

THE INTERVIEW COULDN'T have gone any better. Tom's ideas about expansion in the Middle East had led to a number of the panel, including the VP, nodding in agreement.

Tom managed to keep his excitement reined in until he'd left the building. Once he was a few yards away, he stopped and punched the air. *Yes!* He'd like to see Dhidre top that. He grinned, feeling tension unravelling by the minute. A celebratory coffee and little break reading a newspaper was in order. He couldn't exactly celebrate with his work colleagues, so maybe Og would be up for a drink after work.

Letting out a whoosh of breath, he entered a coffee shop. Of course, the outcome of the interview wasn't a given. He shouldn't underestimate Dhidre. She might just pull a rabbit out of a hat. She was very bright, if devoid of any personality.

Tom sighed. Maybe it was best if he got his coffee and returned to work.

The idea planted during her conversation with Alice had been growing slowly in Stevie's mind. The only thing that was causing her pause was the fact that she would have to talk to Jane. Still, there was less than two weeks left before the ball, so if she was going to do it, it would have to be now. She took a deep breath and punched out her brother's number. No, she reminded herself, it wasn't just Marsh's number. It was Jane's home too. And would soon be the baby's.

Jane answered after two rings.

'It's Stevie.'

There was a pause. 'Stevie. How are you? We've been worried about you.'

'I'm fine thanks. How are you? Everything still going okay with the baby?'

Jane gave a little sigh. 'Yes. We've got another scan coming up soon. We'll be able to see more then. But so far, touch wood, it all seems to be okay. No more scares.'

'That's good.' The rush of relief that the baby was okay, surprised her. She hadn't even realised she'd been worried. Stevie cast about for more pregnancy related chit-chat. There were standard questions you were supposed to ask, but she couldn't think of any. She should have Googled this before phoning Jane.

'Stevie.' Jane took what sounded like a deep breath. 'I'm so sorry about what happened. You really shouldn't blame Marsh for not telling you. He wanted to. I asked him not to. If you're angry with anyone, it should be me.'

Stevie closed her eyes with the effort of not responding the way she wanted to. She and Marsh had argued before and they'd always worked it out between them. That was easier when Marsh had time for her. Which he no longer did now that he was married. Jane didn't need to know about all that. She had enough on her plate without adding Stevie to her problems. Whatever there was to discuss, would have to be discussed with Marsh. Through gritted teeth, Stevie said, 'I understand.'

'Good.' The relief in Jane's voice was clear, even over the phone. 'Marsh is out at the moment. He'll be really glad that you phoned. Are you at home? He'd love to talk to you.'

'Actually, Jane. It's not Marsh I wanted to talk to. It's you.'

'Me?'

'I ... er ... need a favour.' She knew this was a very cheeky thing to be doing, but was going to do it anyway. She needed this gig to go well. It might be the springboard to the whole of her career. Before Jane could reply, she ploughed on. 'I'm organising this charity ball in Oxford. It's to raise money for a children's hospital in Sri Lanka. Maybe even equip the baby care unit ...' She was hoping to appeal to Jane's maternal instincts.

'I know. Louise told us.'

'I need to do some publicity work. And I was hoping you could put me in touch with your friend Pete.'

'Pete? What do you need Pete for?' For someone who was normally so on the ball, Jane was being really dim.

Stevie rolled her eyes. 'I was hoping I could persuade him to come. That would be great publicity for us and it would look good for him too.'

'You want me to give you Pete's private number, so that you can rope him into doing some free publicity for you?'

That wasn't quite how Stevie would have put it, but it did cover what she meant. 'In a manner of speaking. Yes.'

'And you might happen to mention the fact to a couple of magazines, maybe?'

'Er ... maybe.'

'No.' There was no hesitation in Jane's voice. 'No way.'

'But Jane ...'

'Stevie, you know how I feel about the press. I can't let you throw Pete to the press hounds like that.'

In the past Jane had been the focus of a magazine campaign. It had caused her untold grief and had nearly ruined her relationship with Marsh. However, Stevie felt it was a little unfair of Jane to assume that everyone else felt the same way about the press as she did.

'Jane, Triphoppers aren't doing as well as they used to. You hardly hear anything about them these days. Besides, isn't Pete trying to launch a solo career? He might relish the chance to raise his profile a little bit. Maybe rebrand himself as a more grown up celeb with a social conscience. I know his lyrics have been tending towards more serious subjects.'

'No, Stevie.'

Stevie sighed. 'Okay. Okay. I'm sorry I asked. I just thought you'd be able to help out, you know, with it being my first job. Now I know otherwise. That's fine.'

'Don't try to guilt trip me, Stevie. That's not fair.'

What's not fair is you pushing me out of my own brother's life.

She didn't say anything. The silence stretched a little beyond a comfortable gap in the conversation.

'I'll tell Marsh to call you as soon as he gets back,' Jane said.

'Actually, I'm going to be quite busy in the next couple of weeks. I have to try and drum up some support for this ball somehow. Tell Marsh I'll call him sometime after.'

'Stevie ...'

Stevie hung up.

TOM CHECKED FOR LAST minute emails. None. Now that he was certain that his projections for the next phase were up to date, he saved the latest version of the presentation for the Pickering project onto his USB stick. He had barely slept the night before and the pressure around his head was barely kept at bay by the strongest painkillers he'd managed to buy. Pocketing the USB stick, he grabbed the file and went up to the meeting.

Dhidre was already there. Talking to ... Matthias Groenberger. Matthias spotted Tom and nodded a greeting.

'Ah, Tom,' he said. 'I thought I would come and see the close of this important project. It is always good to see how things are going on the ground level.'

Tom glanced at Dhidre, who gave him a polite smile and took her seat. He understood. Matthias had come to observe him and Dhidre in action. This meeting had now become part of the interview to find out which one of them was going to Doha.

'Of course,' he said. 'Great idea. Excuse me. I'll just make sure my presentation is loaded up.'

While he was checking on the presentation, Og walked in. She introduced herself to Matthias and told him that she was there from legal to handle the actual contract.

Reception called through to say their visitors had arrived. Both Tom and Dhidre sprang to their feet, but Og beat them to it and went to meet the visitors.

The meeting went smoothly. Tom was surprised that Dhidre hadn't tried to cut across him or undermine him. He was careful to be courteous to her in return. The tension gripped him tighter and tighter with each passing minute. He rose to give his presentation. He covered the salient points swiftly. He could see the client looked pleased and Matthias was nodding. His shoulders loosened a fraction. Just the projections now.

He had turned towards the projector screen to point at the diagram, so it took him a few seconds to realise that something wasn't right. He turned. The atmosphere had changed. The relaxed faces now wore frowns. Tom stopped talking. 'Is something wrong?'

'Those are the old timelines,' said one of the clients. 'We asked for new projections based on the up to date timelines.'

What? He had checked. There had been no changes. 'These are the most recent timelines we have ...'

'No. We sent them in ...' he tapped into his phone. '... last week.'

'But I have no record—'

'It's okay. I have them,' said Dhidre. 'Perhaps, we should move on to my presentation. I'm sure we can sort this out.' She stood up and approached the laptop at the front.

Tom stared at her. The air felt thin. His head throbbed. 'How can you have the new details, if I don't?'

Dhidre lifted her chin. 'I'm sure I sent them to you Tom.'

'You did NOT!' Tom's hand slammed onto the table. The crash was loud enough to break through the throbbing noise that had filled his head. There was a gasp and movement. He looked up to see that he'd upset one of the glasses of water on the table, the contents of which was dripping off the edge and onto the leg of one of the visitors.

His gaze flew to Matthias, who had leapt forward with napkins to soak up the water. Then to Og, who was staring at him, eyes wide. Mouth an O.

'Are you okay Tom?'

He turned to see Dhidre, gazing at him with apparent concern.

'Perhaps you should take a moment ...' she said, smiling at him.

He opened his mouth. There was nothing he could say that wouldn't make things worse. She had stitched him up. He closed his mouth, jaws clenched.

'Yes,' said Matthias. 'Perhaps that is a good idea.'

Tom nodded, mumbled his apologies and left. Out of the meeting room. Out of the office. Out of the building. He kept walking until he came to a stop outside a small coffee shop. It was relatively quiet at that time of day. He ordered himself a coffee and flapjack, found a seat as far from the front as he could and buried his head in his hands. He'd blown it. Not only had be screwed up the last meeting with the Pickering project, he'd completely wrecked his chances of getting the job in Doha. He dropped his head on the desk and swore into his hands. His phone vibrated as a message arrived.

Olivia:

All okay?

He responded to say he was. Another message from her told him that Dhidre had given an impressive presentation (with up to date projections) and that the meeting had gone relatively well.

Tom groaned. Of course she had.

Tom:

Bloody Dhidre. Masterstroke of epic deviousness. She deserves to win.

Olivia:

Yes, well you didn't do yourself any favours with your reaction. What the actual F***, Tom? Get your arse back in here and sort it out. The longer you leave it. The worse it's going to look.

She was right. Tom groaned and dropped his head back onto the table again.

THE MORE SHE THOUGHT about it, the more annoyed Stevie got with Jane for not letting her have Pete's contact details. Surely, it wasn't up to Jane to police how Pete conducted his publicity. It was almost as though Jane didn't want Stevie to succeed in her venture. She pulled up the Triphoppers website. There was, of course, another way to get in touch.

From: Stevie Winfield

To: Pete Gosling

Subject: From Jane Porter's sister-in-law

Hi Pete

Apologies for emailing you through the fan club site, but I didn't know how else to get hold of you. I met you at Marshall Winfield and Jane Porter's wedding. You said to contact you if you could help with anything.

I have a suggestion for you, it could generate some valuable publicity for a very good cause (specifically, Project PEDS, which aims to raise money to equip a children's hospital in Sri Lanka.)

It would also be a nice way to improve your profile as a more thoughtful and caring person, rather than some airhead pop star (and, from having spoken to you at length at the wedding, I know you're not a shallow person!)

If you're interested, please get in touch with me as soon as possible. My contact details are attached.

Best Regards

Stevie Winfield

It was a long shot to email Pete at the website. Chances were that some junior minion would read it and bung back a standard email reply. On the other hand, Jane's name would hold some clout. The whole saga of *Cause Celeb* magazine's campaign to get Jane and the Triphoppers' lead singer Ashby back together had been instrumental in getting their second album catapulted up the charts. As an interested observer, Stevie had watched countless interviews of the band and the *Cause Celeb*/Jane issue got almost as much coverage as the music. Stevie leaned back in her chair and took a sip of wine. She'd set the ball rolling. All she could do now was wait and hope it would have the desired result.

OG CAME ROUND FOR A quick visit after work, bearing a bottle of wine. Tom got down a couple of glasses and poured the wine. It suddenly occurred to him that he hadn't used his kitchen for anything more that making a bowl of cereal in a long time.

'So, what's going on?' said Og. 'Dhidre's spreading rumours that you've had a nervous breakdown.'

Tom handed her a glass and took his out into the living room. He had bought the furniture in the place off the previous owner, who had been moving to the US. It was furnished in standard vanilla for a bachelor's flat. Black leather sofas, chrome legged tables, big TV stand. He'd not bothered changing anything. He didn't need to.

'Dhidre's not totally wrong,' he said. 'The doc offered to sign me off for stress, but I can't do that. I may as well start wearing a big sticker staying "unstable mental case" on my forehead as far as my job prospects are concerned. So, I've taken two weeks off as holiday instead.' He sank into the sofa. 'It has been suggested that I access the company's counselling service for anger management counselling.'

Og shrugged. 'Maybe a break will help.' She took a big sip of wine. 'Don't worry about Dhidre. I'll spread a counter rumour that you're off building hospitals in Africa.'

'I bet they'd prefer the "Tom's cracking up" line.'

'Nah. No one likes Dhidre.' Og waved her glass dismissively. 'They know she stitched you up. No one can trust her now.'

'Doesn't matter. She'll be off to Doha soon.' *Aargh.*

'Never mind that. How are you going to spend your glorious time off?' said Og. 'Exotic holiday?'

Tom flopped back against the cushions. Two weeks stretched ahead of him like a black tunnel. 'I could do that,' he said. 'But I'll only go obsess about this stuff somewhere else then. And drink far too much.'

'Why don't you stay home for a bit. Take some of those hefty pills the doc gave you and catch up on your sleep. You don't have anything to get up for.'

'Actually, I do have something to get up for. I promised Mum I'd drive some stuff up to Oxford for her.'

'Ooh, I know,' said Og, sitting up straight. 'Why don't you go spend the time at your mum's house. A change is as good as a holiday, right? You need a break. What better way to get that than to spend a week with some barmy old ladies who are organising a ball?'

'For a start, that ghastly Beryl woman might turn up. She gives me a headache anyway, even without the stress and sleep deprivation. Also, Stevie will be there and I don't want to see any more of her than I have to.' He glanced across at

Og and caught her puzzled expression. 'You remember my housemate at uni, Marshall?'

Og grinned. 'How could I forget. The delectable Marshall. I'd have loved to have corrupted him.'

Tom rolled his eyes. 'You tried, remember? Anyway. Stevie is Marsh's sister. You remember what happened the last time I got anywhere near Marshall's sister.'

Og winced. 'I see.' She took another sip of wine. 'I can't see how you're going to avoid her though. You'll be going to the ball.'

'Yeah, but there'll be lots of other people there. And Vienna will be around to keep me on the straight and narrow.'

'Oh yes. I'd forgotten about her.' Og pulled a sour face.

'Do you want to come to the ball?' asked Tom.

'Sure. Why not. You know I love supporting whatever crazy cause Evelyn's supporting.' Og looked at the wall clock. 'I'd better get going,' she said, draining her glass. 'I've got a hot date.' She stood up. 'A second date, no less.'

'Wow. For you, that's quite a commitment.' He rose too and followed her to the door. 'Must be a special guy.'

Og laughed. 'Not that special. Good for fun.' She grabbed her handbag and coat. 'Tom,' she said, her face suddenly serious. 'Look after yourself. Go see you mother. Don't spend two weeks by yourself.'

He looked away. 'I'll think about it.'

Chapter Eight

ON SUNDAY, STEVIE ARRIVED at the shop early. A heavily pregnant young Sri Lankan woman was sitting at the counter, leafing through a baby clothes catalogue. 'Ah yes, Priya's order. It's all here, in the back.'

'Congratulations,' said Stevie indicating the bump. Goodness, the girl was huge. Was Jane going to end up looking like that? What on earth would that do to her figure?

The woman gave her a tired smile. Stevie realised, with some surprise, that this young woman wasn't much older than she was.

'Come, come,' the girl said. 'You need to check that everything is as Priya wanted.' She ushered Stevie into the back room of the shop where several boxes were on a table, with Priya's list on top of them.

It took a few minutes to go through the list. They removed everything from each box then counted it back in again, ticking it off as they went. The smell of spices wafted from the various packets. It was a good job Priya knew how to cook with this stuff. If nothing else, this job would teach her some new recipes. Her repertoire tended to be heavily pasta based.

She was almost done when the shop bell rang. The girl waddled out. She returned a moment later. 'There's a man here. He also says he's here to collect Priya's order ...' She looked doubtfully at Stevie.

'That'll be Tom,' said Stevie. 'He's okay.'

Tom entered, instantly making the room feel smaller. He nodded towards Stevie and gave the woman a warm smile. 'Hi. I'm Tom.'

She gave him a flustered smile. 'Here are the boxes.' She got out of the way, glancing sideways shyly at him. Stevie blinked. This must be Tom in charming mode. The woman moved to pick up a box.

'I'll do that. You shouldn't be lifting stuff, you're carrying enough already.' Tom grabbed a box and closed it. The girl gave a little giggle and retreated back into the shop.

'Stevie,' Tom said, not looking up. 'Can you settle the bill, please?'

Stevie sighed and returned to the shop. Evelyn had given her money to pay for everything the night before. Not used to carrying that much cash around, Stevie had felt like she had a neon 'mug me' sign attached to her jeans pocket all morning. It was a relief to hand the cash over.

After giving Stevie a receipt, the girl glanced at the door to the stock room. 'Is that your boyfriend?' she whispered.

'No!' Stevie was taken aback. 'Definitely not.'

'Shame,' said the girl. 'You two would make a cute couple.'

Before Stevie could reply, Tom emerged carrying a box. He rested it against the counter and freed one of his hands, which he used to dig out his car keys. 'Here,' he tossed them to Stevie. 'Can you open the back door of the car? It's the black one parked outside.'

The car turned out to be a black sports car. 'I'm not sure I'll be able to fit it all into the boot,' said Tom. Sure enough, the tiny boot only had enough room for about half the stuff. Tom sighed and put the latest box down on the pavement. 'The rest will have to go in the back seat.' He opened the door, put down the front seat and manoeuvred a box in, presenting Stevie with an admirable view of his jeans-clad behind.

She didn't even realise she was staring until he started backing out and asked her to pass him another box. She did so, blushing slightly. She looked up to see the shopkeeper raise her eyebrows and wink at her.

As they drove out of London, she noticed how the car smelled of a disconcerting combination of leather and spices. She took a deep breath.

'It's going to take me forever to get the smell out,' Tom grumbled. He overtook someone aggressively, weaving out at top speed.

Stevie clutched the edge of her seat and didn't reply.

Tom cast a glance at her. 'What?' He pulled back in sharply, making Stevie gasp.

'I'm ... a little nervous in cars,' said Stevie. 'My parents died in a car accident.'

'Oh, shit. Sorry.' He slowed down a fraction. 'I forgot. I always drive like that. I'm very careful though. Never had an accident.'

Stevie nodded. 'Right,' she said faintly.

After a while, she started to relax. Tom was making an effort to drive smoothly. Now that she'd stopped holding her breath, Stevie became more aware of her surroundings. The sports car was lower than most vehicles she was used to and the bucket seats made her lean back slightly. This stretched Tom's limbs out so that she was treated to a good view of his long legs. A brief vision of him mowing the lawn crossed her mind. Tom, who had been concentrating on overtaking gently, gave her a quick glance. She turned away, flustered.

'So,' said Tom. 'What have you been doing since the bad old days?'

'Since I was thirteen, you mean?' said Stevie. 'School, uni. The usual.'

'Are you still living with Marsh?'

Stevie laughed. 'God no! He's married now. I live by myself.' Did she imagine it, or did Tom's shoulders just relax a tiny bit?

'Marsh got married?' said Tom. 'I didn't know that. I guess we aren't really in touch after ...'

'After I got stoned in your room?' Stevie grinned. She remembered it well. People kept telling her that one of the great advantages of having an older brother was the access to older boys. But when they were eight years older than you, they treated you like you were an irritating insect. Besides, her brother was Marsh and all his friends were ... Well, a bit boring.

Tom had been different, even then. Even with the stupid hair and the gangly limbs, there had been something cool about him. A sort of fire in him that made him that extra little bit sexy. He hadn't bothered being super nice to her or treated her like she was made of glass, like everyone else did after her parents died. He had just acknowledged her exis-

tence and carried on treating her as though she was just another normal person.

Thirteen years old and vulnerable, Stevie immediately
developed a huge crush on him. Marsh had guessed this,
which went part way towards his incandescent outburst
when he found her stoned out of her mind and semi-con-
scious in Tom's room.

Stevie risked another glance across at Tom. She had been
right, even as a teenager. He was sexy. Even more so now that
he'd grown into his body.

'Has Marsh got over that yet?' said Tom.

'What? The getting stoned thing? Yeah. I think so. He
gave me hell about it at the time though.' Stevie smiled to
herself. 'You should have heard him go on. We had a spectac-
ular row about it.'

Tom nodded. 'And then you both moved out of the student house.'

'Yeah.'

There was silence as they both followed their trains of
thought. After a while, the silence began to feel like it was
settling in for a long wait.

Stevie cleared her throat. 'What happened to him – the
guy with the space cake?'

'Jeremy the Spliff?' said Tom. 'He's a surgeon now. Urology, I think.'

Stevie contemplated the thought of spaced out Jeremy
the Spliff being in charge of opening up people's private parts
and stitching them back together. The thought was so hor-
rifying it was almost funny. 'Urology? I'd have thought you
need a steady hand for that sort of thing.' She giggled.

Tom grinned. 'Well, I wouldn't trust him anywhere near mine.'

Stevie laughed. 'Mind you, I bet he needs a smoke after looking at that sort of thing all day.'

They both started to laugh. Tom had a nice laugh, a deep chuckle that somehow managed to warm Stevie up from the inside. The atmosphere inside the car changed subtly. Tom turned the radio on. Stevie glanced at him as he hummed along to the music. He seemed to be slowly uncoiling from the tightly wound state he was normally in. Perhaps she had misjudged him. Perhaps he was just a nice guy who was a bit stressed out.

Outside, the traffic slowed down, forcing Tom to decelerate. He scowled and muttered under his breath. Okay, thought Stevie. Perhaps not then.

Tom staggered in under yet another fragrant cardboard box. 'That's the last of it,' he said, plonking it down on the long table at the centre of the kitchen. 'I'll just go lock the car and come back to help.'

Priya had everyone organised from the minute the stuff arrived. She was unloading packets and jars, reading out labels and descriptions to Alice, who cross checked the list and sorted everything into piles.

The whole room smelled of cinnamon and coriander. It was making Stevie hungry. She had already been allocated the task of peeling several bags of onions that were going to be fed into the food processor. She decided to peel them all first and chop them later, not wanting to have sore eyes for any longer than she had to. She was sitting on one of the benches that lined the table with two piles of onions and a bucket for the peelings lined up in front of her. She snapped on the blue latex gloves that Priya insisted on everyone wearing.

Evelyn sat next to her, cheerfully peeling her way through several hundred cloves of garlic.

When Tom returned, he was given some root ginger and told to get chopping.

'As small as you can.' Priya smiled and handed him a knife.

Tom dropped into a seat opposite Stevie and bent over his work.

As she peeled onion after onion, her attention wandered. Her gaze drifted towards Tom's hands as he peeled and chopped. She couldn't help noticing that his hands gave the occasional tremor, making him pause in his work so that he didn't chop off a finger. Odd.

She looked up at his face. He was frowning, concentrating on what he was doing, so didn't notice her scrutiny. His eyes looked pinched and had dark shadows under them. His mouth was turned down at the corners. A general aura of unhappiness hung around him. How had she not noticed it before? She had spent the whole car journey trying not to stare at his profile and, admittedly, being rather distracted by his legs. Now that she had paid attention to his face, it was obvious something was wrong.

She looked around to see if anyone else had noticed. Evelyn was talking about the seminar she had to give later in the week and seemed to be oblivious to any change in her son. Alice was too busy helping Priya to pay much attention to her uncle. So it seemed that only Stevie had noticed. She glanced at his hands again. Yes, there was a definite tremor. Not all the time, but often enough.

Suddenly Tom's hands stopped moving.

Stevie looked up to find him staring at her.

'What?' he whispered.

'Are you okay?' Stevie whispered back. She glanced at his hands again.

He clenched them into fists. 'Yes thanks.'

'You look tired.'

She must have spoken louder than she intended because Evelyn said, 'What's that? Oh, I say, she is right, darling. You look shocking. Are you alright?'

Tom gave Stevie a glare that said *See what you've done now*. 'Yes, I'm fine. I've just not been sleeping very well lately. That's all.'

'You work too hard, darling. You should ease up a bit. Maybe take a few days off. I mean, when was the last time you had a whole weekend off? Including the Saturday?'

'Mum—'

'It's not good for you to work six days a week like that. Not for so long at a stretch anyway. Honestly, if I didn't drag you down here on the odd Sunday, you'd work the whole seven days.'

Evelyn reached for another head of garlic. 'I used to have the same problem with your father. Once that man started on something, it was nigh on impossible to get him to take a break.'

Her focus shifted back to the present. 'He suffered from terrible headaches you know. They disappeared completely once he retired though, which just goes to show.'

Tom's brow had furrowed even further. He removed his blue gloves and rested his fingers against his temples. 'Mum?' When Evelyn didn't appear to hear him, he practically shouted, 'Mother?'

'Yes?' Evelyn raised her head. 'There's no need to shout darling, I'm just here.'

'Mum.' Tom sighed. 'I am taking a few days off. A whole two weeks in fact. Okay?'

'Oh, you never mentioned.' Evelyn turned her attention to her cloves of garlic again. 'What are you going to do with all that time? Not go skiing I hope. Not after what happened to poor Olivia. How is she, by the way? Is she back at work?'

Tom sighed again. 'Yes.'

'Terribly dangerous, skiing,' Evelyn continued, without looking up from her work. 'So, what are you doing in those two weeks?'

Stevie's gaze swung back to Tom, who looked uncomfortable.

'Um ... Week after next, I've got a couple of things to do in London. Next week, I'm just going to chill out. In the flat.'

Evelyn finally looked up. 'In that little flat, for a whole week? You'll go mad with boredom. Tell you what, why don't you come and help us out with the ball. There's an awful lot that needs to be done in the garden. You could get that sorted out faster than any of us could.'

Everyone looked at Tom. He scowled at his pile of ginger.

'Evelyn, that wouldn't be very relaxing, would it?' Priya spoke mildly. 'I know my daughters' idea of relaxing is sitting in front of a rom-com and eating popcorn.'

Alice chuckled in agreement.

'It'll be a complete change of scene,' said Evelyn. 'That's what holidays are all about.' She gave her son a radiant smile. 'What about it Tom? It would be a great help.'

She turned to Stevie. 'Wouldn't it, Stevie?'

Stevie jumped, surprised to be included in the conversation. She felt sorry for Tom. It was clear that he wasn't going to get out of staying and helping with the ball. She was sure he didn't want to. He probably had plans with that Vienna woman. On the other hand, the garden did need a lot of work and it would solve a range of problems if Tom were to sort it out. Besides, thought a small, less professional part of her, it would mean more opportunities to see Tom with his shirt off. She nodded and gave Tom an apologetic smile.

He glowered at her.

'Excellent. That's settled then,' said Evelyn cheerfully. 'You can have one of the upstairs rooms. Best save the good rooms until the night of the ball. We might have a few guests staying overnight.'

She gasped as though struck by an idea. 'Come to think of it, Stevie, why don't you stay here too? It's silly to have you bussing to and fro when there are perfectly good rooms you can use here. You can have the old flower room? It's pretty self-contained, so you'll have lots of privacy.'

Stevie felt at a loss for words. It was knackering, catching the bus in every day. Staying over in such a beautiful place would be beyond wonderful. But it seemed a little above her professional role to be accepted as a houseguest. 'Oh, I couldn't possibly accept—'

Evelyn waved her objections away. 'Don't be silly. It would be a pleasure. Besides, we'll be paying for all those bus rides, so we may as well save the money. And it'll be so much easier for you to get things done when you can get hold of any of us whenever you want to.'

The small part of her that was wired to her libido pointed out that would mean seeing Tom every day. What a fantastic accompaniment to one's morning Weetabix. She told herself to stop it.

There was a lot of truth in what Evelyn had said. It would make sense for her to stay. Evelyn was clearly waiting for a response. 'If you're sure. That would be lovely. Thank you.'

'That's settled then,' said Evelyn. 'Tom can give you a lift back to London tonight and bring you back here tomorrow.'

Stevie glanced at Tom, and saw him draw a rebellious breath.

'Actually,' he said, 'I've got plans in Oxford for tonight. I'm meeting Vienna for a drink at the Randolph.'

There was a small silence. Stevie's mind filled in the implication that he'd either be leaving Oxford very late, or staying over in Vienna's hotel room.

'I'm fine on the bus,' said Stevie. 'Honestly.'

Stevie didn't recognise the number on her phone, but she answered it anyway.

'Is that Stevie Winfield?' a woman said.

'Yes. Who am I speaking to?'

'My name's Sharon of MST publicity. I'm phoning regarding a message you sent to Pete Gosling, about a charity ball.'

Her heart picked up speed. If she could get some sort of celebrity endorsement, even if it was just Pete, without the rest of the band, she could shift some of those tickets that were cluttering up Evelyn's desk. 'Yes. How can I help?'

'I was after more information, really. How high profile is this event?'

'The charity itself is international, but the profile of the event is fairly select. It caters for the tasteful end of the charity ball circuit. The venue is a beautiful stately home on the outskirts of Oxford and the ball will be attended by a high brow mix of Oxford literati.' Stevie rattled off the statement that she'd been preparing for just this eventuality. She hoped it sounded competent and not too forced. She also hoped that Evelyn would forgive her for calling the house a stately home, although it certainly would have fit in with the National Trust.

'Okay.' The woman sounded like she was writing it all down.

'We thought that Pete might find such an event would fit in well with his new image of being a lyrical poet and an altogether more grown up celebrity figure. I know he turned down a stint in *I'm a Celebrity* because he wasn't that desperate, so this might be just the sort of thing he wants his name associated with.'

'Right.' Another pause. 'And what sort of press coverage are you likely to get?'

'Well, we're in discussions with a number of publications at the moment,' Stevie crossed her fingers and hoped she wouldn't be struck down by lightning for lying.

'So you have no actual press coverage arranged at the moment?' The note of disdain in her voice was unmissable. Stevie sensed the opportunity slipping away.

'Actually,' she said quickly. 'We do have at least one press person coming.' She took a deep breath. '*Cause Celeb*.'

'Ah.' The quickening of interest was palpable. 'Is that a reporter only? Or a photographer as well?'

'Um ... both, I believe.'

'Okay. Thank you for all the information you've given me, I'll have to get back to you.'

'So, is Pete going to be coming then?'

'Like I said, we'll get back to you. Thanks. Bye.' The woman hung up.

Stevie disconnected the call and stared at the phone. She hadn't even tried phoning any magazines and press, apart from the local ones. Oh dear.

Picking up her notebook she flicked through until she found the number of *Cause Celeb*. Marsh would kill her if she contacted them. But in her panic, she'd just told Pete's publicist that they would be there. Sighing, she dialled the number.

'*Cause Celeb*.'

'Hi, I'm phoning to tell you about a charity ball in Ox—'

'I'm afraid we're mostly interested in celebrity sightings and events that involve celebrities ...'

'Yes, that's why I'm phoning. Pete Gosling is going to be coming. He endorses the charity and the work they do.'

'Pete Gosling? From Triphoppers?'

'Yes. That's him.'

'Is Ashby going to be there?'

'At the moment, it's just Pete, but you never know, Ashby might come round to it.'

'Can you give me dates and times and I'll see what we can do,' said the girl.

Stevie gave her the information.

Phew. That had been easier than she'd thought. Now she just needed the Triphoppers' publicist to agree to send Pete along and she'd be well away.

Chapter Nine

EVER SINCE HER DRIVE up to Oxford in his car, Stevie's feelings towards Tom had been oscillating. On the one hand, he was arrogant and treated her like she was young and incompetent. On the other hand, once he let his guard down, he could be quite nice. He was undeniably handsome in a way that made her stomach tingle every time she saw him.

She had felt that way about men before. They had all ended up being unsuitable for her. Her last serious boyfriend, Buzz, had been the sexiest man in the world, but he turned out to be a money-grabbing rat fink. Since then, she'd had a string of hot, but not serious boyfriends, which worked out fine, so long as neither party wanted more. The trouble was, now that she was out of the university environment and trying to be a grown up, the idea of a fling no longer held as much appeal.

She was standing by her bed, with a bag open in front of her, trying to pack for a week away in Oxford. It was difficult knowing what to pack. She was there to work, so comfortable old clothes were a good idea.

Stevie sighed again and scanned the flat. Even though the summer sun was starting to fade, the building was still warm. If the weather continued to be this good for the ball, it would be lovely.

She chucked a few light blouses in on top of her jeans. It could get quite hot if she ended up helping in the garden. Or even the kitchen. And she looked good in them. Of course, she wasn't seriously interested in Tom. But it didn't hurt to look nice. It could do wonders for her self-confidence.

She was carefully folding her gown, bought in the days when her trust fund had been worth something, when someone thundered on the door.

'I wonder who that could be,' she said to the postcard of Indiana Jones, and went to the door. Through the spy hole she could see Marsh. Scowling.

'Marsh.' She opened the door. She hadn't seen him since she made him give his keys back.

Marsh strode in and swung round to face her. 'What are you playing at Stevie? Are you deliberately trying to upset Jane?'

'Nice to see you too, Marsh.' Stevie shut the door. 'What are you talking about?'

'*Cause Celeb.*' Marsh folded his arms and glared at her. Challenging her to deny it. 'You contacted *Cause Celeb.*'

Stevie tried to keep her face from looking guilty. 'It's only stuff to do with the ball. Nothing to do with Jane.'

'Really? Pete emailed her and told her that you mentioned her name in order to get your email past the front door.'

'Well, yes. She didn't give me Pete's email, so I thought I'd use my initiative.'

'You know how much Jane hates being involved in the press. She's very fragile at the moment. Imagine if they came after her again. She's feeling delicate and ill and not sleeping. Imagine what it could do to her?'

Despite having had similar thoughts herself, Stevie wasn't going to admit that sort of thing to her brother. Especially if he didn't feel he could tell her about her future niece or nephew until after he'd told their friends. 'Oh yeah? What makes you think she'll have any trouble? It's years since she went out with Ashby. She's happily married now and pregnant. Do you really think the press will be the slightest bit interested in her? Get real!'

Marsh's lips parted, but no sound came out. He stared at her as though too stunned to speak. Stevie closed her eyes and stifled a groan. Marsh adored his wife. She had managed to make it sound as though she was accusing Jane of being unattractive and uninteresting. She opened her eyes again to find Marsh turning to leave. She grabbed his arm.

'I'm sorry,' she said. 'I didn't mean that. I meant ... I meant that Jane's been out of the limelight for a few years now. The press won't be interested. They didn't even cover your wedding. I honestly think she's safe now.'

Marsh didn't turn round. 'And what if you're wrong?'

'Then I did a terrible thing and I totally deserve it if you never speak to me again.'

He sniffed, part disbelieving, part amused. 'You never cease to amaze me.' He turned to face her. 'You just do stuff without thinking.'

Stevie relaxed, relieved to be on familiar ground. 'And you think about everything, but don't *do* very much.'

'Yes, well it works for me.'

They stood in silence for a minute as the argument simmered down inside.

'So, how's the ball organising going?' Marsh straightened his sleeve, avoiding eye contact. They had argued enough over the years for Stevie to know that this was a peace offering. He was trying to make small talk while he calmed down. Eventually they would part and tomorrow they'd both feel sorry and peace would return. All she had to do was keep up the conversation and not needle him and everything would be okay.

'It's going okay, actually. It's hard work though.'

Stevie wondered if he knew whom she was working for. Given his interaction with Tom in the past, it was probably best to steer clear of that topic too.

'There's only a week to go. I'm going to stay over there for the next few days, so that I don't have to keep bussing it up from London every day. Evelyn wants to open the place up as a B&B, so they've got plenty of rooms available.' She pointed to the bag that had clothes poking out of it. 'I'm in the middle of packing.'

'That's a good idea. It means you'll be a lot less tired too. Do you want me to give you a lift up there?'

'Oh, no need,' said Stevie. 'Tom's picking me up in a bit.' Immediately as she said it, she knew she'd slipped up. She bit her lip and hoped Marsh wouldn't pick up on it.

But her brother knew her better than she'd realised. Her slight hesitation gave her away. He raised an eyebrow. 'Tom?' he said. A small smile appeared. 'Tell me about this Tom.'

'Oh, he's not important,' she said, in what she hoped was a nonchalant tone. 'He's Evelyn's son. He works in the city and is giving me a lift in his car, which now smells of curry since he took the ingredients for the food up to Oxford.'

Marsh was watching her intently. 'Stevie,' he said. 'What is it that you're not telling me?'

Damn. She should have looked him in the eye. Stared him out. Damn. 'Nothing. Why?'

'Come on. I know when you're being cagey.'

That was true. He did always know when she was hiding something, just like she normally knew when he was. She'd always thought it was her superior intuitive powers. Perhaps it was just a side effect of growing up with your brother as your best friend and guardian rolled into one. 'I don't know what you mean.'

Marsh thought for a moment and then shrugged. 'If you say so. I guess you're entitled to a few secrets.'

Just like you feel entitled to yours. 'Yes. Actually, I am.'

There was another silence.

'How's Jane?'

'She's okay. She's starting to show now. It's not too obvious yet, but she's definitely getting a tum.'

'She'll probably have a tiny designer bump,' said Stevie. 'Has she stopped feeling sick?'

'Yes, that's much better now, which is a relief.'

'Good.'

More silence. Stevie shifted her weight. 'Listen, Marsh. I've got to finish packing and do some stuff ...'

'Right. I guess I should be getting back too,' said Marsh. 'Look, I'm sorry I flew off the handle.'

'And I'm sorry I brought Jane up again with the press.'

'Please don't do it again. She really was very upset.'

Stevie nodded. Marsh put his hand on the door. 'By the way,' he said. 'What's does Evelyn do? Lou said she was an academic.'

'She is. And quite a good one, by the sound of it. She's giving a lecture that's going to be taped for Radio 4. That's why she needed to get someone to take over the ball work.'

'Sounds interesting. What's the full name? I'll have to listen out for it.'

'Evelyn Blackwood.'

Marsh froze in the act of opening the door. 'Blackwood?' Slowly, he shut the door again. He turned round. 'Tom. Blackwood?'

Damn. Damn. Damn.

'What about him?'

'The same Tom Blackwood that I was at uni with?'

Stevie shrugged.

'Stevie, are you out of your mind?'

'What? He's my employer's son. So?'

'SO? Don't act all innocent with me, Stevie. You fancy him. I can tell from the way you talked about him. Don't you remember what happened the last time you met? He got you stoned. You were only thirteen.'

'Exactly. I was only thirteen. In case you hadn't realised, I've grown up a bit since then.' She turned away. 'Besides, it wasn't him that got me stoned. It was Jeremy the Spliff.'

'That's immaterial. He shouldn't have let you have anything in his room. He was an adult. You were a child. It was irresponsible and ...'

'But I'm *not a child anymore*!' Stevie stamped a foot and immediately realised how childish that seemed. 'I'm twenty-two, Marsh. Old enough to make my own decisions. Even my own mistakes. You don't get to tell me what to do anymore.'

'You're going to get hurt. That's what Tom does. He uses women and then drops them. It's what he's always done. He's not good boyfriend material.'

'You don't think anyone's good boyfriend material for me. Just because you don't want to take any risks doesn't mean I have to live like that too. I want to do things *my* way. So you can bloody well take your advice and shove it up your anally retentive arse.'

There was a stunned silence from Marsh. He glared at her. She glared back.

'Fine,' he said, icily. 'Be like that. Throw yourself at Tom. Don't expect sympathy when he spits you out like a worthless piece of rubbish. I warned you. It's not my fault you're too pig- headed to listen.'

'Oh spare me the holier than thou speech.'

Marsh's lips tightened. He turned to leave.

'It's a good job you're having a child,' Stevie shouted at his back. 'That way you'll finally have someone else to stifle.'

Marsh paused, but didn't turn round. Without a word, he left, slamming the door behind him.

Stevie stared at the door for a moment then stamped her foot again. Spinning round, she grabbed a cushion and threw it across the flat at the postcard of Indiana Jones. It hit the board hard enough to dislodge the push pin. Both Indiana Jones and the photo of her family slid to the ground. Stevie sank into the sofa and started to cry.

She was still crying when Tom phoned to say he was downstairs. Stevie managed to control her voice enough to say 'I'll be right down.'

She dashed into the bathroom and washed the tears off her face. Her bag was only half packed, so she shoved handfuls of underwear and her toothbrush in. At least she knew her clothes for the ball were good to go. She looked down at the light summer dress she was wearing. She had intended to change into jeans and t-shirt, but there was no longer enough time. Sighing, she stuffed those into her bag too and zipped it shut. Tearing round the flat, she closed windows and made sure things were locked and ready to be left for a week before grabbing her stuff and pelting downstairs.

Tom was sitting in the car, tapping away into his phone. He saw her come out of the building and glanced irritably at his watch.

'Sorry,' said Stevie. Despite running around as fast as she could, she knew she'd kept him waiting a good quarter of an hour.

Tom said nothing, merely popped open the boot of the car and put her bags in it. Feeling sheepish, Stevie let herself into the passenger seat and sank into the leather. Tom slid back into his seat and pulled out. He hadn't said a word to her. Clearly, he was annoyed. She hoped he wasn't going to sulk all the way to Oxford.

Stevie's eyes still felt raw. She rubbed her hand on her cheek, trying to get rid of the starchy feel left by the tears. The movement brought with it a fresh wave of loneliness and her eyes filled up once more. She blinked the tears back and inadvertently sniffed.

Tom threw a glance at her and then focused back on the road. Stevie pretended to stare out of the window and quickly wiped away a tear that had leaked out of the corner of her eye. The silence in the car seemed to get heavier and heavier.

Finally Tom said, 'Are you okay?' Rather than sounding annoyed, he actually sounded concerned.

'Fine,' said Stevie, her voice quavering.

'Sure?'

She turned to look at him. He raised his eyebrows.

Stevie sighed. 'Just had a small argument with my brother, that's all.' She wiped her eyes. 'I'll be okay in a minute.'

Tom nodded. 'Do you argue a lot?' he said after a moment. 'With Marshall, I mean?'

Stevie shrugged. 'I guess.'

Tom nodded again. 'My brother and I never really got on either.' He paused to manoeuvre round a roundabout and get them onto the motorway. 'That's one of the advantages of growing up. We moved out of home and don't have to see each other anymore.'

How strange, that the very thing Tom thought was an advantage was making her feel like she'd lost everything. She didn't say anything aloud, but a little snort escaped her. She resumed staring out of the window.

'Marshall really upset you, huh?' said Tom. 'I guess he has got a temper on him.'

'No he hasn't.' She was allowed to complain about her brother, but that didn't mean other people could. 'He's just very protective of ...' she was about to say 'his family', but realised she wasn't sure who that meant anymore. Did it still include her? Right now she didn't feel very protected by

Marsh. '... of some people,' she finished. 'Anyway, I don't want to talk about it.'

'Okay. Just trying to help,' said Tom.

Now she'd offended Tom as well. Stevie sighed. 'I'm sorry. I shouldn't snap at you. It's just that Marsh and I manage to wind each other up so well. Years of practice.'

Tom nodded. 'I know that feeling. Dan and I were similar.'

'Do you still argue?'

'Not really. I only see him on Mum's or Alice's birthday. He's always away on expeditions and conferences and things. That's why poor Alice has to spend her holidays with her grandmother.'

Stevie filed this piece of information away to think about later. 'Alice seems happy enough to stay with Evelyn.'

'She doesn't have much choice. She's been dumped on Mum and Dad often enough though, so they're all used to it. It was okay when she was little, doing up a house can be lots of fun when you're seven or eight years old, but now she's a teenager, she's probably missing her friends and dying of boredom.'

Which might explain why he'd bought Alice an iPhone? 'You're fond of her, aren't you?'

For the first time that day, Tom smiled. 'She's a great kid. We used to have lots of fun when she was little. It's harder now that she's older and trying to be cool, but I think we still get on quite well.'

Stevie looked at him in surprise. His voice was warm and full of affection. She had never heard that before.

'What's it like?' she said, slowly. 'Having a niece?'

'Great fun. You get to play with them and they think you're wonderful. Then you can hand them back when they get tired and cranky. Best of both worlds.'

Stevie wondered if she should be feeling some sort of bond with this unborn child of Marsh and Jane's. She felt nothing towards it at the moment, merely resentment towards its parents. Perhaps there was something wrong with her. Perhaps there was a vital Aunty gene she was missing.

'Why do you ask?' said Tom. 'Is this part of your party planner research? Trying to see how best to get work out of me and Alice?'

Stevie gave a little giggle. 'No,' she said. 'I've already figured that one out. It's just that I'm going to be an aunty. I hadn't really thought about it before, that was all. It doesn't feel real yet.'

"It won't feel real until she ... or he ... is actually born.'

'Oh. That's good.'

There was a pause. 'You said you'd figured out how to get work out of me and Alice,' said Tom. 'How do you propose to do that?'

'I was going to get Evelyn to ask you.'

Suddenly, Tom laughed. 'I see I've underestimated you. You're a devious one. I'll have to watch you.'

Stevie stole a glance at his laughing face, handsome in profile. She smiled. She knew she would be watching him. With pleasure.

Chapter Ten

STEVIE WOKE UP FROM the dream with tears on her cheeks and immediately scrambled for her phone. It was 2.00 a.m. Even if she'd felt inclined to call Marsh, there was no point doing it at this hour. Looking around the unfamiliar room, she remembered she was in Oxford. Absolutely no point calling Marsh, then.

She lay back down, clutching the phone to her chest. Under her fist, her heart still thundered. She tried to breathe slowly. Eventually, her heart settled down to a more normal pace. Now all she had to do was get back to sleep. She closed her eyes. Behind her eyelids was an imprint of a white lily. In gloved hands. Her eyes flew open again.

Her room was up near the attic. It was small, but comfortably furnished with a lovely skylight that let her watch the moonlit clouds without leaving her bed.

After a few moments of staring at the night sky, Stevie felt a little better, but was no closer to returning to sleep. She might as well go make herself a hot drink. Pulling a dressing gown over her short pyjamas, she stepped out into the corridor.

The house was eerie in the dark. Moonlight slanted in through undraped windows, leaving a patchwork of light and dark. Clutching the banister, she took the stairs slowly.

She hadn't managed to count all the rooms in the house. Some were part of the original building, some later additions as people had extended it to suit their needs. The corridors that connected them all looked similar, making it impossible to keep track of where she was. There was a real danger of getting lost and spending hours wandering down corridors. She made a note to suggest that some signs be put up to guide guests around.

She only knew one way to and from her room and that was through the kitchen. Ignoring the unfamiliar corridors and doorways that she passed, she stuck to her route. As her eyes adjusted to the dim light, she realised she could actually make out a lot of detail – doors, light switches, fire exit signs, the outlines of pictures on the walls. Getting to the kitchen using her special route involved crossing the small courtyard. As she stepped out into the warm night air, the ground was cool and gritty under her bare feet. A light was on in the kitchen.

It was bright enough to hurt her eyes. She blinked. There was no one there. Pots, which had been scrubbed clean after the day's cooking were stacked on the side ready for when they would get together to finish making the snacks. Passing Evelyn's enormous fridge, Stevie resisted the temptation to check on the bowls of ingredients and fillings inside.

When she picked up the kettle, she realised that the water was still hot. Someone had been down not long before. She refilled it and set it to boil while she hunted through the cupboards. After some cursory searching, she located a jar of Ovaltine.

Once she'd made herself a drink, she looked around. Warm and comfortable though the kitchen was, she didn't feel like sitting there under the clinical strip lighting. Turning the lights off behind her, she padded up to the library.

She poked her head round the door. Huge swathes of moonlight fell into the room, silhouetting an armchair pulled out to face the window. The room appeared to be deserted. She debated turning the light on, but the moonlight was enough to see by as she made her way towards the window.

Suddenly something stirred in the armchair. She shrieked and hot Ovaltine slopped on her wrist.

A figure leaned out of the chair. 'It's only me.'

Stevie stood still, getting her breath back, too shocked to speak. Tom rose from the armchair.

'Sorry,' he said. 'I didn't mean to scare you.'

She hesitated. Should she go back to her room and leave him alone? Or would that be rude. She nervously moved the mug from one hand to the other.

'You can sit down, you know. I don't bite.'

'Why are you sitting in the dark?' Stevie placed her mug on the window sill so that she could pull up a chair, and sat down, a little unsteadily. 'If you don't mind my asking.'

Tom shrugged. 'I was looking out of the window.' He gestured towards it. 'And I have a headache. The light makes it worse. What are *you* doing wandering around in the dark?'

'I couldn't sleep.' She didn't mention the nightmares. It was too personal a thing to discuss with strangers.

'You can turn the light on, if it makes you feel better.' Tom sat back down again. Now that the moonlight caught him, she could see his face and limbs, pale and slightly hazy against the dark.

'No, that's okay.'

Tom in the daylight was distractingly attractive and quite irritating. This slightly spectral Tom was somehow easier to deal with. She retrieved her drink and settled back. The chair was an old-fashioned one with deep wings either side. There was something comforting about being surrounded by thick velour.

The garden glowed through the window. The moonlight was bright enough to make out a hint of colour. The white gazebo and night flowers shone ghostly against the dark green foliage. 'Oh. It's beautiful.'

'Isn't it? There's something wonderful about the garden at night.' He smiled, making the shadows move on his face. His voice was soft, almost reverential. 'It's pretty during the day too, but at night it's something special. The night jasmine and honeysuckle smell wonderful too.'

'Why are you looking at it from inside then? Why not go outside and enjoy it properly.'

'I did. I got cold.'

She took another look at him. He was wearing boxer shorts and a T-shirt. So, not much. Her face flushed. She was even more grateful for the darkness.

Under her gaze, he self-consciously crossed his legs. 'I wasn't expecting to have company. I don't normally when I'm up in the middle of the night.'

Stevie was glad of her dressing gown. She hadn't been expecting to see anyone either, but had opted for sensible short pyjamas and a spaghetti top because she was in a client's house. At home she would have been in a large T-shirt and nothing else. She wondered if Tom would normally have bothered pulling a T-shirt on over his shorts. Probably not if he was in his flat.

For a moment neither of them spoke. The silence made her uncomfortable. She had to say something. 'Do you often wake up in the middle of the night?' Oh dear. That sounded too personal. Her face suddenly felt very hot.

Tom shrugged. 'I have trouble sleeping sometimes.' He frowned. 'Well, quite a lot, actually. These headaches don't help.' He rubbed his temples.

'You get them a lot then?'

He nodded, still rubbing his temples.

'Have you seen a doctor about it?'

He opened one eye and nodded.

'And ... '

'You're not nosy at all, are you?'

She said nothing and kept watching him. She was on safer ground now. Headaches were easy to talk about. And not embarrassing.

He held her gaze for a moment, his eyes glittering. Then he sighed and looked away. 'Stress apparently.'

She nodded. That tied in with what she'd seen the day before. It would also explain the grumpiness. She took a sip of Ovaltine. Having lived with a workaholic brother for so long, she knew the signs of burnout.

What had driven Marsh to work so hard was the pressure of suddenly being responsible for himself and his sister. But what drove Tom? He didn't seem to have any major insecurity that she could see. His mother was still alive and he clearly came from a fairly wealthy background.

There was only one way to find out. He'd already decided she was nosy. What did she have to lose?

'Why do you do it?' Her voice sounded unnaturally loud. She lowered it. 'If working so hard is making you ill, why not slacken off a little?'

His eyes narrowed. 'What?'

'I mean, you've got a good job, a nice home to come to. It's not like you've got a family to look after ...'

He leaned forward. 'You want to know why I do it?' He stood up in one swift movement. 'Here,' he said, his voice taut with annoyance. 'I'll show you.'

He strode over to the other side of the room and turned on a small reading lamp. The room was instantly flooded with a warm yellow glow. He crouched down, his long legs folding underneath him. 'Here. Look.' He pointed to a shelf.

Abandoning her drink, Stevie hauled herself out of the comfortable cocoon of the chair and joined him, taking care not to get too close. He was pointing to a row of books that seemed to be of random shapes and sizes.

'Look at the authors,' he said.

Stevie knelt on the floor and looked. Every single one had the name 'Blackwood' on the spine.

'All of those are Dad's. These are Mum's.' He pointed out economics and politics textbooks and academic discourses. 'These,' he said pointing to a slim volume and a fat binder, 'are Dan's. He writes mainly papers, but he's co-authored some texts.'

So his family wrote a lot of books. 'And?'

'And I'm the only Blackwood who isn't an expert on something.' Tom sat down on the floor, his back against a bookcase, his legs stretching out in front of him. 'When I was young, my parents said they didn't mind what I did, so long as I did it well.' He sighed. 'I've been trying to live up to that.'

'I'm sure they didn't mean—'

'Yes, they did. They were both brilliant in their fields. Even after they supposedly retired, they were still asked to give talks and lectures. Or to chair seminars, like Mum's doing next week. Dan's pretty much the same. To them, being good means being the best.'

He rubbed his palms over his eyes. 'I don't think I'm cut out to be the best. I'm damned good at what I do, but I'm not the best.' He looked up, not really seeing her. 'Not yet.'

For a moment Stevie didn't know what to say. A dozen responses went through her head, most of them involving pointing out that he was just being pig-headed and self-centred. None of them seemed the sort of thing that would give him comfort.

'Perhaps,' she said, while feeling her way to the end of the sentence, 'you're judging yourself too harshly.' She eyed the assorted books. 'You say you're good at what you do. You've still got years to climb the corporate ladder. You're still relatively young.'

'Relatively?' There was a trace of something in his voice. Was it amusement? She risked a glance at him. He was staring at her.

'You're the same age as my brother. Thirty isn't that old.'

'No,' he said quietly, 'I suppose not.'

Stevie shifted position so that she was kneeling more comfortably on the floor. 'Besides, your mother loves you. I'm sure your parents didn't think their request that you be good at what you do would make you drive yourself to the point of a nervous breakdown.'

'Who said anything about a nervous breakdown?' The sharpness of his reply made her look at him again. Something akin to fear crossed his face before he got his expression under control.

Oh dear. That meant that something had happened. Something he hadn't told Evelyn about. Come to think of it, it was very unlikely that someone so driven as Tom would suddenly decide to take a two week holiday with no plans whatsoever as to what to do with that time.

'Tom,' she said gently. 'Why do you really have two weeks off?'

'I was owed the time and it seemed a shame to waste it—'

She continued to stare at him, not believing a word.

His mouth became a firm line. He looked like a petulant child. 'You look as though you don't believe me.'

'I don't.' She smiled. 'I know a stressed person when I see one. You've got persistent headaches, your hands shake periodically. You look like you haven't slept in weeks. If I were to make a guess as to why you were taking time off ...' She wondered if she'd gone too far.

His mouth was still pressed into a line and he was glowering. He indicated she should go on.

'I'd say you'd been signed off for stress.'

He opened his mouth as though to protest, and then shut it again. He gave a huge sigh and something in him seemed to deflate. He stared at his feet.

For a moment Stevie forgot that Tom was annoying, or even that he was a sexy man she was trying her best not to be attracted to, and wondered whether she should give him a hug. He seemed lost and sad and in need of comfort. For some reason, her argument with Marsh popped into her head. She looked away. With the remnants of her nightmare still fresh in her mind, it was hard to be angry with Marsh. She wondered what he would say if he could see her now.

'Don't tell Mum,' Tom said, suddenly.

'Of course I won't.' She resisted the urge to pat his hand. 'Although, you might find she's more helpful than you think.'

Tom shook his head. 'No, I don't want her to think I'm a failure.'

'Why would she think that? So you're stressed. People get stressed. Especially in high pressure jobs like yours. Evelyn might be able to help you relax. Maybe even help you get over this rod you seem to have made for your own back.'

Tom gave a snort. 'You've only just met my mother. You don't know her like I do. She's always seen me as the inferior one. Dan was always the one who won prizes at school and got top grades for his exams. I was always the other one, who did okay, but nothing special. It was always ...' He sighed again. 'Oh, you wouldn't understand.'

'Wouldn't I? I've got Marsh for a brother. He does everything and does it well. He did his finals, bought a house and fought to be my guardian, all in the same year our parents died. If he were a woman, they'd call him Super Mum of the Year.'

Tom's gaze moved over her face, as though he were seeing her properly for the first time. 'Yes,' he said slowly. 'I see what you mean.' He looked down at his hands. 'You think I'm being childish.'

Well, yes, she did, but she couldn't very well say that without hurting his feelings further. 'No, I think you've chosen to take your parents' comments in a very negative light. You think they wanted you to outshine everyone, when they probably just wanted to give you the freedom to do whatever you wanted.'

He considered it for a while. When he looked at her again, he seemed less annoyed.

'You know,' he said, and gave her a small smile, 'you actually talk a lot of sense.'

She smiled back. 'I do my best.' They stared at each other for a long moment.

When he wasn't scowling, Tom's face was remarkably open and attractive. His eyes, which were so blue in the daytime, were dark as midnight ink in the lamplight. His hair was tumbling over his forehead, making her want to push it back.

Suddenly, Stevie was very much aware that she was wearing very little underneath her dressing gown and that she was sitting on the floor of her client's house, having a fairly intimate conversation with her client's son. She was supposed to be proving she could be professional.

She tore her gaze away from him and back to the books. The brilliance of the Blackwoods took up a whole shelf in front of her. The father, the mother, the son. She remembered the photo in Evelyn's office of a family – two parents, two grown-up sons.

She thought of the photo of her own family, hidden behind a postcard of an archaeologist with a bullwhip. Stevie had never known what her parents expected from her. They may have told her, but she didn't remember. All her memories of them were now reduced to a few fractured images, and she was having trouble separating things she'd actually seen from things Marsh had told her. Would Tom ever realise how lucky he was to know what his parents wanted for him, even if he had let it screw him up?

She cast a quick glance at him. He was staring into space. Sitting there in silence was nice, but she felt somehow it was safer to be talking to each other.

'So, if you could have anything or do anything in the world,' she said, 'what would it be?'

'Pardon?'

'If you could do anything you wanted, what would it be?'

He looked surprised, then smiled. 'Haven't you psychoanalysed me enough for one night?'

She turned back to the books, which managed to appear slightly accusing. 'Sorry.'

'Actually,' he said. 'It's rather nice to talk to someone about it.'

She was becoming more and more aware of how close he was. It was making her skin tingle. This wasn't a good thing. She should go back to bed right now. Alone, she added quickly to her thoughts. Definitely alone.

Tom shifted position slightly. 'What about you? What do you want?'

Stevie thought of her nightmare and the tugging loneliness that still hadn't left her. She thought back to her teenage years, of Marsh trying to be a parent and her not wanting to be a child. Of well-meaning youth workers who asked strange questions. Of the new school she'd moved to where she was no longer the poor girl who lost her parents, but the weird girl who lived with her brother. Of all the things she missed about having her parents. Of the flat she'd called home that she'd watched Marsh sell.

When she considered all that, the answer was easy. 'I want to have a normal life. A home, a family, a pet. All that stuff. Just something nice. And normal.'

She took in that he was now marginally closer to her than he had been, that his hand was halfway into the space between them, paused en route to hers, that his eyes were wide with surprise and something else she couldn't place. Too late she realised she'd misunderstood the question.

'I should be going.' She scrambled to her feet. 'I'm never going to get back to sleep if I don't even try.' She went over to the window and retrieved her Ovaltine, which was now tepid. When she turned, Tom was on his feet, leaning against the bookcase, his arms crossed. 'Goodnight, Tom.'

'Goodnight, Stevie.'

She almost ran from the library. It took a few minutes for her to retrace her steps back to her room. She drained the Ovaltine and lay on the bed. The encounter had taken her mind off her dream, but it was going to take a long time before she got back to sleep.

Tom:

Og. I know it's the middle of the night and I hope that this doesn't wake you. I just have to talk to someone.

I've just had a weird conversation with Stevie. I told you how she's very young. Well, she's also had a very hard life. When their parents died Marsh was pretty cut up, but that was nothing compared to the impact it had on his sister. Yet here she is, nine years later, a perfectly normal, functioning human being. And here's me, who's had nothing but comfort and normality all my life, and all I can do is feel sorry for myself. She made me feel like a child.

But that's not the weird part. The weird part is that she asked me what I wanted from my life and I realised I have no idea where I'm heading. All I can see is the next promotion, the next bonus, until I retire and then what? I've never thought beyond that. Life has just been all about work. No wonder it's been making me ill.

Is that strange to you, Og? You love your job and you work hard. I know you have a better work-life balance than me with your crazy holidays. Do you know what you want in the end?

Does everyone? Is it just me who doesn't?

T

Olivia:

Jesus. That must have been some conversation to bring this midlife crisis on! Don't worry about me, I'm awake. And sober, more's the pity. I'm not sure what to say, Tom. Yes, you work too hard. Yes, you've got a weird hang up about never being good enough to please your parents (you KNOW what I think about that). As for knowing what you want in the end ... well that rather depends on the way things pan out, doesn't it?

Personally, I'd like to be swept off my feet by someone tall, dark, handsome and loaded, please. While I'm waiting, I intend to have as much fun as possible from my life as it is.

I work hard enough to keep my job. My job pays for my fun.

Do I want kids? Not particularly. House with the picket fence, no thanks. Give me a life of champagne and caviar and I'll grow old a happy hedonist.

See. I've thought about it. The dream is within my grasp.

Tom:

Really? That's it? You just want life to carry on just like it is now?

I've never had a girlfriend I'd want to settle down with.

Apart from Vienna, none of my girlfriends have been that interesting. Vienna and I were a disaster as a couple, but at least she's intelligent and good company.

Olivia:

That's because you always go for women who are long on leg and short on brains.

As for Vienna, please tell me you're not thinking of getting back with her. Have you forgotten the fallout from the last time?

Chapter Eleven

IT WAS HOT OUTSIDE, but inside the kitchen was sweltering. Under Priya's careful instructions, Stevie, Alice and Evelyn were busy making Sri Lankan nibbles. Evelyn and Alice were carefully wrapping lamb filling and lightly curried vegetables in pastry, while Stevie and Priya stood next to the stove, deep-frying them until golden brown. The little patties looked delicious, but the heat near the stove was making Stevie sweat. Even the little cotton vest she was wearing seemed like too much clothing.

Priya, dressed in white cotton and linen, seemed to be suffering the heat with much more grace, although Stevie noticed her wiping the odd bead of sweat off her face using a hanky.

'Last batch.' Alice handed Stevie a plate of neatly pinched triangles full of vegetable filling.

'Thanks.' Stevie pulled out the current batch and dropped them gently onto paper towel to drain before easing the fresh ones in.

'Do you need a hand, Gran?' Without waiting for an answer, Alice returned to the table to help Evelyn with the circular nibbles that contained meat.

Through the open windows came the chimes of an ice cream van. In the simmering kitchen, the idea of ice cream sounded unbelievably welcoming.

'Ooh. Ice cream,' said Alice.

Priya looked up from her frying. 'Why don't I treat us all?' She nodded towards her coat, which was hanging off the back of a chair. 'Can you get them Alice, please? My purse is in the right hand pocket. I'll have a Magnum.'

'Priya, you don't have to do that.' Evelyn passed her friend a stacked plate.

'After all this hard work you're doing, it's the least I can do.'

Alice grinned and skipped off. Evelyn watched her leave, smiling. 'She thinks she's so grown up,' said Evelyn. 'But show her an ice cream van and she's ten years old again.'

Stevie laughed. 'Isn't everyone?'

They took their ice creams to the garden, Alice carrying a spare one. As they clattered down the metal steps, Stevie could see Tom, who was supposed to be sorting out the rose garden, lying on the grass underneath one of the magnolia trees, his arms folded underneath his head and his eyes shut. His T-shirt had lifted up to reveal a small stretch of toned stomach. A few wisps of hair lead to the waistband of his jeans. She looked away, seeking out the rose garden instead.

Tom thought she was too young to do this job. Drooling over him like a lovesick teenager was not going to help her change his mind. No, Tom was out of bounds until well after this job was over. Any consideration of his attractions had to be squashed quickly and efficiently.

Alice skipped across and laid the packet on the exposed skin of Tom's stomach. 'Hi Uncle Tom, we bought you an ice cream.'

Tom yelped and sat up. He made a lunge to grab Alice, who jumped nimbly out of the way.

'Cheeky mare.' He gave his niece a mock frown before picking up the ice cream. 'White chocolate. Nice. Where did these come from?'

'Present from Priya.' Alice flopped onto the ground next to him.

Stevie smiled at the picture of family familiarity. She turned back towards the rose garden. The plants had been cut back and tied up so that the pathways were clear. It must have been hard work getting all that done. At this rate at least the rose garden would be useable come the night of the ball.

'Does it meet with your approval?'

Stevie turned round to find Tom watching her.

'I was just thinking it looked lovely. You've got through much more than I expected.'

Tom seemed pleased. 'That's me. A regular He-man when I put my mind to it.' He tore the wrapper off his ice cream.

'What's a He-man?' Alice pulled out her phone. With her ice cream held in one hand, she checked her phone with the other.

'He-Man,' said Tom. 'Like the cartoon.'

Alice looked at him blankly. They both turned to Stevie, who shrugged. 'Before my time. Although I think Marsh had some toys. There was a tiger and some sort of skeleton thing.'

'Skeletor,' said Tom. 'One the scariest villains ever.' He glanced from one girl to the other and threw up his hands. 'I can't believe you've not heard of them. Kids. Honestly!'

'Whatever.' Alice continued using her phone.

Stevie sat on the other side of Alice, where she felt she might be free from the temptation of staring at Tom. His comment about kids rankled. It meant he still thought of her as very young, despite the fact that she was now an adult. It seemed to be a curse on her that all men would think she was still a child. She stretched her legs out in front of her and closed her eyes. A breeze passed, cooling her down. She tilted her head back and let it waft over her, revelling in the feeling.

For a moment there was silence, apart from the rustling breeze and the muted beeps from Alice's phone. Stevie opened her eyes. Her ice cream was starting to melt, she took a long lick to catch the drip that was making its way towards her hand. Hearing what sounded like a cough, she turned, just in time to see Tom's gaze move away from her. He turned to eating his ice cream with ferocious concentration.

Stevie wondered if he was thinking about their conversation the night before. Judging by the deep shadows under his eyes, he hadn't slept much at all. Her glance flicked to his hands. No sign of a tremor. Perhaps gardening was doing him good.

There she was, thinking about him again. She forced herself to turn her attention to the far end of the garden and think about what else needed to be done for the ball. They still had a lot of tickets to sell if they were going to make any money.

Beside her, Alice gave a little snigger.

Tom reached out a foot and poked Alice with his toe. 'What's funny?'

'Dad,' said Alice, still giggling. She read off the screen. 'Apparently he thinks he's found a new sort of beetle. He's all excited about it. He's wondering whether to call it ...' She read it off the screen. '*Acilius danieli* or *Acilius blackwoodus*.' She shook her head. 'My parents are so lame.'

When Stevie looked at Tom, he rolled his eyes.

'I guess it would be rather nice to have something named after you,' she said to Alice.

'The Blackwood Beetle?' said Tom.

Alice giggled. 'That's really funny. I'm going to message Dad and suggest that.'

'Don't tell him it was my idea. He'll think I'm taking the piss.' Tom's gaze flicked to Stevie and back. 'Which, of course, I would never dream of doing.'

Alice slurped up the last of her ice cream and started munching on the cone, while still typing with one hand. 'There. See what he says to that. He'll be all about beetles when he gets back. You have no idea how boring he and Mum can get when they talk about bugs.'

Stevie thought of her brother, but refrained from saying anything. For a moment there was silence. Tom's face had clouded over. She wondered if he was thinking about his successful older brother.

'When are your parents back?' she asked Alice.

Alice waved a sticky hand. 'A few weeks. They'll probably go home for a week and then to the institute before they come here to get me.'

'They seem to go to some exotic places to look for these things,' said Stevie. 'Don't you ever wish you could go with them?'

'Ugh. And sleep in a tent in the middle of the jungle? With, like, huge spiders and mosquitoes and things? No thanks.' Alice sighed. 'Most of my friends go to fun places like skiing in the Alps.'

'Dangerous sport, skiing.' Tom gestured with his Magnum. 'Og broke her collar bone last year.'

'Og?' Alice frowned. 'Is that your friend from school? What's her real name? It can't possibly be Og.'

'Olivia.'

'I bet she has a cool job.'

Stevie had to smile. 'What qualifies as a cool job, in your opinion?'

Alice stared into space. 'Well, something interesting and cool. I mean, your job's pretty cool – organising parties. I bet you get to go to lots of interesting people's houses and meet famous people.'

'I guess so. I did when I worked for my friend Louise.' She'd met one famous person. And then there was Pete, but she'd met him at a wedding, not in the course of work, so perhaps that didn't count.

'Your job's pretty cool too, Uncle Tom,' said Alice.

'It is?'

'Yeah. You know, working in the city. Power lunches. Corporate do's.'

'It's not all like that. We have to do some work in-between too.' Tom's eyes were twinkling.

Alice waved a dismissive hand. 'Yeah, but I'm sure it's worth it.'

Stevie didn't hear Tom's reply, because her phone rang. It was a woman from the Triphoppers' office. 'We'd like to buy two tickets to your ball.'

'Okay. Where do you want me to send them?'

The woman rattled off an address.

Stevie checked around her. There wasn't a pen or paper in sight. 'Um, I'm really sorry, but can I call you back for the address? I don't have a pen on me at the moment.' Oh God, this was embarrassing.

The woman sighed. 'Why don't you email me and I'll send it to you. It's Sharon at triphoppers dot com.'

'I'll do that, thanks.'

'And *Cause Celeb* will be there?'

'Absolutely.'

She hung up and punched the air. 'Yes!'

'Who was that?' said Alice.

'Guess who is coming to our ball?' Stevie was grinning so widely her cheeks hurt.

Alice sat up a little straighter. 'Someone famous?'

Stevie nodded. 'Someone you like.'

'Ashby? Off Triphoppers.'

'Er ... no. Very close though. Pete,' said Stevie. 'And someone from *Cause Celeb*. Hopefully with a photographer in tow.'

Alice shrieked. 'Oh my God. Oh my God.' She pulled her phone out and started typing frantically.

'What are you doing now?' Tom wore a puzzled frown.

'I'm telling people on the FB group.' Alice held up a hand to stop him saying anything else. 'In a minute.'

Tom shook his head. 'That's pretty impressive. How did you manage that?' he said to Stevie.

'I phoned up Triphoppers and told them *Cause Celeb* were coming,' said Stevie.

'And how did you get *Cause Celeb* to agree?'

'I told them someone from Triphoppers would be coming.'

Tom stared at her for a moment. 'That's ...'

'Devious?' Stevie raised her eyebrows. 'Cheeky?'

'Well, yes, but I was actually going to say "genius".' He gave her an appraising look. 'It must take some balls to pull off a stunt like that.'

Stevie inclined her head modestly, accepting the compliment. 'Mind you,' she said. 'It did help that I had some contact with Pete already. He's a friend of Jane's.'

'Jane is?'

'My sister-in-law.'

'Oh yes. Marshall's wife.' He made a face. 'Marsh was always such a quiet, spoddy sort of guy. I can't imagine him married to someone who used to hang out with pop stars.'

'Who's Marsh?' Alice still had her head bent over her phone.

'My brother.'

Alice looked up. 'Hang on.' She pointed her phone at Tom. 'You know her brother?'

Tom shrugged. 'We were at uni together.'

Alice's head swung round to look at Stevie. 'So your brother is the same age as Uncle Tom? I thought you were, you know, young.' She looked Stevie up and down, as though searching for signs of aging.

Stevie laughed. 'I'm twenty-two,' she said. 'There's an eight-year age gap between me and my brother.'

Alice frowned as she did a mental calculation. 'So he's thirty.'

'Nice to see that expensive education isn't wasted,' said Tom.

Alice gave him a playful kick.

Tom smiled. His gaze moved towards Stevie and his smile faded. He stood up and dusted off his jeans. 'I'd better get back to work.'

@LuvAshbysEyes:

OMG! I've just had the BEST news. PETE GOSLING is coming to my Gran's for a charity ball. And I get to meet him!! Squeeeee!

@Penguin82:

When and where is this party? Do U need tkts? R there any still available?

@LuvAshbysEyes:

It's a charity ball.

Tix – DM me and I'll send you the email addy for the organiser. I SO need a new dress. And shoes.

@Penguin82:

I've emailed. I hope there are still some tix left. Pete's my favourite!

TOM WENT BACK ROUND to the bit of the garden he'd been working on. He had cut things back far enough to figure out which plants he wanted to keep. He found his father's old kneeler and got down to ground level to tidy things up.

With his hands busy, his mind drifted to Stevie. The sight of her, dressed in a little vest and shorts, her hair escaping from its ponytail, had done funny things to him. He was used to being attracted to women, but this was something different. This time, he couldn't do anything about it. He didn't do commitment and he was perfectly open about that. The women he dated knew that from the start. Most of them were fine about that ... and if they weren't, things never went any further. But Stevie. She wasn't someone you could date for a bit and then leave. So, even without the Marshall complication, she was effectively out of bounds.

He wished she wasn't so damned attractive though. She positively glowed with it. Thank goodness Alice had been there earlier, otherwise the temptation to touch Stevie might have got the better of him. He needed to get a grip. Accept and move on.

Tom sighed and dug his fork into the ground to lever out a stubborn weed. It wasn't often he met a woman he wanted, but couldn't have. Maybe that was what was getting to him. Once he went back to work, he would probably forget all about her. The thought of work made his chest constrict. Forcing himself to breathe slowly, he gripped the offending plant and wrenched. The weed came out of the soil with such speed that it almost knocked him over. Tom steadied himself and tossed the tangle of plant and root into the wheelbarrow. Somehow, that made him feel better.

STEVIE RETURNED TO the kitchen to find Evelyn and Priya frowning at the trays laden with food.

'What's the matter?'

'I think we've got too much food and nowhere to store it,' said Evelyn, pulling a face.

'I thought you'd sorted out fridge space with a number of people.'

'I think we underestimated the amount of food,' said Priya. 'We can house this lot, but we don't have anywhere for the rest of it.'

All three of them looked at the food. It was a lot to waste. Not to mention the fact that they needed it in order to cater for the event. Stevie felt panic starting to rise in her throat.

Tom came into the kitchen and filled a pint glass with water. 'What's the matter?' he said, over his shoulder.

'We're running out of fridge space to store the food.' Stevie glanced again at the samosas. She knew this was only part of the food mountain. They were supposed to be preparing fish cutlets the next day. They would need to be stored too.

Not to mention all the stuff that was to be made fresh on the day. Given the summer heat, everything would dry up and go off if left lying around in the kitchen. And the food poisoning risk didn't bear thinking about.

Evelyn groaned and sank into a chair. 'This is awful. All this lovely food and all that effort gone to waste.'

Priya said nothing, but looked like she might burst into tears. Stevie sat down next to Evelyn. As the party planner it was her job to sort out things like this. She closed her eyes. They needed somewhere cool. It didn't have to be a fridge, just something under five degrees. She opened her eyes. 'You don't have an ice house here, by any chance?'

Evelyn glared at her like she'd gone mad. 'Of course not. This is a house, not a stately home.'

'Right. Sorry. How about a cellar of some sort? Somewhere cool.'

Evelyn frowned. 'I don't think so.'

'What about the wine cellar?' said Tom, from near the sink. 'That's pretty cold. It's practically underground.'

The wine cellar. Of course. A house this size would have a wine cellar. 'Is it rat free and safe for food?'

'It's definitely rat free,' Evelyn said. 'I can't stand rodents. I've put traps and poison down anywhere that's likely to house them. I'm not sure about safe for food. What do you mean?'

'I mean, is it cold and dry and reasonably clean.'

'It's a bit dusty,' said Evelyn. 'It is a wine cellar.'

Stevie stood up. 'Show me,' she said. 'We might be able to clean it up and use it. We only need the food to keep for thirty-six hours.'

'Tom darling, could you get the key from my office?' said Evelyn, perking up. 'You know where it is.'

'Better still,' Tom drained his glass of water. 'I'll show Stevie the wine cellar. Come on, Winfield.'

Winfield. That's what Marsh's friends used to call him. For some reason Stevie felt a shiver of resentment. It meant Tom still saw her as Marsh's baby sister. Pulling her thoughts back to the task at hand, she followed him down various corridors via Evelyn's office.

He led her round the back of the house into a sheltered area beneath the fire escapes that she'd never noticed before. It was gloomy in contrast to the bright sunlight on the courtyard outside. Steep steps ran downwards to a door. Only a few inches of the door was visible from ground level. If Tom hadn't pointed it out, she would have walked straight past it.

Tom put the old-fashioned iron key in the lock and gave it a good twist. The door rasped open, revealing a dark room. He disappeared into it.

'There's a light in here somewhere,' he muttered. Stevie could just about make him out as he ran his hand along the wall searching for the switch. She stayed firmly outside.

'Ah.' The light came on.

Stevie descended the last few steps. Tom moved along to make space for her inside.

The drop in temperature was immediately obvious. She would have to bring a thermometer in to be sure, but Stevie felt that it was probably cool enough for their needs. The room was roughly rectangular and lined with shelving. Light was provided by a single naked bulb in the middle of the room. The shelves contained a scattering of things. Stevie took a jar down and read it. 'Blackberry jam,' she read. 'From last year.'

Tom was farther down the room. 'And here's Dad's wine collection.' He moved aside so that she could come and stand next to him. The back wall was a huge wine rack full of bottles. Judging by the dust on them, the bottles had been put there a few years ago.

Tom touched a bottle, almost reverentially. 'This was my Dad's other hobby. He'd buy wine when on holiday in France and lay it down.' His hand moved purposefully to one side of the rack. 'Here,' he said, pointing to about half a dozen bottles with little tags on them. 'These were laid down when Dan and I were born. We used most of Dan's bottles when he got married and when Alice was born.' He pointed to the ones just below. 'These are mine.' He ran a finger along one of the bottles. 'We haven't found an event worthy enough to open these yet.'

Stevie felt the tone of sadness in his voice and felt sorry for him. It must have been hard trying to struggle out of the shadow of his brother. She would have liked to have put an arm around him and comforted him, but she didn't trust herself. Or him.

Leaving Tom still standing in front of the wine, she turned her attention to the shelves. There was plenty of room. The trays of food could be stored here, provided they were well covered. She ran a finger along the shelf. It was bare wood and in need of a good cleaning. She frowned.

'What do you think?' Tom turned round so quickly that his elbow brushed her back. His touch sent a bolt of electricity through her spine. Suddenly, she had goosebumps.

'It'll do for the food,' she said. 'But it'll need to be cleaned out. We'd have to wipe the shelves clean and line them with paper, just to be sure.'

'Shouldn't take too long,' said Tom. 'I'll do it if you like.'

'Oh no, you've got lots to do—'

'It'll do me good to get out of the sun for a few hours,' he said with a grin. 'And I'm sure you've got more important things to attend to.'

Stevie nodded and rubbed her arm. The goosebumps had very little to do with the cold, but covering up would be a good idea, especially if Tom was going to be around.

From: Human Resources

To: Tom Blackwood

Dear Thomas

A panel from our Middle East HQ will be visiting on Thursday afternoon. We are arranging for an informal meeting for the shortlisted candidates. The meeting is scheduled from 11.30 until 15.30. Lunch will be provided.

Regards

Anne Weston

HR Assistant.

TOM STARED AT THE EMAIL. Did this mean he was still in the running for Doha? Clearly, Dhidre hadn't been given the job yet. He responded confirming that he could come. Then sat there, drumming his fingers as he tried to keep a lid on the rising tide of excitement and anxiety. He couldn't talk to anyone here. No one would understand ... or care. In the end, he messaged Og to see if she was free for a quick chat.

She messaged back 'ten minutes'.

He should really go downstairs for dinner. While his mother and Alice wouldn't wait for him, it would be polite to show up. He paced his room for a few minutes. He should brush up on what he'd said at the interview, in case they wanted to quiz him about his ideas. Where had he put his notes? How come they hadn't just handed the job over to Dhidre after his performance? He should ask Og about whether there was some HR thing about discriminating against someone who was technically mentally ill. Was the company keeping him on side until they made sure he couldn't sue them?

The pain above his eyes was worse by the time Og called.

'Why are you coming in on Thursday?' she said, without preamble. 'You're supposed to be on holiday.'

He quickly explained what was happening.

Og listened quietly and said 'hmm'. He could almost hear her lawyer brain working things out.

'I think,' she said, 'that you're still in with a good chance for the Doha thing. They're struggling to decide, so they've decided to put you and Dhidre in the same room as the people you'll be working with and see how you get on.'

Tom grinned. 'That's brilliant.' He could outperform Dhidre in a personality contest any day.

'Is it though? You're off work for a reason, Tom. Are you sure you'll be okay?'

'I feel much better for having a bit of time off. Don't worry. I won't lose it again.' He wished he was as confident as he sounded.

Chapter Twelve

WITH TWO DAYS TO GO to the ball, Priya had solved the lack of entertainment by getting a nephew to DJ for them. Stevie and Alice surveyed the front room. This room had the least furniture to move out. Stevie picked up the corner of the rug that covered most of the floor. There were polished floorboards underneath. Perfect for a dance floor.

'We need to block out the windows somehow.' Stevie pulled out her tape measure. Blackout cloth could be expensive and these windows were so tall they would need quite a lot of material. She ran her fingers over the sill. 'Why is there a hinge here?'

Alice looked over her shoulder. 'I'd never noticed those.' The hinges were small and were about half way across the width of the sill, a few inches from the edge. Stevie put her fingers on the edge of the sill and pulled. Nothing happened. Alice crouched down and checked under the sill. 'I think there's a lid of some sort. It's been painted shut,' she said.

'Do you think Evelyn would mind if we unstuck it,' said Stevie. 'I've got a feeling this might be the solution to our light problem ...'

A few minutes later, she was running a knife along the edge, trying to dislodge as little paint as possible. She gave the sill another good tug. Protesting slightly, the wooden flap came open. Inside was a compartment containing two boards, one of which had bronze hooks on the top.

She pulled one partway out. Wisps of dust curled from it.

'What is that?' Alice said.

'I'm not totally sure, but I think they're blackout boards. From the war.' Stevie pulled the board all the way up. 'I've heard of these. They should fit on the windows.' She spotted the two corresponding hooks on the top of the window frame. They too had been painted over. 'The one with the hooks fits on top and this one fits the bottom. They should seal out the light completely.'

She laid the board on the floor. Her hands were covered in grime. 'We'll have to give them a good cleaning.'

'It's going to make a real mess of the paintwork,' said Alice dubiously.

'Doesn't matter for the ball. It'll be dark in here. We can sort it out after.' Still, it was probably best to run it past Evelyn.

'I'd forgotten about those. Frank was really excited about them. I think we tried them out in the library, just for fun. They do work really well,' Evelyn said, when they asked. 'Of course you can dig them out. So long as you touch up the paintwork afterwards.' She smiled. 'It'll be rather nice to have those accessible. Make a feature of it.'

So Stevie and Alice spent the rest of the day in the back courtyard, wiping years of dust off huge wooden boards, which were painted white on one side and black on the other.

As they worked, Stevie commented on the number of emails that she was getting requesting tickets.

'That'll be some of the people from the TripHoppers' forum,' said Alice. 'I posted a note on there.'

'That would explain it,' said Stevie. 'I've sold nearly all of them now.' She paused to turn her board round. A sudden thought occurred to her. 'Alice, these people on your forum, would they mostly be teenagers?'

'Dunno,' said Alice. 'Suppose so.'

'Um ... You might want to mention that they can't have any alcohol unless they've got ID.'

Alice snorted. 'Seriously? That's a bit lame isn't it? It's a party after all.'

'It's illegal to sell alcohol to under-eighteens. Your gran could lose her license.'

Alice said nothing.

'So, will you pop something on there, just so that they're aware? Please?'

'Okay. If you think we need to,' Alice said. 'I think you're fussing over nothing.'

'I'm not. Trust me.'

Alice merely grunted. She pulled out her iPhone and put on her earphones. Stevie could hear a tinny version of the latest TripHoppers album seeping out. She shook her head. Teenagers! They were all so full of attitude. She wondered if she'd been like that at her age. She realised that Alice wasn't much older than she had been when Marsh became her guardian. And Marsh had been about the same age as she was now. She'd been a lot less sunny than Alice. Goodness, what must Marsh have had to cope with!

Stevie scrubbed, trying to get rid of the black spots where muck from the boards had splashed on her skin. She had abandoned her shoes and decided that her clothes would have to go in the wash that night. Or the bin. On the other hand, the boards were nearly done. Once they were dry, they could be hung back up in the right place.

She smiled at her reflection and retied her hair in a firm knot. Despite the dirt, she was enjoying the feeling of a job well done.

The tiles in the hall were cool underfoot as she padded back. The doorbell rang, and she decided to answer it. After all, she knew just about everyone who came to the house now.

Vienna stood on the doorstep, impossibly elegant in pressed linen trousers and blue cotton blouse. She pushed her sunglasses to the top of her head. 'Hi. Is Tom in?'

'No.'

Vienna looked Stevie up and down. 'Can I come in?' she said. 'Leave him a note?'

'Oh yes, of course.' Stevie opened the door fully and stepped out of the way.

There was an antique letter desk in the hall where Evelyn kept the guest book and a stack of notelets for messages. Stevie gestured towards it. She felt something more was required of her, she said, 'Tom's gone to work. He had a meeting.'

'Oh. I see.' Vienna dug a silver pen out of her Lulu Guinness handbag and started to write. She was wearing blue strappy sandals the exact same shade as her top, and had sparkly toenails.

Stevie shuffled her bare feet and tried to hide the tide-marks left by the black dirt. She really needed to do her toes.

'How are the preparations going? Everything under control?' Vienna's hair fell in a perfect glossy curtain by her face. She pushed it back and continued writing.

'I think so.'

'It must be terribly tiring for you.' Vienna folded the note paper and put her pen away. 'Working hard all day.' She eyed Stevie's spattered T-shirt. 'And then having to take the bus back to London. Must be exhausting.'

'Oh no, I'm staying here for the moment.' Stevie crossed her arms. 'Evelyn's kindly let me have one of the rooms.'

Vienna's eyebrow went up. 'Oh, that's lovely!' When her eyebrows had returned to their normal place, she looked around the sun-filled hall. 'This is *such* a gorgeous house. We used to come and stay here some weekends. I've got some beautiful memories from back then.

'Of course, it wasn't done up like it is now. Evelyn and Frank have done wonders with the old place.' She smiled, her eyes far away. 'We used to have lovely dinners on a trestle table in the garden, drinking Frank's wine. Frank was Tom's father.'

Her focus returned to Stevie. 'He had the most wonderful wine collection. I suppose it's all gone, now that he's no longer around to collect it.'

Was this her way of telling Stevie that she was part of the family? Stevie decided she really disliked Vienna.

Alice appeared, also barefoot and grimy. 'Oh, hi. It's Vienna, isn't it?' She smiled and pushed her fringe back. 'Are you after Uncle Tom? He's out.'

'Yes I know. I've left a message.' Vienna, lowered her sunglasses. 'Well, I guess I'd better let you get back to whatever you were doing. Tell Tom I'll see him tomorrow.' Vienna gave them both another dazzling smile and left with a waft of something that smelled delicate and expensive.

Stevie shut the door behind Vienna and fought the urge to stick her tongue out at it.

'She pees me off,' said Alice. 'And Gran's looking for you.'

Stevie frowned. 'Any particular reason?'

'Dunno.' She put her headphones back in. 'I'll come help you finish off in a minute. I've just got to phone someone.' She sauntered off before Stevie could reply.

Olivia:
How did the meeting go?

Tom:

It went very well thank you. I'm on the train home now.

There was some discussion about the things Dhidre and I had suggested in our presentations, but mostly, it was a personality contest – like you said. Dhidre may be formidable and sneaky, but she doesn't have a personality. Besides, I get the impression Matthias didn't like the way she

stitched me up. He made some pointed comments about 'team players'. So, it's all good.

Olivia:

Tom Blackwood! I never thought I'd hear you being so bitchy. And about a colleague too!

You should never underestimate that woman. I'm
sure she has hidden shallows.

How did you bear to tear yourself away from the
lovely Stevie for a whole day?

Tom:

You're right. I probably am underestimating
Dhidre. It wouldn't surprise me if she pulls a sense
of humour out from somewhere, just so that she
can dazzle them with it.

Re: Stevie. I managed fine, thanks.

On the other hand, I've got a headache again. It
must be London that makes me feel ill. Hopefully, the sunshine in Doha will cure me of that.

STEVIE WENT BACK TO the boards. At some point in
the afternoon Tom went past, back from London. She was

aware of him before she saw him and felt the hairs on the back of her neck stand on end.

'Where's Uncle Tom going?' Alice said.

'He's cleaning out the wine cellar, hopefully.'

'Good. It won't be just us covered in dust then.' Alice returned to her task.

It didn't take them much longer to finish off the boards. In the library, Stevie and Alice attached all the lower boards, immediately dimming the room. The higher boards would require a ladder.

Alice eyed the heavy oak panels dubiously. 'They're quite heavy. Might be better to see if Uncle Tom can help.'

Stevie had to admit she was right. The boards were heavy and slotting the lower ones in had taken considerable effort. To try and lift the upper ones to the tops of the windows would pose a serious risk of putting their backs out. Perhaps if she and Tom were to take a side each, it could be done safely.

'Okay, but before we do anything, I think we deserve a break.'

'Good idea.' Alice pulled her phone out of her pocket. 'I'll see you in a bit, right?'

Stevie smiled. 'Right.'

In the kitchen, Evelyn and Priya were having tea and eating Sri Lankan sweets. 'Here, try one.' Evelyn gave her what looked like a rolled up pancake.

Stevie bit into it. Warm, sweet, coconut filling flowed into her mouth. She chewed, letting the flavours mix. 'That is heavenly. What is it?'

'Pancakes with cinnamon, coconut and treacle,' said Priya. 'One of my favourite things ever. They're best served warm so we'll pop them in the oven before we set them out.'

'Mmmm.' Stevie was barely listening as she took another bite.

'How are the boards doing?' Evelyn poured the tea.

'All done. We've fitted the bottom ones. We're going to need Tom's help with the top ones.'

'I'm glad Tom's been here this week,' said Evelyn. She absent-mindedly stirred a tea bag round and round a mug. 'It's nice to have a man around the house again. There are some jobs that are just more suited to the male of the species.' She blinked, as though surprised she'd said anything out loud. She fished out the tea bag and flicked it into the bin. 'I daresay he's been enjoying himself. Could you be a dear and take a mug of tea for Tom. And one of those pancake things?'

Stevie nodded, her mouth full of pancake.

'You can see how the cellar is getting on too.'

The door to the cellar was ajar. Stevie knocked before entering carefully, in case he had put anything by the door. 'Tom. I've brought tea and nibbles.'

When her eyes adjusted to the dimness, she saw Tom standing on a stepladder, taping liner to the top shelf. He held the Sellotape in his teeth, making it impossible for him to reply. Rather incongruously, a blue and white feather duster was sticking out of his jeans pocket.

Stevie grinned. 'There's something you don't often see,' she said, knowing he wouldn't be able to reply. 'A man with a feather duster.'

Tom narrowed his eyes at her and spat the tape out from between his teeth. 'I've dusted the wine rack.' He sounded pleased with himself. 'So everything in here is clean now.'

Stevie looked around. Everything on the shelves was neatly boxed up. The floor had been swept and even the rat poison containers had been wiped clean. The room smelled of disinfectant. Tom was clearly a perfectionist in whatever he did. She found herself watching his hands as he smoothed down the lining paper and taped it. There was not a hint of tremor. They were big, capable hands. And probably very sensitive. And thorough.

She reminded herself that he was out of bounds. 'That's great,' she said, trying to sound like the professional she should be. 'Thank you for doing that.'

'No problem.' He finished the last bit and descended the ladder, giving Stevie a view of his behind, which was quite nice, despite the feather duster. 'Now, you mentioned tea?'

Stevie held the mug out to him, as though trying to ward him off with it. With the stepladder in the way, the cellar seemed suddenly very small and he was now within touching distance. She could see the tiny smudge of dust on his cheek and smell the antiseptic soap on his hands. She fought the urge to take a step back. It would never do to let him know she liked him. He had a girlfriend. Oh goodness. Vienna. She'd forgotten all about that.

'Your girlfriend came round.'

Tom's forehead furrowed. 'What girlfriend? I don't have a girlfriend.'

'Vienna.'

'Vienna's just a friend.' He gave a small smile. 'We're not together.'

'Really? You seem pretty together to me.' It came out before she'd had time to think about it. Damn. It sounded like she cared.

Tom took a step closer to her. He was so close she could barely breathe. There was nothing between them but a few inches of air and one hot mug of tea. She found herself focusing on his mouth. There was a hint of stubble on his cheeks and chin. She wondered if it would scratch if he kissed her. She forced herself to look up into blue eyes.

'I told you the other day,' he said, softly, 'I don't do commitment. All my relationships are on a strictly casual basis. I have lots of lady friends, but I haven't had a steady girlfriend in years. I just don't have the time.' He took the mug from her hands, his fingers grazing hers and making her jump and spill some of the tea. He moved the mug to his other hand and shook the first one. 'Ow. That's hot.'

'Sorry, sorry.' Stevie backed up. 'I'll go get you some ice.'

'No. I'm fine.' He examined his hand. 'I'll live.'

She practically ran out of the cellar and up the few steps. As Tom bent over to retrieve the plate with the pancake, she saw him smile, a tiny, knowing smile. He knew she fancied him. And he'd expected it. The arrogant, supercilious ...

She turned round and stalked back to the kitchen, ignoring him as he followed her.

When they reached the kitchen the others looked up.

Alice was leaning against a counter. 'Uncle Tom, your floozie came round.'

'She's not a floozie,' said Tom. 'She's a solicitor.'

Alice grinned. 'Oh yeah? Where does she solicit then? King's Cross.'

Stevie grabbed her own tea and stormed off before she could hear his reply. She needed a moment to herself.

Chapter Thirteen

STEVIE SAT ON THE TOP metal step leading into the garden. She could smell a faint scent of wisteria on the breeze. After a few minutes, she felt the thumping in her head ebb away, and with it her anger at Tom.

Of course he realised she fancied him. She was acting like a total idiot around him.

Taking up her mug, she frowned. On the other hand, she had thought he fancied her, too. It had certainly looked like it that night in the library. Perhaps he just couldn't help playing games. He obviously wasn't after a girlfriend. He couldn't have made that any clearer. And if he was after an easy lay, he'd bloody well have to think again.

She took a thoughtful sip of tea. Even if she had been tempted to have a short fling with him, which, she quickly reassured herself, she wasn't, she certainly wouldn't want to be second fiddle to that Vienna woman.

Ugh. Vienna. Stevie shuddered. The idea of being someone's booty call was just a little ... seedy. Or needy, if you thought of it that way.

The worst thing about all this was that Marsh had been right. Again. It was infuriating how he always managed to be right. She pulled her phone out and looked at it thoughtfully. She was tempted to phone him, like she always did when anything went wrong. He had always been able to swoop in and help. Or at least give her a brotherly shoulder to cry on. But this was supposed to be her chance to show that she was a grown up. She couldn't very well go crying to her big brother because she'd fallen into the very trap he'd warned her about in the first place. She sighed and put her phone away.

She looked down at her tatty cut-off jeans and made a mental note to schedule in some pamper time before the ball. If Vienna was going to come round and be glamorous, the least she could do was try and look fresh and youthful. Besides, it was important for her to be cool and professional as the party planner. The ball was just as much an advertisement for her services as it was a fundraiser.

The thought reminded her that she needed to check if anyone else had emailed for tickets. Since Alice's announcement on her forum that Pete was going to be there, the tickets were flying out. At the rate they were selling, they would be sold out in time for the ball. Which meant that the ball would more than break even. Given the fact that they'd budgeted for a shortfall and done as much as they could on a shoestring, the charity could make a small profit.

Opening her email, she found a few more requests for tickets. She sent them payment details and added the standard disclaimer about alcohol, just in case.

Listing on eBay.co.uk posted by penguin82

You are bidding for the exclusive opportunity to meet Pete Gosling from Triphoppers in an informal setting. Pete will be attending a charity ball held in Oxford to raise money for Project PEDS, which is trying to buy equipment for a ward in a children's hospital in tsunami-struck Sri Lanka. There are only a limited number of tickets being issued to the public for this ball.

All proceeds will go to this charity.

Happy Bidding!

OUT OF THE LIBRARY windows, Tom could see Stevie sitting on the metal steps, hunched over her phone. She looked sad and fed up. Louise had told him how Stevie had taken the news about Marshall's baby. He was no fan of Marshall, but he understood why Stevie would feel the way she did. Marshall was her constant. The one fixed point in a kaleidoscope world. No wonder she was having trouble adjusting to not having Marshall to herself.

Outside, Stevie ran a palm over her eye, as though squashing out tears.

Had he done anything to make things worse? He thought back to their conversation. No. Not really. Okay, he might have been a bit heavy-handed with warning her off, but really, it had been more for his benefit than hers. There had been something there. An insistent tug of attraction that he couldn't ignore and he knew she felt it too. But he couldn't do anything about it ... because, heaven help him, he liked her too much. He had seen her, as he came in, scrubbing grime off ancient window blinds. Her hair was piled messily on her head and she was smattered in muck and he still fancied her. He was smitten by the curve of her neck, by the way she walked around with no shoes on, the way professional polish had to fight to win over natural exuberance. She was so completely unlike the other women he knew ...

Which was why he had to keep his distance. She needed someone stable. Consistent. That wasn't him. For all he knew, he might be going off to Doha in a few weeks.

If only there was something he could do to cheer Stevie up a bit. Tom sighed. There was nothing that couldn't be misconstrued. The best he could do was to sort out the garden for the party, as he'd promised.

He watched as Stevie stood up, stretched and went back into the house. He remained where he was, looking out of the window at the garden. The rose garden was ready. The gazebo needed some attention ... hang on. He stared at the fading white building in the middle of the rose garden. Suddenly, he knew the perfect thing to cheer up Stevie. He was going to need some help from his favourite niece.

Getting the upper boards hung in place took them several hours, with Stevie standing on the stepladder and Tom on a chair. Once they were done, Tom and Alice waited while Stevie turned the lights out. The room became instantly dark. Only the few rays of light that forced their way through small chinks round the edges of the boards showed how bright the day was.

'Oh wow!' Alice spun round. 'That's amazing! There's, like, no light coming through.'

'Not surprising since they're blackout boards,' Tom said. Alice ignored him.

Stevie turned the lights back on. 'That is pretty effective.' She was so pleased with her discovery.

'Those boards are quite thick.' Tom rapped the wood. 'They'll probably give very good sound insulation too, which should keep the neighbours happy.'

'If we close the serving hatch, we can put a table there for Priya's nephew to do the DJ bit,' said Stevie. 'We can always put a table across the other door to the make a makeshift bar.'

'Good idea. That'll limit the number of people crowding round at any one time,' said Tom.

'We'll need some sort of lighting system though.' Stevie glanced dubiously at the old iron light fitting. 'Something a bit more ... disco.'

'Like a mirror ball?' Tom said.

'A mirror ball! That is *so* lame, Uncle Tom.'

'Actually,' said Stevie. 'A mirror ball would work. We'd still have to have something that shone some lights onto it. Preferably coloured lights.'

'Gran's got a couple of strong lights that she got when the kitchen was being redone,' said Alice. 'They've got pretty powerful beams.'

'I wonder if she's still got that bubble machine thing that you used to love so much when you were younger, Alice.'

'That was years ago.' Alice gave him a withering look.

'Only a few years.'

'I don't think bubbles would be appropriate ...' Stevie began.

'I wasn't thinking of bubbles. This gizmo had a rotating bit in front. If we could attach some coloured acetate, you could have different coloured lights coming through—'

'And they'd reflect off the mirror ball.' Stevie finished the sentence. 'That's brilliant! We should try that.'

Alice looked from one to the other. 'You seventies people are *so* weird.'

'I wasn't alive in the Seventies.'

'Neither was I.'

'Whatever,' said Alice.'Do you want me to go to the party shop to see if I can find a mirror ball then?'

'I'll come with you.' Stevie looked down at her grime-spattered clothes. 'Although, it might be an idea if we changed first.'

They returned a few hours later carrying, not just a mirror ball, but a whole disco lighting set.

'Stevie talked to the guy.' Alice ushered in Priya and Evelyn while Stevie plugged in the lighting and Tom hung the mirror ball from the middle of the old light fitting. 'She gave him all this chat about how it was for a good cause and everything and he said he'd loan the whole kit out to us for free! It was incredible.' Alice's eyes glittered as she gazed at Stevie with open admiration.

'Not quite.' Stevie slotted the coloured filters into place. She still felt uncomfortable when Alice looked on her as some sort of role model. It just didn't seem right.

'We paid a deposit. And we have to have a notice some-where saying "lighting supplied by ..." and mention his shop to people who ask. But he said if we brought the kit back in one piece, he'd give us all of our deposit back, seeing as it was for a good cause.' She stood up. 'Okay. I think we're ready.'

She glanced at Tom, who gave her the thumbs up.

Alice turned the lights off and Stevie flicked a switch. The room filled with dancing spots of multi-coloured light.

Alice gave a little shriek. 'That's *awesome*!'

Evelyn started to laugh. After a second Priya joined her.

Alice leapt into the middle of what would be the dance floor and struck a pose.

'All we need now, is some music,' said Priya.

'Hang on.' Alice dashed out. A minute later the serving hatch from the bar opened and Alice pushed a set of mini speakers to it and connected up her phone. Suddenly the room was full of Triphoppers music.

Alice ran back in and started jumping around to the mu-sic. Tom dragged the coffee table into a corner to give her more room. Priya and Evelyn applauded, still laughing.

'Come on.' Alice grabbed Stevie's hand and dragged her onto the makeshift dance floor.

She looked self-consciously at Tom, who was now busy pulling a comfy chair back. He wasn't paying attention to her.

Oh, what the heck. She laughed and threw herself into dancing.

Chapter Fourteen

IT WAS STILL RELATIVELY early when Stevie walked around the garden and everything was damp with dew. Tom had done a great job, but there was still quite a lot to do. It was mostly small but irritating jobs like weeding and making sure there were no stray bits of rose to snag passing skirts or shawls. As she walked around, she jotted down notes.

The gazebo was now covered in pink rosebuds and cleared of stray branches. Its benches were clean, but the paint was peeling. There was still time to paint them before the ball, provided it didn't rain.

Sitting on the bench, she closed her eyes and breathed in. A faint scent of roses enveloped her. Birdsong filled the perfectly still morning air. It was almost possible to believe she was in a country house and there wasn't a city just five minutes away.

On the other side of the house, a car drove past, shattering the illusion, but the garden was still quieter than London ever was. She would miss this place when she had to go back to her own little flat. She would miss the house, the work and most of all, the people. In the past week she'd got to know Evelyn, Alice and Priya well. She felt like she belonged in their little group. It was a feeling she hadn't had in a long time.

The sound of someone clattering down the metal steps made her open her eyes. She stepped out of the gazebo to see Tom sauntering along wearing his work jeans and a T-shirt, with a pair of gardening gloves in his hand.

'Hello,' he said. 'Checking up on my work again?'

'It's my job.'

He came close and studied her list. 'Is that all the stuff you've found fault with?'

'Hardly that. It's just a list of things we might want to see to before tomorrow.'

He pulled his phone out of his back pocket. 'You're not the only one with a list.' They compared her paper list to his digital one. Standing next to him, Stevie felt her skin screaming to touch his. She sneaked a sideways glance at his handsome profile.

The need to touch him suddenly got worse.

'That's a good idea,' said Tom, pointing at her note that said 'paint gazebo bench'. 'Let me just make a note of that.' He tapped it in. 'Even if I don't paint it, I can at least brush it down so that the peeling isn't obvious.'

Stevie tried to subtly move away.

Tom put away his phone. 'As you can see, I've got the garden covered.'

'True.' She had to admit he'd thought of most things, including some that had never occurred to her.

'So how about you leave the garden to me? That way, you can get on with the millions of things you need to do inside the house.' His eyes met hers, intense and playful.

Stevie took a step back. 'That's a very good idea.' If she spent too much time close to him, she was going to cave in and fall for his considerable charms. This was no time to get distracted.

'You trust me then?'

Sensing the challenge in his voice, she raised her chin. 'Of course.'

'Good. Off you go.'

She gave him her most sparkling smile. 'Thanks.'

'By the way,' Tom called after her. 'Lady Beryl phoned. She's coming round this evening.'

Stevie groaned.

From: EBay seller Penguin82
To: EBay buyer Farrier29
Congratulations! You are the winning bidder for this item:
Two tickets to exclusive event with Pete from TripHoppers
Winning bid £480.

PRIYA TURNED UP MID-morning with her nephew, a young man with short black hair and golden brown skin. He took one look at Stevie and his eyes lit up. His face was cheerful and handsome.

'Hi, I'm Dilan.' He shook her hand and grinned.

'Stevie.' She smiled back. 'So, you're the DJ?'

'I am indeed.' His eyes sparkled.

'Let me show you where you'll be working.' She led him into the front room. 'Thank you for agreeing to do this.'

'It's a pleasure. It's for a good cause. Besides, my aunty can be very persuasive.'

'Aunties always are.' Stevie thought of her own aunt, one of the few relatives she had. Her thoughts immediately spun towards her brother. This event was turning out to be all about family and she hadn't spoken to the only remaining member of her family in weeks. She missed Marsh. But she had to do this one on her own, if only to prove to herself that she could.

They checked out the room and discussed what he needed. Stevie showed him the disco lights and he laughed. 'That's brilliant,' he said. 'I can do a whole cheesy disco theme. That's very Sri Lankan.' He glanced at her questioningly. 'Unless you have objections?'

Stevie returned his smile. 'Not at all.' She felt Dilan's interest in her. Ordinarily, she would have flirted back, but right now her head was too full of Tom to think about anyone else, no matter how attractive.

Dilan's gaze stayed with her for a moment, and then he nodded as though he'd got the message. 'I think you've got a great set-up here. I'm looking forward to this gig.'

The day was spent sorting out myriad little things. Precious objects had to be moved. Bookcases had to be covered before the disco. Sponsors and suppliers had to be telephoned and delivery or pickup times organised. The inventory for the bar had to be double-checked.

Somewhere in the middle of all this, the last ticket was sold and Stevie had to send several emails saying she was very sorry, but the event had sold out. Each time she did this, she couldn't help grinning.

In the evening, everyone convened in the kitchen for last minute discussions. Evelyn was still dressed in her trouser suit; Lady Beryl was talking loudly to a bored-looking Priya; Alice was glowering at the soft drink she was forced to have while everyone else had a glass of wine and Tom was slouching in his chair and kept casting glances out of the window.

Stevie cleared her throat. 'Okay, everyone.' They all turned towards her, apart from Lady Beryl who was still talking. Priya gestured to her that Stevie wanted her attention. Lady Beryl finally turned to Stevie.

'Firstly,' Stevie said. 'I wanted to thank everyone for the hard work you've been doing.' She made a point of not looking at Lady Beryl. 'You'll be pleased to hear that all the tickets have now been sold.'

There was a small cheer round the table.

'I thought you said we were behind on sales,' said Beryl.

'We were, but Alice and I did some judicious advertising,' Stevie said.

'How, exactly?'

'Stevie got Pete from Triphoppers to come. He's this awesome pop star,' Alice said. 'And I mentioned this on a forum and suddenly everyone wanted tickets.'

'What? You mean you sold tickets to any old riff-raff?'

'Oh come on, Beryl,' said Evelyn.

'You have, haven't you? I knew it was a bad idea to enlist an amateur who had no idea of the sort of—'

'Lady Beryl,' Stevie said. 'When I was told about the remit of this ball, I was informed it was to raise money for a charity. You explained the budget and the cause.' She gave Lady Beryl her sternest glare. 'At no point did you mention how "exclusive" you wanted this event to be, nor did you give me any criteria on which you wished the attendees to be vetted.'

'Well, I'd have thought it was obvious to anyone with half a brain—'

'Actually,' said Evelyn. 'It isn't obvious to anyone. Just because you're—'

'Ladies. Ladies,' Tom said, 'I'm sure this is merely a case of crossed wires.' He turned to Lady Beryl and gave her a charming smile. 'Lady Beryl, you have, as we all know, taste and style that is superior to most people's.'

'Well ...' Lady Beryl seemed less affronted than charmed.

'Now, we're not all as gifted as you are,' Tom continued, with his gaze never leaving her. 'So you must make allowances.'

'I suppose—'

'And it is true that we never stipulated what social standing the guests should have. So I don't think it's fair to criticise Stevie for that. It isn't her fault if she was given incomplete information.'

'I'm just saying this wouldn't have happened if we had Sally helping us,' Lady Beryl said.

Evelyn made an explosive noise.

Stevie remembered that the reason Sally left was a disagreement with Lady Beryl.

'Actually,' said Priya, quickly. 'Considering the position we were in a few weeks ago and where we are now, I think Stevie has done a great job. She's managed to sort out the menu, the entertainment, the ticket sales and all sorts of bits of sponsorship, which we'd never have thought of. She's managed to sell all the tickets, and I couldn't help noticing that she was happy to get down to it and do whatever odd jobs that needed doing, no matter how hot or dusty. I, for one, am glad we enlisted her help and I don't think we could have done half as much without her.' She stopped speaking and took a gulp of wine.

There was a moment of silence as everyone absorbed this long speech from the normally quiet Priya.

'Hear, hear. She's certainly worked as hard as any of us.' Evelyn looked pointedly at Lady Beryl, who ignored her.

Stevie smiled, slightly embarrassed. 'Thank you.' She checked the notes in front of her. 'Now that's cleared up, there are a few things we need to go over.' She glanced round the table for any dissent. Sensing none, she carried on. 'First of all, there are tasks for the event itself. Lady Beryl, I'd like you to do the meet and greet.'

'What? Like some sort of butler?'

Stevie gave her the sweetest smile she could muster. 'Not at all. More like the hostess. After all, you will know all the important people who will be coming. It would be best if you were there at the entrance, greeting people and setting the tone.'

'Ah.' Lady Beryl appeared mollified. 'I see what you mean. Of course.'

'We will need you to be here an hour or so before the ball starts, so that you can go through the list of attendees and to catch any early birds.'

'Of course.'

'I'm sure Tom will be on hand to help you out if anything goes wrong.' Stevie glanced at Tom, whom she hadn't got round to asking.

He gave her a nod. 'I doubt there'll be much that Lady Beryl can't handle.'

Lady Beryl preened.

'Priya, can you be in charge of the food leaving the kitchen? We'll all help put out the cold stuff, but the warm stuff will need someone supervising. Also, once you're done, you could do some PR work for the charity, you know, mingle and talk to people.'

'Gladly,' said Priya.

'Tom, can you man the bar?'

'Sure.'

'Alice, Evelyn and I will do things like circulate the food, help people flow through the different rooms, introduce people to each other, that sort of thing. Of course, Lady Beryl will be able to do a lot of that too, once most of the guests have arrived.'

There were nods all round.

'Have you arranged serving staff?' said Lady Beryl.

'No,' Evelyn snapped. 'Unless you've got a fleet of volunteers hidden up your sleeve.'

'I could ask a couple of my nieces. They might not do it for free though,' Priya said.

'We have to rely on volunteers,' said Stevie. 'It won't hurt to ask.'

She ran through a few other points on her list, answered questions, made notes on last minute things to be done. After a while, Alice excused herself and left the room, already on the phone.

Tom took another glance out of the window. 'Stevie. Can I have a word?' He nodded towards the door leading to the main house.

Stevie saw that the others were chatting amongst themselves. There was nothing more she needed to say. 'Of course.' What on earth did Tom need to talk to her about?

'Follow me.' He led the way up the stairs.

'Actually, Tom. I need to talk to you about manning the bar.'

He said over his shoulder, 'I've been a barman before.'

'It's not that.' Stevie lowered her voice. 'A lot of these tickets were bought by fans from the Triphoppers forum. They're likely to be quite young.'

Tom frowned. 'Okay. I'll bear that in mind. I suppose we'll have to have some non-alcoholic punch or something to hand out then.'

'It's on my list of things to do tomorrow.'

'You seem to have thought of everything.' He sounded impressed.

Stevie felt a surge of pride. She had done a good job so far. 'It's my job. Now, what was it you wanted to talk to me about?'

'It's more something I want to show you.' He lifted a finger. 'Just a sec.' He pulled out his phone and made a call. 'Alice? Two minutes.' He put the phone away and grinned. 'Follow me.'

She started to follow.

He stopped. 'Actually, better still, close your eyes.'

'What?'

'Close your eyes. I'll guide you.'

She stared at him, perplexed for a moment, her common sense warning against this. But the red wine was starting to have its effect. 'Okay.' She was still suspicious, but she closed her eyes.

He took her arm. The touch of his palm against her elbow was like a jolt of fire. It was all she could do not to gasp. His fingers curled gently round her arm, he guided her through the house.

With her eyes closed, the warmth of his skin was all the more intense. A tingle of arousal spread through her body. She had to concentrate hard on walking without stumbling. A slight breeze told her they'd gone outside.

'Stairs,' he said. 'Keep your eyes shut.'

He helped her down the metal stairs, one hand still on her arm, the other near the small of her back. A careful touch, Stevie thought. Low enough to be suggestive, but too high to be accused of being sexual. At the bottom of the stairs he led her across the gravelled path.

'Okay.' When he released her arm, she felt bereft. 'Open your eyes.'

The moon, though no longer full, was bright enough for her to see that she was in the rose garden. The gazebo loomed up, an ethereal monument in the rose-scented air.

Suddenly fairy lights twinkled from amidst the plants and along the gazebo walls. Hundreds of points of light, shining and dimming, turning the rose garden into a magical fairyland.

'Oh!' Stevie took a step forward. She had known the garden would look lovely in the daytime, but she hadn't arranged anything for lighting it at night. This was exactly what she would have done. It was like Tom had read her mind. She clasped her hands together. 'It's ... amazing!'

She spun round, taking in the beauty of it.

Tom was standing there, his hands on his hips, a smile on his face. 'D'you like it then?' His smile widened.

'It's beautiful.'

He took a step closer and it suddenly occurred to her that the garden was also incredibly romantic. Was he trying to lower her defences by creating this fantastic spectacle? If he was, she decided, he was succeeding. In the soft glow of the lights, his face was gentle and gorgeous and so, so kiss-able.

'I told you I'd take care of the garden,' he said.

'Where did you find so many lights?'

'Alice and I did a frantic ring round for outdoor Christmas lights.'

'Wow.'

'Impressed?' He seemed closer than ever now, even though neither of them had moved noticeably.

Stevie realised she was leaning towards him. Her gaze moved from his lips to his eyes and back again. 'Very.' Her voice was barely a whisper. She could feel the warmth of his breath and smell his shampoo. Her lips tingled with antici-pation. She closed her eyes.

Evelyn's voice cut through the night air, making them jump apart. 'Tom!'

Stevie's eyes flew open. Tom's face, wearing a slightly horrified expression, was moving away from hers.

'I'm sorry,' he whispered.

Before she could ask him what he meant, Evelyn arrived. 'My word, is this your handiwork, Tom? It looks wonderful.'

'Thanks.' Tom had retreated to a safe distance and shoved his hands in his pockets.

'Is this why you were looking for Christmas lights?' Evelyn looked inside the gazebo. 'Very nice indeed.'

'Did you want me for something in particular?' Tom's voice held a trace of impatience.

'Oh yes,' said Evelyn, from inside the gazebo. 'That girlfriend of yours. What's her name? Austria? Anyway, she's here. Seems to have brought a garment bag with her. Said you were expecting her.'

Tom muttered something under his breath. 'Right. Yes. I'd forgotten. She was going to drop her dress off here tonight, so that she could come straight here from her client meeting tomorrow.'

He set off back to the house. At the edge of the roses, he paused and half turned, as though he was about to say something. He seemed to change his mind and stomped off, taking the metal steps two at a time.

Stevie watched him go, torn between annoyance and relief. She really couldn't afford to fall for Tom. Clearly, for all his talk of non-commitment, Vienna clicked her fingers and Tom responded. She sighed and sat down next to Evelyn.

'I wish he'd get shot of that girl,' said Evelyn suddenly.

'Pardon?' She looked at Evelyn in surprise.

'That Vienna girl. She's not good for him. As long as he's got her at his beck and call, he's never going to find himself a proper partner. It's almost the opposite problem to Dan. He married Laura as soon as they finished their degrees and he was just starting his PhD when Alice was born.' Evelyn sighed. 'It's all worked out in the end. Dan doesn't spend as much time with Alice as he should, but she seems not to mind.'

Stevie continued to stare. Evelyn had always seemed disinterested in her sons' lives. To the point that Tom thought she found him a disappointment. She wondered if she should mention the nervous breakdown.

'Don't look at me like that,' said Evelyn. 'I may be scatty, but it doesn't mean I don't care.' She gestured towards the library, where Vienna was visible, talking animatedly. Tom was out of view.

'Dan was lucky. He found his calling at first attempt. Poor Tom. I know he's good at his job and he works hard at it, but I don't think he loves it. And it does so make a difference to love your job.'

Not knowing what to say, Stevie remained silent.

'What makes it even more of a shame is that he seems to have put his personal life on hold to devote himself to his job. It's a thankless way to be. He's going to burn himself out soon, if he's not careful.' She stopped and looked at Stevie. 'What do you think?'

'Me? About Tom?' Obviously she couldn't say what she really thought. Not to his mother. 'I think ...' she began carefully. 'You're right that he's too obsessed with work and it doesn't make him happy.'

'Poor Tom.'

'Evelyn,' said Stevie. 'I know it's none of my business, so tell me to butt out if you want to, but have you tried talking to Tom about it? I think it would mean a lot to him if he knew what you think. That you are proud of what he's achieved so far.'

Evelyn looked astonished. 'He knows I'm proud of him. I don't need to tell him that, surely?' She shook her head. 'I don't hold with that sort of touchy-feely, "Let's talk about our feelings until everyone's sick of hearing about them" nonsense.'

'Ah,' said Stevie. 'I see. Sorry.'

'You young people watch too much American TV.' Evelyn patted her arm. She looked around at the gazebo. 'Tom and Alice have done a lovely job with the garden, haven't they?'

'Yes, they have. It looks wonderful.' She had trouble feeling anything but sad.

'Ah well. Best get back to the house. Paperwork to do, you know.' Evelyn sprang up and headed off. 'Coming?'

'I'll be along in a minute.' Stevie looked at her twinkling, dream-like surroundings. What had seemed like such a beautiful and romantic setting a few minutes ago was now reduced to mere rose bushes and fairy lights. Yes, it was lovely. But it was no longer special.

She shook her head and sighed. She had done her best not to fall for Tom Blackwood, but it looked like it was too late. The best she could do now was accept that she'd made a mistake and keep a lid on her feelings until this ball was over.

Making her way back to the house, she paused at the top of the stairs. She could easily see into the library windows. Tom had moved close to Vienna and appeared to be picking something up. He straightened up and Vienna reached out to tuck a stray curl of his hair behind his ear. It was such an intimate gesture that Stevie felt like she'd been punched. She willed Tom to move away. He said something, turned and moved out of view and Vienna, flicking her hair over her shoulder, followed him.

Stevie reached the conservatory door in time to see Tom, carrying a garment bag over his arm, open the door leading to a staircase she'd never explored. He said something to Vienna. Her laugh tinkled as she followed him up the stairs. No prizes for guessing where they were going. Stevie hadn't realised her heart could sink any further, but it did.

Feeling unbearably sad, she went back to the kitchen to gather her things. She made her excuses to the ladies and, pleading exhaustion, took herself off to bed before Tom returned from his tryst with Vienna.

OLIVIA: HOW DID THE surprise go? Did she love it?

> Tom: She did love it. She was so pleased it seemed
> to fill the whole of her body. Seeing her so pleased
> made me feel like I'd achieved something wonder-
> ful. It was quite a buzz. I could get addicted to see-
> ing that look on Stevie's face.

Olivia: Oh my God. You're in love. Finally. After all these years of breaking hearts, you've lost yours.

That's so sweet, I don't know whether to laugh or throw up!

What happened after that? Did you try to kiss her? Bet you did.

Tom: No. I didn't get the chance. Vienna turned up and Mum came to find me.

I was pissed off at first, but I guess it's best that nothing came of it. I can't give Stevie the sort of commitment she needs and I don't want to hurt her.

Olivia : You keep saying that, but what's stopping you? Don't tell me it's work. Only an idiot would give up on love because of work.

Tom: If I get the Doha job, I'll be leaving in the next couple of months. I can't start something and then just leave. That would make me a total shit. I know I'm not great boyfriend material, but I like to think I'm not a total shit.

Before you go off on one, my work is important to me. This job in Doha is exactly the right next step for my career plan. The job with Lambert Kassel would be nice too, obviously, but Doha is the big one.

Olivia: Whatever. It's your life.

So, what did the delightful Vienna want then?

Tom: Vienna was just dropping her dress off so that she didn't have to bring it round tomorrow.

Actually, she was coming on a bit strong this evening, even for Vienna. She's normally so laid-back. Not sure what's going on with her.

Olivia: Laidback? Vienna? You mean 'laid often'. She's one of the most ruthless women I've ever met.

As to what's up with her, could it be that she smells competition from a certain young party planner?

Tom: Vienna's not like that. We've always been totally open about the fact that there is no commitment involved in our relationship. Obviously, if either of us started dating someone, we'd stop seeing each other, but until then, it's just as and when. That was the deal. No questions asked.

Olivia : But you did have a relationship involving commitment with Vienna once, remember? Maybe she wants that again? Or, now that she's sensing her regular shag slipping away, it's starting to bother her.

Tom: Vienna and I were a terrible a couple. We're not really the relationship type, either of us. When we weren't in bed, we just bickered the whole time. It was only after we decided to split up that we started to get on.

Olivia: It amazes me that someone so bright can be so DENSE.

Let me spell it out for you. You love this Stevie girl. She may even love you back. Vienna is being a jealous bitch.

Question is, what are you going to do about it?

Tom: Oh shut up. Even if you're right, which you aren't. Vienna hasn't got anything to worry about.

I'm going to go turn those lights off and go to bed. Alone (before you ask).

Chapter Fifteen

THE DAY OF THE BALL Stevie did little but rush around tying up loose ends, calming down a panicky Evelyn and curtailing annoying phone calls from Lady Beryl.

At five that afternoon, she was still in her jeans and flip-flops. She had spent the last half hour minding things in the kitchen while Priya went home to shower and change. Now that the cooking was finally done, she was washing pans so they could be put away, making the space available for laying the trays out. She really needed to have a shower and do her hair before the guests, or worse, Lady Beryl, turned up.

Alice burst into the kitchen. 'Stevie. I can't do the nails on my right hand properly! I've done these, look.' She waved a purple painted left hand. 'But the other hand keeps going wonky.'

Stevie sighed. A party organiser's job seemed to entail a huge range of duties. 'Give me a minute and I'll do them for you.' She pointed to the pile of dripping dishes. 'If you could dry those and put them away, that would make my life easier.'

Alice glanced dubiously at the dishes and then at her hand.

'It won't damage your nails.' Stevie fought to keep the impatience out of her voice. 'It's not like you're washing up.'

Unlike me, she thought, looking at her own hands, which were submerged past the wrists.

Alice picked up a tea towel. 'What are you going to do with your hair?'

'I was going to put it up.' Stevie dunked the last of the pans in the sink. 'I'm not sure I'll have time though. I have to go have a shower in a minute.'

'What colour's your dress?'

'Blue. Yours?' Her mind was only half on the conversation. Most of it was occupied with ticking things off a mental checklist.

'I'm wearing this hipster skirt and a sparkly top,' said Alice. 'The top's the same colour as my nails.'

Stevie let her talk without actually listening.

Evelyn raced in. 'What do you think?' She was wearing a red floaty summer dress and linen jacket, with pearls. She looked neat and tidy and every inch the retired academic.

'You look lovely,' said Stevie. 'Very elegant.'

'You look amazing, Gran.' Alice sounded impressed.

'Thank you, both. Now then, I'm going to make a start on laying out these trays. Oh, nearly forgot.' She tossed a small box onto the table. 'If Tom passes through, tell him that's his father's bow tie. He's forgotten his.' With that, she swept out.

Stevie and Alice finished clearing up and sat at the end of the long table. Stevie was busy concentrating on applying even strokes of nail varnish when Tom appeared.

'Have you seen Mum?'

'She's in the wine cellar,' said Alice. 'She left you a bow tie. She said to say it's Gramps.'

'Right.'

Stevie felt a prickling between her shoulder blades as he walked behind her to pick up the box. She forced herself to concentrate on Alice's fingers.

'Damn,' Tom said. 'It's one of those real ones. I've only ever used clip-on ones.'

There was silence. Stevie didn't look up. She finished the last nail.

Tom was standing barely a foot away from her shoulder and she was trying not to look at him. He was bound to look gorgeous in a tux. He looked gorgeous enough in jeans.

'I don't suppose you know how to tie a bow tie, Stevie?'

As it happened, she did. One of her ex-boyfriends had chatted her up by showing her how to tie one. Did she really want to admit to that? It would mean being closer to Tom than she really wanted to be. She had to concentrate on the ball this evening. She was, after all, a professional.

Tom took her silence to be a denial. 'I wish I'd thought of this earlier. I could have gone out and bought one. What am I going to do now?'

Stevie sighed. 'I'll do it. Give it here.' She finally looked at him and all thoughts fled from her head.

He did indeed look wonderful in a tuxedo. The jacket showed off his broad shoulders while the cummerbund emphasised his trim waist. His hair had been washed and tamed so that it no longer tumbled lazily over his forehead, somehow making his eyes bluer. The top button of his collar was undone. He hastily did it up so that she could put the tie on.

Stevie blinked and tried to concentrate on the job at hand. She could feel the warmth radiating from his skin as she slipped the tie round his neck. Tom put a hand on the back of a chair and lifted his chin.

She concentrated on pulling the fabric of the silk bow tie through the correct knot. After a moment she found herself staring at the freshly shaved skin on his throat. There was a tiny nick just under his chin. All she wanted to do was kiss it better.

Blood was pounding in her head and she felt hot all over. She couldn't possibly be this close to him and not have her head explode out of sheer lust.

Tom swallowed. The movement of his throat reminded her that she was supposed to be tying his tie, not staring hungrily at his throat like some demented vampire. She noticed that he was breathing faster than usual. She forced herself to look away, and saw that he was gripping the back of the chair so hard that his knuckles were white. Could he be finding this as difficult as she was?

She finished tying the bow, barely able to think for wanting him. As she finished, she gave into temptation and let her finger lightly brush his throat. Tom inhaled sharply and his eyelids fluttered shut. Stevie pulled the knot tight, straightened it and let her hands drop.

He lowered his chin and his eyes met hers. For a moment he gazed at her with such pure naked lust that she forgot to breathe.

The moment stretched. They were only inches apart, yet he made no move to close the gap.

Alice's phone beeped. They both jumped. Stevie had completely forgotten about Alice.

Tom cleared his throat. 'Thank you.' His voice was deeper than normal. 'You're a star.' He took a step back.

Stevie was suddenly embarrassed that Alice might have witnessed the look that had just passed between Tom and herself, but the teen, who was still blowing on her nails and texting with one hand, seemed oblivious.

Evelyn came in, carrying a large tray of canapés still wrapped in cellophane. 'There you are darling. You found the bow tie then.' She carefully put the tray down.

'Yes. And Stevie tied it for me.'

'Ah,' said Evelyn. 'It suits you.'

There was something in Evelyn's voice that made Stevie look at her and mentally change gear. Evelyn's normally steely eyes were misted. 'You look so handsome.' She stepped close to Tom and straightened the already straight bow tie. 'So much like your father.' Her voice cracked completely then. There were tears in her eyes.

Tom kissed his mother on the cheek. She put her arms around him and hugged him. Stevie felt a lump form in her throat. She knew that Evelyn, normally so capable and business-like, was seeing this ball as a tribute to her late husband. It would launch the house in its new incarnation as a B&B. The culmination of a project he'd started. It was clearly an emotional moment for her.

A chair scraped as Alice went over to hug her grandmother too. Tom put his arms round both of them and they stood together in the kitchen, a tableaux of family affection.

Stevie quietly left them to it.

Back in her room, Stevie showered quickly. The incident in the kitchen had left her feeling unsettled and very much alone. She missed Marsh. She even missed having Louise around to bounce ideas off.

Sitting in front of the mirror to dry her hair, her thoughts turned to Tom. She now had no doubts that she wanted him. Madly. And after the look he had given her, she was sure that he wanted her too, just as much. Yet something was holding him back.

If he'd wanted to kiss her, he'd had plenty of opportunity. Something was bothering him, but what? Stevie brushed out her wet hair. With it pulled away from her face, she looked fresh and young.

Tom kept making comments about youth. Was that it? Did he think she was too young for him? Eight years wasn't that much of an age gap. By the time he was seventy, she'd be sixty-two. That was barely a difference.

Or maybe it wasn't that at all. There was also Vienna. Despite Tom's protests that Vienna wasn't his girlfriend, she obviously had some power over him. Perhaps some sense of loyalty to Vienna was stopping him.

She freed a knot in her hair with a vicious tug. 'Ouch!'

She would have to try to watch Tom and Vienna that evening and see how they interacted. She'd only seen them together fleetingly. Maybe seeing them in a setting like a ball, which they claimed was the sort of thing they did together, might shed some light on how Tom really felt about Vienna.

Stevie sighed and raised her hands to her hair to tie it up. Suddenly she remembered the night in the library when Tom had asked her what she wanted from life. She thought back to her answer. Was that it? Had her suggestion that she wanted something stable for her life made her sound like some sort of needy sad case?

If Tom thought she was after a husband and nothing else, no wonder he was running away. She studied her face in the mirror. A year ago, she would have had no problem with jumping on Tom and having a few days of fun and then moving on. It would hurt, but she'd go in accepting the risk. But now, the idea of a frivolous relationship seemed wrong for her. What had happened in a year to change her so much?

Pursing her lips, Stevie returned to doing her hair. She knew the answer to that question. In the last year, she'd left uni to start work in the real world, moved into her own flat and her brother had got married. She had taken for granted the fact that Marsh would always be there for her and now suddenly, he had his own family to think about. It was as though a safety net that she'd not even been aware of relying on had suddenly winked out of existence. It left her feeling shaken and vulnerable. Needy, even.

She tethered her hair with a clip and loosened a few tendrils to frame her face. Reaching for her make-up, she told herself to stop being silly. She wasn't needy. Even if she was, she didn't have to let it show. And anyway, she told herself as she swiftly applied her mascara, tonight was all about setting herself up as a professional. This ball was important to her future and more than that, it meant a lot to Evelyn, who had been nice to her. She couldn't let her down.

After slipping on her dress and matching shoes, Stevie gave herself one last check in the mirror. The dress was blue silk and fell in a flattering swish around her hips. Coupled with her subtle make-up, she looked smart, fresh and professional. She gave herself a reassuring smile and stepped out to take over her job as organiser.

Tom carried a crate of wine up to the bar area, deep in thought. Seeing Evelyn upset had shaken him. She showed weakness so rarely that he'd almost forgotten she was capable of it. His parents had loved each other with a passion that he had never seen in anyone else. He and Dan, although well loved and looked after, were an add-on to the unit that was Evelyn and Frank. He had assumed that all parents were like that, until Og's family imploded. Now he knew that such devotion was a rare thing in a marriage.

Tom put the crate down. Turning, he caught sight of his reflection in a mirror that hung on the wall. He paused. Dressed in black tie, he did look a lot like a young version of his father. No wonder the sight of him had upset Evelyn.

When his father passed away, Tom had worried that his mother might die of grief, but after a short while, she had rallied and seemed to have found her purpose again in finishing work on the house. Now he realised that it had just been a distraction. A way of pretending that Frank was still alive, just working somewhere else. Maybe Stevie was right. Maybe he should tell her about his breakdown. Maybe she would understand more than he thought.

Stevie. He fingered the edge of the bow tie and thought of Stevie tying it. Just thinking of her fingers skimming his throat made his skin warm up. It had taken all his will power to stand so near and not kiss her. Tom sighed. They say what doesn't kill you makes you stronger. He should have been approaching superhuman strength by now.

STEVIE REACHED THE landing and found Tom and a tall girl with spiky blonde hair manoeuvring a board under Priya's direction. The girl gave Stevie a grin, before turning back to her task. They put the board by the front door where everyone would have to walk past in order to get to the main rooms.

Priya had created a display showing the devastated site of the old hospital and the plans for the new one. Photos showed the construction that had already taken place. There was a price list showing what various sums of money would buy and explaining how the equipment would save lives. Finally, there were some pictures of children who would benefit from the hospital, all heart-rendingly cute.

Stevie nodded with approval. 'That's good. We need a collection box.' She dragged Evelyn's writing desk out so that part of it stuck out beyond the display. 'In case people want to make a donation.'

Tom turned and saw her for the first time. He seemed to freeze in place.

The blonde girl glanced at Tom, and then looked Stevie up and down. 'Have you got a bike chain or something?'

'Pardon?' She was completely thrown by the question.

'You might want to lock the collection box down. In case it walks.'

'That's a good point. I'll sort that out.' Tom placed a hand on the girl's arm and tried to move her along.

She stayed where she was and smiled at Stevie. 'I'm Olivia. You must be Stevie. I've heard a lot about you.'

Stevie wondered who this woman was. Olivia was nearly as tall as Tom and wore a smart trouser suit and killer heels that made her seem even more willowy. She and Tom were clearly very comfortable in each other's presence, but Stevie sensed no chemistry between them.

Tom gave her a quick grin and turned back. 'Come on Og, I thought you were helping.'

Og. The friend from school. That made sense.

'I'll see you later.' Olivia allowed Tom to shoo her out of the room.

Priya was straightening up the display. She was wearing a beautiful red and cream sari and had her hair up. The image was spoiled somewhat, by the large apron she'd tied over the front. She was frowning slightly.

'You okay, Priya?'

Priya nodded. 'Yes. We're all good to go in the kitchen. I've press-ganged one of my nieces into helping with the food. Apparently, she's a fan of this pop star you have coming.'

Stevie nodded. She glanced at her watch. 'It's nearly time for people to start turning up. Is Lady Beryl here?'

'No.'

Stevie rolled her eyes. 'I need her to do door duty.'

'I know. Beryl doesn't really do "helping out". She thinks it's beneath her.' Priya gave Stevie an apologetic smile. 'I know Tom buttered her up again this morning, so perhaps he helped changed her mind.'

Stevie hoped so. Lady Beryl was a royal pain, but she needed her approval if she was going to get more commissions based on this ball. If Lady Beryl was late, Stevie would have to step in and do the meet and greet without a murmur of disapproval. She sighed and ran off to do a last check that everything was under control.

By the time the first guests arrived, Stevie had checked that all was in place and that private areas were cordoned off and, where possible, locked. She flew to answer the door. The early birds were friends of Evelyn and Priya. Stevie ticked them off her list and marked their tickets. She had time to direct them to the bar where Tom was waiting with glasses of champagne, wine or juice, all ready and poured out.

A text arrived. It was from Marsh. Stevie opened it with some trepidation.

Good luck with the ball. Hope all goes well. Marsh. x

She stared at it for a moment. She had behaved very badly towards Marsh lately. She hadn't called or texted. This was the longest time she'd been out of touch with him. And it was the longest time she'd stayed angry with him. She'd been a real shit to him and Jane, dragging Jane's name back into contact with *Cause Celeb*, yet here was Marsh, thinking of her and wishing her luck. A lump rose in her throat. She missed him. She really, really missed him.

She pressed reply and stared at the blank screen. The doorbell rang. Stevie pressed *cancel* and answered the door.

Vienna stood there, dressed in a perfectly cut pinstripe suit and stilettos.

'Hi,' said Stevie. 'Have you got your ticket?'

Vienna stared. 'Um. Damn. Not on me. It's in Tom's room with my dress.'

Briefly Stevie thought about turning her away. The idea of being able to bar Vienna from the ball was delicious. But she wasn't that petty.

'Tom will vouch for me,' said Vienna, while watching her carefully.

Stevie took a deep breath. 'Okay. You're lucky you got here before Lady Beryl took over door duty. Can you bring me your ticket once you've found it though. I need to mark it and cross you off the list before Beryl checks.'

'Absolutely,' said Vienna, giving her a toothpaste advert smile. 'Thanks. You're a star.' She picked up her briefcase and headed in.

'Tom's in the bar,' Stevie shouted after her. 'In case you need his keys.'

Vienna raised a hand in thanks, but didn't turn round.

Stevie returned to her task, smiling. She knew it was childish, but it was fun to bait Vienna.

Lady Beryl arrived a few minutes later. Stevie opened the door to find her glowering. 'There is nowhere for me to park.'

Stevie peered past and saw that the large forecourt was full of cars. Tom, Priya and Evelyn's cars were well and truly hemmed in by those of later arrivals. Stevie hoped that none of them would need to get out before the guests left, or there would be chaos.

'You should have reserved me a space.' Lady Beryl glared at her.

Stevie resisted the temptation to point out that had Lady Beryl showed up when she was supposed to, parking would not have been a problem. Instead she said, 'I do apologise Lady Beryl. I should have thought of that. Perhaps Evelyn has a visitor's permit she can give you.'

Lady Beryl stood there, glaring at her. Obviously expecting Stevie to run in and find Evelyn.

'Evelyn's in the kitchen, I think.' Stevie kept her tone pleasant. 'I'm on door duty, so I can't really leave. Unless you want to take over immediately, of course.'

Lady Beryl sniffed and swept off. She returned a few minutes later, looking even crosser. 'Evelyn hasn't got any parking permits, or so she says.' From her expression, Stevie surmised that Evelyn may have said a bit more than that.

'Oh dear. I'm sure there's plenty of spaces in the roads nearby. And it's free after 9.00 p.m., so you only need to pay for two hours.' She smiled as sweetly as she could. 'I'm so glad you're here. We need someone with authority around.'

Looking slightly mollified, Lady Beryl went to park her car. When she returned, she hung her coat up carefully in the cupboard under the stairs. The cupboard usually housed assorted junk, but tonight it had been cleared and a clothes rail put in, so that it would take coats.

'Lord Grayingham will be arriving shortly,' she said, as she shut the cupboard door. 'He will be accompanied by some friends.'

Stevie consulted her list. Four friends. Two double-barrelled surnames, one Major and a Mrs. 'In that case, it's brilliant that you'll be here to greet them.' She smiled. 'I'm happy doing door duty, but it would look so much better if you were here instead. It would lend the event so much more *gravitas*.'

Lady Beryl nodded in acknowledgement of the compliment. 'Let me see that list.' She scanned down the names. 'Who is this Peter Gosling? Why has he been marked with a star?'

'He's a VIP. Can you let me know when he arrives? He's the reason we managed to sell all the tickets in the end.'

'Lord Grayingham has not been marked with a star.'

'Hasn't he? Oh dear. He should have been.' Stevie whipped out a pen and drew a star next to the name. *Anything to keep the old bat happy.*

'And this person?' Lady Beryl pointed to another highlighted name. It was the reporter from *Cause Celeb*.

'Er yes, another important person. All part of the publicity campaign that sold the tickets.' Stevie pointed at the sheet. 'As people come in, check off their ticket numbers and names. That way we know which tickets have already passed through here and we know whom we need to locate, in case of a fire alarm.'

Lady Beryl nodded her understanding.

'Just point them in the direction of the bar. If they loiter in the hall, suggest they check out Priya's display on the charity ...' Stevie rattled off the instructions she'd given the others earlier in the day. She could tell Lady Beryl wasn't really listening. 'Any problems with anything, anything at all, just call me. Here are the useful phone numbers, including mine.'

Lady Beryl took the piece of card and dropped it into her handbag. 'I'm sure there won't be any need.' The doorbell rang.

'I'll leave you to it.' Stevie fled before Lady Beryl made her act as door maid for her.

As she rounded the corner, she nearly collided with Alice.

'What time's Pete arriving?' said Alice. She was dressed in a purple outfit and wearing far too much eye make-up. It was a look that could only be carried off by someone in her teens.

'I don't know,' said Stevie. Pop stars liked to make an entrance. Even someone relatively down to earth like Pete would leave it until fairly late, to ensure they turned up when the party was in full swing. 'Not for a while yet, I should think.'

'Can I help with door duty?' Alice's eyes sparkled. 'Gran said she could spare me.'

Stevie looked her up and down. She looked kooky and young, but she would be a nice counterpoint to the overbearing Lady Beryl. 'Okay. That's a good idea. Can you let me know if there are any problems and make sure Lady Beryl doesn't insult anyone?'

Alice pulled a face. 'I'll try. Lady Beryl can insult most people without even trying.'

'Precisely. I think a friendly face to counterbalance that would be a good thing.' Stevie gave her a conspiratorial smile. 'Besides, I can count on you to recognise Pete.'

Alice flushed.

'There's a reporter coming from *Cause Celeb*. I think her name is Amber Jackson. Make her welcome and let me know she's here. Whatever you do, don't let Lady Beryl figure out she's from a gossip mag.'

'Okay.'

'Brilliant. Off you go then.' Stevie watched Alice skitter off in ridiculously high purple sandals and suddenly felt very old. Shaking her head, she went to the bar to check that everything was under control.

AS STEVIE NEARED THE bar, Vienna came down the side stairs. She was wearing a figure-hugging red sequined dress that sparkled when she walked. Her blonde hair flowed to her shoulders, and her make-up was glamorous and perfect. She smiled at Stevie and entered the bar just ahead of her.

Stevie couldn't help noticing that as soon as she did so, Vienna's stride lengthened slightly, making her hips swing suggestively with each step.

Tom was busy pouring champagne and talking to Olivia, who was sitting to one side. He paused in his work when he spotted Vienna. His eyes rested on her briefly before they looked past her and found Stevie. He smiled.

Vienna cast the briefest glance over her shoulder.

Yes! Stevie one. Vienna nil.

'Hello Vienna,' said Olivia.

'Hello Og,' Vienna replied. 'Still telling other people how to run their business?'

'Oh yes. How about you? Still parting fools from their money?'

Vienna laughed. 'You haven't changed a bit,' she said, with ice in her voice. 'It's lovely to see you.'

'You too.'

Vienna turned to Tom. 'Darling, thank you *so* much for letting me use your room. Did you want your key back now? Or later?' She left the comment hanging in the air.

'You keep hold of it,' Tom said. 'It'll save you having to track me down when you need it.' He handed her a glass of champagne. 'You look nice, by the way.'

Stevie couldn't help noticing the slight stiffening of Vienna's shoulders. She smiled.

'Is everything okay, Stevie?' said Tom.

'Just checking if you needed anything.'

'Actually, yes. We could do with some tea towels or something in here, for spills and things.'

'Right. I shall sort that out right away.' Stevie gave him a business-like nod. *Stevie two. Vienna, still nil.*

Most people seemed to drift towards the garden. They sat or stood in groups, sipping their drinks and chatting. The summer evening was warm and mellow. Stevie went out to check whether the food trays needed replenishing.

As she approached the table, an elderly man with a handlebar moustache helped himself to a couple of buns that had been helpfully labelled 'Hot and Spicy'. He looked at her with narrowed eyes.

'You the party planner girl?'

'Yes sir, I am.' Stevie smiled pleasantly, noting that the less fiery nibbles were almost gone. She began to gather empty trays.

'Splendid buns these,' he said.

'I'm glad you like them, Mr …?'

'Major. Major Cosham.'

Ah, Lady Beryl's friend. 'I'm glad you like them, Major Cosham. I see they're a bit strong for a lot of people.'

'That's why I like 'em,' he said. 'Reminds me of my time in India. Good stuff, this. Not like the nonsense you get in curry houses.' He paused for a moment, his eyes far away.

Stevie carried on gathering plates.

'I say,' said the Major. 'What's the name of your caterer?'

'There isn't one. We made all these nibbles here, under Priya's excellent supervision.'

The Major bit another bun in half and gulped it down. Stevie was impressed. She'd tried one of those and it had made her eyes water.

'You mean to say, Evelyn and Beryl made these? Well, I'll be damned.'

'Evelyn and Priya, yes. Of course, the rest of us helped out.'

'Hmm.' The Major eyed the food. 'Excuse me.' He wandered off bellowing 'Darling!' at a woman who was standing at the other end of the lawn talking to someone.

Stevie watched him go and then returned to her task.

A middle-aged woman appeared at her elbow. 'The garden looks fabulous,' she said. 'Has Evelyn got a new man?'

Stevie was about to reply that she wasn't privy to the details of Evelyn's love life, when she realised the woman was talking about a gardener.

'Evelyn's son, Tom, did the garden,' she said. Just saying Tom's name sent a little thrill through her chest.

'Which one's Tom?' the woman said.

'The younger one,' said another woman. 'Who works in The City.' She glanced at Stevie for confirmation.

'That's right.' Stevie picked up the empty trays. 'He's doing the bar this evening.'

'Oooh. He's quite a dishy specimen. I'd happily watch him doing my garden.' The first woman giggled and knocked back her wine. 'Why, I believe I need another drink.' She giggled again and wove off towards the house.

Stevie's fixed smile was starting to hurt her cheeks, but she had to maintain it. She started back towards the house.

The Major's voice boomed. 'That young lady there.'

Stevie turned to see a small, trim lady approaching her. 'Hello. Did you want me?'

'I'm Mrs Cosham. I was wondering, do you have a card? We will be organising a ruby wedding anniversary soon and—'

'Of course. Just a second.' Stevie scurried back to the table to put the trays down and retrieved a card from her bag. 'Do call me. Whenever you need.'

'Thank you.' The lady scanned the card. 'I must say, you seem to have done a lovely job on Evelyn's house.'

'It was a group effort.' Stevie's heart skipped. With any luck, this conversation would lead to another commission. This was what it was all about.

Mrs Cosham put the card in her clutch bag. 'Thank you.' She gave Stevie a perfunctory smile and returned to her conversation.

Feeling hopeful that this party was going to start her career, Stevie picked up her trays again.

She heard the excited voices as she got to the hall. Three teenage girls, all dressed in variations of Alice's outfit, were all talking at once, despite Lady Beryl's efforts to speak over them. Alice, who should have been helping Lady Beryl, was jiggling up and down and yapping excitedly too. Stevie guessed that the girls from the forum had arrived.

'Oooh, ooh,' said Alice, when she spotted Stevie. 'Everyone, this is Stevie. She's the one who organised it for Pete to come.'

Stevie put the trays down next to the collection tin. 'Hi.'

'Hiyeee.' It was a chorus of three. Stevie immediately singled out the girl who was the leader. She had a mass of blonde curls and too much make-up on. Her skirt was so low slung it was almost obscene.

'These young ladies have not shown me their tickets,' said Lady Beryl, finally making herself heard.

The girl in the lead rolled her eyes. She dug the ticket out of her handbag. A rather large handbag, Stevie noticed. 'Here.' She thrust the ticket at Lady Beryl. 'Happy?'

Lady Beryl glared at her and ticked off the number. 'I need your name.'

'What for?'

'Only so that we know who's here, in case there's an emergency,' said Stevie, smoothly. 'Like a fire, for example. I know it's a pain, but it's a health and safety thing.'

The girl's eyes flicked to Stevie and back to Lady Beryl. 'Veronica Smith.'

Stevie knew immediately that she'd just been given a made up name. She didn't even bother listening to the other two girls, who would probably give fake names too. She knew trouble when she saw it. A quick glance at the three girls' faces told her that under all that make-up, they were probably very young. She would have to warn Tom at the bar.

'So is he not here yet then?' said Veronica to Alice.

'Not yet.'

'You're sure he's coming?'

Alice looked at Stevie.

'Of course,' said Stevie. 'He's just waiting for the best moment, I'm sure.'

'There's a reporter from *Cause Celeb* coming too—' Alice caught Stevie's eye and clamped her mouth shut.

'What,' said Lady Beryl, 'is that?'

'Oh, just a magazine.' Stevie gave Alice a warning glare. 'Like *Tatler*.'

Lady Beryl looked unhappy, but let it pass. Stevie wondered if she approved of *Tatler* or not.

Stevie ushered the girls inside. 'The disco is through there,' she said. 'There's food in there. And the bar is here. If you'll excuse me.' She left them exclaiming about the impressive hall and ran to find Tom.

Tom and Olivia were serving wine and beer as fast as they could. Vienna was nowhere to be seen. He looked up when Stevie ran in.

'What's up?'

'There are three girls just arrived. I'm pretty sure they're under age and they're bound to have fake ID. They seem that sort,' she whispered.

Tom nodded. 'Right ho. I'll see what I can do.' He tapped a sign behind him that read 'We reserve the right to refuse to serve alcohol at our discretion'. 'If all else fails, I'll use that.'

'Okay. The one with the blonde curls just gave her name as Veronica,' said Stevie. 'In case it's useful to know. According to my list, at least one of them is called Jemima Eustace something'

Tom nodded. For a brief moment, he looked into her eyes. 'Don't worry. It'll all be fine.'

Stevie wished she could just stand there, gazing into his eyes and allowing her fears to be allayed, but she forced herself to pull herself together. 'Thanks.'

On her way out, she passed the girls going in. They were giggling at something and completely ignored her.

As she passed the door to the front room, Stevie could hear the muffled music from the disco. She popped her head in.

Opening the door immediately increased the volume. Only a few people were on the dance floor. Dilan was busy at his decks, but was looking a little bored.

She gave him a wave. He waved back and gave her the thumbs up sign. Things would hot up soon enough. She nodded and returned to her original errand.

Chapter Sixteen

SHE PUT DOWN THE EMPTY glasses she was carrying to answer her ringing phone. It was Lady Beryl.

'There's a man here with a ticket, but his name is not on the list. Come here immediately.'

'Er ... right.' Stevie ran to the front of the house. When she slewed around the corner, she saw Lady Beryl nose to nose with a short man in a loud houndstooth jacket.

'I paid two 'undred and fifty pound for this ticket!' He was red in the face and neck. Behind him a tall woman in a mustard-yellow catsuit was tugging at his arm.

'I seriously doubt that.' Lady Beryl was at her haughtiest.

Stevie put on her brightest smile. 'What seems to be the problem?'

'Who're you?' said the man.

'The organiser. Can I help?'

'I paid a fortune for these tickets and this woman says I can't come in.' The man thrust a pair of tickets at her.

'May I?' Stevie took the two tickets and examined them. They looked genuine. She checked the numbers against the list. They had been allocated to a Mr F. Howerd.

'Are you Mr Howerd?'

'No I bloody well aren't.'

The woman in the catsuit coughed.

He seemed to take stock. 'I mean. No. I am not,' he said, smoothing out his accent. 'I'm Farrier. Bill Farrier.'

Stevie cranked the smile up a notch. 'Pleased to meet you, Mr Farrier. I'm Stevie.' She handed the tickets back to him. 'I take it you bought these tickets from Mr Howerd?'

'Yes. On eBay.' He rummaged inside his jacket pocket. 'Paid two hundred and fifty pounds for each of them. Here.' He shoved a print out at her.

Stevie read the text with mounting dismay. It clearly implied that the tickets were for a private meeting with Pete. What's more, it suggested that the proceeds of the eBay auction were going to the charity, which seemed unlikely. If Triphoppers found out about this, there would be serious trouble. She wondered if she and Evelyn could be done for fraud. Really, she rationalised, they'd sold the tickets in good faith. If anyone could be sued, it would be the eBayer who sold them on under false pretences. But still, even if nothing came of it, the bad publicity could be fatal to her fledgling business. Chewing her lip, she looked up to see all three people watching her.

'Is something wrong?' Lady Beryl sounded uncharacteristically worried. 'You've gone pale.'

'Sorry.' Stevie said to Mr Farrier, 'I'm afraid, we didn't know anything about it. Mr Howerd bought these tickets from us at the normal price and sold them on without our permission. I'm sorry that you had to pay such an extortionate amount for them.'

The woman in the catsuit whispered something in the man's ear.

'My wife wants to know if that means that Pete from Triphoppers isn't coming?'

'He is, but we can't guarantee a meeting with him. All I can do is promise to try.'

Lady Beryl grabbed Stevie's arm. 'A word.' She dragged Stevie away from the Farriers. 'You are not thinking of letting those people in, are you?'

'The tickets are genuine.'

'Yes, but they're not the sort of people we want here. Just look at what that woman is wearing.'

Stevie looked. Mrs Farrier, who was a good two decades younger than her husband, had big blonde hair that didn't match the colour of her plucked eyebrows. Red high heels and a matching red diamante belt set off her catsuit. She was what Stevie's friends would call 'Chav totty'.

'I mean, they're so ... *nouveau riche.*' Lady Beryl spat the words out with distaste.

'They still have a valid ticket. We have to let them in.'

'But what will Lord Grayingham say? And the Major?!' Lady Beryl's voice was clearly audible to the Farriers now. Mr Farrier was starting to go red again.

'I'm sorry Lady Beryl. I have no choice.' Stevie strode back to the couple. 'I will do my best to introduce you to Pete,' she said. 'I'm sorry you got caught out by Mr Howerd, but we really didn't promise anything of the sort.'

'I only paid that stupid sum because Cherry here is so keen on Pete,' said Mr Farrier, his voice softening slightly. His wife, if she was really his wife, slipped a hand into his.

'I'm sorry.'

'I'll be complaining to eBay.'

'So will I, Mr Farrier. So will I.'

'I suppose we're here, we may as well stay.' Mr Farrier looked into his wife's eyes. She gave him a delighted smile.

'Wonderful,' said Stevie. 'Why don't I show you to the bar?' She ushered the couple into the house, giving the fuming Lady Beryl an apologetic smile over her shoulder.

At the bar, Olivia and Tom were eating their way through a plate of nibbles. Vienna was decorously perched on a chair. Tom's eyebrows rose as Stevie led the guests in, but he maintained his composure. Mrs Farrier simpered a little and flicked her hair.

'You got any beer?' said Mr Farrier, putting himself firmly between his wife and Tom.

'I do indeed.' Tom produced a bottle and pint glass.

Mr Farrier took the bottle and picked up a glass of champagne. 'Here you go love.'

Mrs Farrier took the glass. In her high heels she towered above her husband.

'There's access to the garden through there.' Stevie pointed to the library. 'Or the disco is through here.' There were muffled sounds of ABBA.

'Ooh, let's dance, Bill.' Mrs Farrier trotted forward, dragging her reluctant husband behind her.

'What,' said Tom, 'was that?'

Stevie quickly outlined what was going on.

'Phew,' said Olivia. 'He made a tidy profit from that.'

'I know. I'm furious,' Stevie said.

Tom grinned. 'Are you annoyed that someone sold the tickets on? Or that you didn't think of auctioning them in the first place?'

Stevie allowed herself a moment to relax. 'Both,' she admitted.

Olivia laughed. 'I like this girl.'

Vienna had been listening to all this in silence. 'It takes a lot of money to make designer-wear look that cheap.' She sounded thoughtful.

Tom gave her a suspicious glance. 'Vienna ...'

Vienna grinned and slipped off her seat. 'Back in a minute.' She disappeared after the Farriers.

'Vienna!' Tom called after her. 'Come back here.' When she didn't stop, he swore.

'What?' said Stevie, alarmed by Tom's reaction.

'Think about it,' said Olivia. 'He's been ripped off. She's a litigation lawyer ...'

Stevie stared at him. Surely, he didn't mean that Vienna would encourage the Farriers to sue? 'But that would reflect badly on Evelyn.' She turned back. 'Your mum!'

Tom scowled and nodded his head.

'That woman has no scruples.' Olivia finished her drink.

@LuvAshbysEyes:
OMG! HE'S HERE!!!!

STEVIE RUSHED TOWARDS the crowd of people in the hall. At its centre was a group of giggling girls, who were being held back by a stern-faced woman, and Pete, who was looking mildly amused.

'Will you sign my bra?' Veronica lifted her top to expose a white lacy bra.

Pete took a step back. Stevie scanned the room for the journalist and photographer, but didn't see anyone who looked likely.

'I'm sorry, I don't sign underwear,' said Pete. 'I'll sign your top, if you like.' He took the marker pen from Veronica, who pulled her top down with a pout. 'If you could let me have your shoulder. It's much easier to write on shoulders – what's your name?' he asked

The girl shot a glance at Stevie and muttered, 'Veronica.'

Stevie grinned. The girl was clearly regretting having lied about her name, but couldn't back out now without losing face.

Pete wrote something on the girl's shoulder. 'There. Anyone else?'

He spotted Stevie. 'Hello Stevie,' he said, with what seemed to be relief. 'I'll be right with you.'

Stevie grinned. 'Take your time.'

Pete's guest sidled up to Stevie. 'I'm Sharon. From Triphoppers' PR department.'

They shook hands.

'Is *Cause Celeb* here?' Sharon looked around the room.

'Not yet,' said Stevie apologetically. She had hoped the reporter would be here before the celebrity. Now she was beginning to worry that the reporter wasn't coming at all.

Sharon frowned. 'We came on the understanding that they would be here.'

'Oh, they will be,' said Stevie.

A flash went off as one of the girls took a photo. Stevie motioned for Alice to take one too. If all else failed, they could pass them on to *Cause Celeb* themselves. Alice seemed to spring into life out of a daze. She pulled out her phone and started snapping away.

Having signed several shoulders and a few pieces of paper, Pete handed the pen back and smiled at his audience. 'Tell me about this charity.'

The other girls looked at Alice, who opened her mouth, but managed to produce only a squeak.

Veronica sighed, tossed her hair and stepped in front of Alice. 'It's a charity based in Sri Lanka.' She guided Pete to the display and talked him through it. Even though it was obvious that she was merely reading what was on the boards, she kept talking with supreme confidence.

Stevie was impressed. It took a lot of bravado to pull that off.

When Veronica had run out of things to read off the board, Stevie stepped forward. 'Hi Pete.'

'Stevie. Lovely to see you again.' He shook her hand and kissed her on the cheek.

'Thanks for coming. Shall I show you round?'

'Yes, please.'

Stevie sent Alice off to get some drinks and ushered them into the library. The others followed, giggling.

She was halfway round showing Pete and his whispering entourage the garden when she remembered the Farriers. 'Oh,' she said. 'There's another fan I'd like you to meet, if you can possibly bear it.'

Pete shrugged. 'All publicity is good publicity. Lead on.'

'Wait here,' she said. 'I'll just go get them.' She went into the disco, where Mr and Mrs Farrier were dancing to Blondie. She caught Mrs Farrier's eye and mouthed 'Pete's here'.

Mrs Farrier immediately grabbed her husband's hand and dragged him over.

When they got back to Pete, he was talking to a woman with a cascade of red hair. 'Stevie, this is Amber, from *Cause Celeb*.'

Amber turned round. 'Hi. You must be the organiser.'

'I am.' Stevie shook her hand, feeling weak with relief. If the magazine had failed to send anyone, she would have lost all credibility with Pete. Remembering her guests, she added, 'I've just got to introduce someone to Pete.' She introduced Mr and Mrs Farrier. The lady in question giggled and went bright red. Her husband stepped up and gave Pete a firm handshake.

'Farrier,' he said.

'Pete Gosling.'

Stevie couldn't help thinking that Pete was utterly charming. So far he'd been mobbed by teenage girls, glowered at by Lady Beryl and was currently being alpha-male eyeballed by Mr Farrier and he was taking it all in his stride.

'I'm from up North myself,' Pete was saying.

Mr Farrier seemed to soften a little. 'Whereabouts?'

'Near Knutsford.'

'Posh.'

Pete laughed. 'Very middle class, I think.'

Stevie left them chatting and turned to Amber, who was taking photos of Pete with a handheld camera. 'Is there no photographer?'

'No.' Amber lowered the camera and gave Stevie a funny look. 'This isn't high profile enough to merit it.' She took another photo, the flash went off.

'Who're you?' said Mr Farrier, glaring at her suspiciously. 'Why are you taking photos?'

'This is Amber.' Stevie stepped in smoothly. 'She's from *Cause Celeb* magazine. She's covering Pete's visit to us.'

Mrs Farrier spoke. 'Are we going to be in *Cause Celeb*?' she said. Her voice was unexpectedly deep and melodious. Stevie had been expecting something more high-pitched and squeaky. She glanced at Amber.

'Could be,' said Amber. 'Depends how the photos turn out.' She looked Mrs Farrier's outfit up and down and raised the camera again. 'May I?'

Mrs Farrier put her arm through her husband's and posed. She was a very pretty woman underneath all the make-up and, apparently, used to posing for the camera. Her husband, on the other hand, appeared stiff and false.

Stevie stepped next to Pete. 'Can I get you another drink?'

'Please. Better still ...' He gave a swift glance towards Sharon, the PR woman, who was watching Amber carefully. 'Where's the bar?'

Gathering that he wanted a moment's quiet, Stevie said, 'Just a second.'

She went to Sharon and said, 'Those girls over there are very active members of the Triphoppers' fan community.'

'And?'

'If you wanted to canvas opinion on what the fan base is into, they'll happily tell you. Veronica, in particular, could be a mine of information. And she'd probably be very amenable if you asked her to post nice things on the forum – things that are better coming as a buzz from inside, rather than as part of a press release, for example.'

Sharon eyed the girls thoughtfully.

Stevie could almost see the cogs whirring in her mind. 'I'll introduce you.'

A few minutes later, with Sharon talking to the teenagers and Amber writing down the Farriers' details, Stevie managed to get Pete out of the room without any of them noticing.

He took a glass of wine and sank into a chair, gratefully. 'Fans are great. But it can be hard work. Especially the young ones.'

Stevie smiled. She had reservations about his young fans.

'So,' said Pete. 'Marsh tells me this is your first gig.'

'You've seen him?'

'I had dinner with him and Jane last week. Your email meant that I had an excuse to get back in touch with Jane, which was good because I'm terrible at keeping in touch. It's very exciting news about the baby.'

So they told him, a relative stranger, a mere few weeks after they'd told her. Stevie pushed the thought away. 'Yes. It is.'

Feeling the need to change the subject, she said, 'Thank you so much for agreeing to come, it means a lot to us ... to the charity.'

Pete waved her thanks away. 'We need the publicity, frankly. I'm not Ashby, he's the one the fans are really after. The rest of us do what we can with smaller things like this. It's all part of the job.'

'Your PR person seems pretty good.'

Pete laughed. 'She is. Her boss, Mike, is a pretty ruthless PR man. I don't always agree with his methods, but they do work.'

Stevie thought of the magazine campaign that had nearly destroyed Jane and Marsh's relationship. Ruthless it certainly was. She was about to comment when she noticed that she no longer had Pete's attention. He was staring at the door. She turned.

Vienna had just undulated in, with another plate of canapés in her hand. She stopped in the doorway, one foot ahead of the other in a perfect pose, and locked eyes on Pete.

Pete stood up.

'Er ... Pete, this is Vienna. Vienna, this is—'

'Pete Gosling. I know.' She held out her hand. 'I'm Vienna Jansen-Verlag. Delighted to meet you.'

'Likewise.'

Vienna handed the plate to Stevie, who took it out of surprise. Vienna opened her clutch bag and produced a business card. 'My card.'

He scanned it. 'You're a lawyer?'

'Yes. And we do have a few clients in show biz.' She gave him a charming smile and slipped her arm through his. 'So Pete, tell me about yourself.'

Stevie watched them leave and took the plate of canapés over to the bar. 'I guess these were meant for you.'

'Yes, until Vienna saw something more interesting.' Olivia helped herself to a meat patty, holding it delicately between forefinger and thumb.

'So that was the famous Pete,' said Tom.

Stevie was surprised that he didn't seem overly bothered about Vienna's flirting with Pete. Perhaps he was still annoyed with her.

Tom was watching her intently.

'What?' Did she have lipstick on her teeth?

'Nothing. I just can't believe you pulled that trick off. I take it the reporter is here too.'

'She is. In fact—' Stevie spotted Amber coming in, her head turning as she looked for Pete. 'Here she is now.' She waved. 'Amber. Over here.'

'Where's Pete gone?' Amber said.

Stevie glanced at Tom. He was best placed to know where Vienna was likely to have gone.

'Garden, probably,' he said. 'If not, you'll have a hell of a job finding them in this house.'

'Do you want to go look for him?'

'Actually, I need to get some details off you first. Like your name?'

Stevie handed her a card.

'How do you know Pete?' A pen appeared from nowhere.

Stevie hesitated. The obvious answer was that her sister-in-law was Ashby's ex. This piece of information might have been interesting enough for Amber to resurrect the old story and make the piece more substantial than a small item in a back page. It would give Stevie's career a decent boost. But

Jane had been upset by the idea of her contacting Triphoppers in any capacity. Mentioning her to someone from the press would cause even more upset. Did she really want to deepen the rift between her and her brother, just when things were looking like they might be getting better?

The pause was long enough for Amber's eyes to light up with suspicion.

'Sorry,' said Stevie, hoping to buy time. 'What was the question again? I got distracted there.'

'How do you know Pete? Is there a mutual acquaintance?'

'Oh. We met at a wedding. My friend, his friend. I got talking to him and he was so nice and said I should contact him whenever ... So I did.' She laughed, in what she hoped was a convincing manner.

Amber scribbled something down. There was a burst of noise as someone opened the door to the disco. As the door swung shut, the noise dropped.

'That's one sound proof door,' said Amber. 'This is an impressive house.'

Stevie grabbed the chance to change the subject. 'Let me show you round.'

By the time Stevie finished walking Amber round the house, it was well and truly dark outside. They had been all over the public areas of the house, but failed to spot Pete. Stevie was beginning to think Vienna had taken him to Tom's room.

The garden was lit up as it had been the previous night. Stevie felt a small rush of sadness as she thought of her close encounter with Tom just twenty-four hours before.

Amber was looking round. 'Wow! This looks stunning.'

'All Tom's work. You know, the barman.'

'A man of many talents, clearly.' Amber seemed distracted. 'Your name ... It's Stevie Winfield, right? Are you by any chance related to Jane Porter's husband, Marshall Winfield?' She raised her eyebrows.

Bugger. Stevie had hoped she'd got away without bringing Jane into it. If this woman decided to follow up what Jane was doing now, both Marsh and Jane would be unbelievably upset. On the other hand, Amber had clearly done her research and lying to her would be pointless.

'Yes, as a matter of fact, I am,' said Stevie. 'It was at their wedding that I met Pete.'

Amber nodded. 'Thought so.' The notebook was back in her hand. 'And how are Jane and Marshall now?'

Happy. Expecting a baby. 'Fine.' Stevie kept her eyes on the garden, wishing there were some way she could escape this conversation before she inadvertently gave something personal away. Why on earth couldn't Lady Beryl pester her now? When she needed her to?

Her eyes fell on the gazebo. She could just make out two figures, their heads close together. One of them moved and the fairy lights gleamed off a sheet of blonde hair. 'I think we've found Pete.'

Amber narrowed her eyes and peered. 'So we have,' she said, a thrill of excitement in her voice. 'Wait here.' Amber took off her shoes and disappeared down the metal steps.

Stevie wondered whether she should make a noise and warn the couple. She thought of how much trouble her brother had got into with his firm when his picture appeared in *Cause Celeb*. Would Vienna get into as much trouble? It would serve her right.

She smiled as the flash went off, illuminating Pete and Vienna's embrace. They both turned, startled by the sudden light.

Stevie drew back out of sight.

Amber reappeared. 'Fabulous,' she said, her eyes shining. She retrieved her shoes. 'Let's go back in.'

Stevie rather thought she'd forgotten all about the conversation about Jane and Marsh.

Chapter Seventeen

PETE LEFT SOON AFTERWARDS, taking Vienna with him. He thanked Stevie before he left, showing no sign of upset at being snapped by Amber. Amber retreated to the bar and was soon chatting to Tom and a few other guests who had left the dark garden to stand around inside instead.

'Stephanie.'

Stevie turned to find Lady Beryl bearing down on her like a galleon in full sail. 'Lady Beryl.'

'I have some questions to ask you. Who is that woman with the red hair that's taking photos of people?'

'That's Amber. From *Cause Celeb*.'

'The magazine that's like *Tatler*?'

'That's the one.'

Lady Beryl drew herself up to her full height. 'She has not taken a photo of me and my husband.'

'Oh dear,' said Stevie. 'I'm sure she meant to. Why don't you go ask her?'

'What? And *beg* to have my photo taken? No Stephanie. You will ask her.'

Stevie sighed. 'Okay. She's in the bar. You find Lord Grayingham. I'll ask her.'

'I would prefer to be photographed in the library,' said Lady Beryl. 'We shall wait in there.'

Stevie considered running off to a different part of the house. She was tired and in desperate need of a sit down and stiff drink. But she knew Lady Beryl would eventually catch up with her and she was too tired to think of an excuse as to why she hadn't found Amber, so she dragged herself into the bar and tapped the journalist on the shoulder.

Amber laughed when she explained the situation. 'You'd be amazed how often that happens. We usually just take a haphazard photo and it keeps them happy.' She stood, grabbing her glass and her camera. 'Lead me to them.'

'Before you go,' Tom said. 'It's nearly midnight. I'm going to do last orders. Is that okay?'

Midnight. Oh good. Only a few more hours to go and she could go to bed. 'Yes, that's fine. Thanks for keeping it going for as long as you have.' She gave him a grateful smile and ushered Amber towards the library.

Once the photo of Lady Beryl and Lord Grayingham, who was red in the face and wobbly from drink, had been taken, Amber made her apologies and said goodbye. Stevie found Amber's coat for her and saw her to the door.

'I'll tell you something,' said Amber. 'I didn't want to come to this, but I'm glad I did. It's been fun. And ...' She patted her pockets to check that she had everything. 'I think I've found the perfect place for my mum and dad to come on their thirtieth wedding anniversary. I spoke to the bar guy. Tom, is it? Sounds like it's pretty reasonable room rates for such a lovely house.'

'Brilliant, I'm glad.' Stevie felt happy that Evelyn's plans were working out as well. She waited with Amber until the taxi arrived and waved her off.

Standing outside the house, Stevie felt reluctant to go back in. Every spare minute she seemed to be wanted by somebody. Still, this was her job. She had to get on with it. She went back inside and shut the door. She was just wondering whether she could take her shoes off and carry on with her duties barefoot, when her phone rang. She checked the display. It was Evelyn. The food was all gone, so there couldn't be anything important that Evelyn wanted now. She ignored the call.

Simultaneously, Lady Beryl's voice shouted, 'Stephanie!'

Stevie groaned. The last thing she wanted to do was to talk to that old bat again. All she wanted was five minutes peace.

'Stephanie? Where is that girl?' Lady Beryl was getting closer.

Spotting the door to the coat cupboard, Stevie darted in and shut it behind her.

The only light in the cupboard was a thin line from under the door. After a few seconds, Stevie's eyes adjusted enough for her to step over the few items on the floor and find a wall to lean against. As the cupboard took up most of the space underneath the large staircase and only had a coat rail in it, there was plenty of room. She slipped off her shoes and closed her eyes with relief. Outside she could hear Lady Beryl.

'Where is she? I told her something like this would happen. I warned her.'

'Actually, I need to speak to her as well.' That was Tom's voice. 'If I see her, I'll tell her you're looking for her.'

'Why aren't you in the bar, anyway?'

'Bar's closed. I called time.'

'Well that's a mercy. I don't want that man to have a drop more.'

Stevie groaned. This didn't sound good. It sounded like Lady Beryl was going to blame her for Lord Grayingham's inebriation. That was hardly fair. She should get out there and sort it out, regardless. But two more minutes wouldn't hurt, surely?

'I'm going to try the kitchen.' Lady Beryl clumped off.

There was a brief silence, followed by a faint beep.

Stevie opened her eyes and stared at the darkness. It was nice in this cupboard. Calm. Besides, she couldn't very well walk out without Tom asking her what she was doing. She might as well stay put for a few minutes. She wriggled her toes and leaned her head back.

Her phone rang, making her jump. She clutched at her bag and tried to fish it out. Outside, footsteps approached the cupboard. Stevie stared at her phone. It was Tom, phoning her. She quickly cancelled the call.

The door opened. 'Stevie?' Tom peered into the gloom. 'What are you doing?'

Stevie sighed. 'Hiding from Lady Beryl.'

Tom glanced over his shoulder and slipped into the cupboard. 'She's looking for you, you know,' he whispered.

'I know. I know. I just wanted a couple of minutes to myself.' She bent her head and turned her phone on to silent. When she looked up, Tom was staring at her, his face ghostly in the light of the phone.

'Poor thing. You've been running around all evening. Have you had anything to eat?'

Stevie had to think about that. She realised she hadn't eaten since lunchtime. No wonder she was feeling awful.

There were footsteps outside. 'Normally, Stevie would do this,' said Lady Beryl. 'But she's disappeared at the moment.' There was a scrape as someone put something into the collection box. 'Thank you very much. Your donation will be much appreciated. Did you have a coat?'

Tom started and put his hand out to catch himself. His arm dislodged a number of coats and hangers, which crashed to the ground.

'What's going on in there?' Lady Beryl said. Footsteps approached the cupboard.

Stevie's heart was pounding. Bad enough she would be caught hiding in a coat cupboard when she should be out there working, but she was hiding in there with a man. Lady Beryl would have a fit.

Hmm. One man in a black suit looked pretty much like another from the back. And he was broad enough to hide her.

The handle turned. Stevie grabbed Tom by the lapels and swung him round so that his back was to the door. Without pausing to think any further, she threw her arms around his neck and pressed her lips to his.

Light fell into the cupboard.

'Oh my goodness!' Lady Beryl made a strangled noise. 'How perfectly disgusting! I knew we shouldn't have sold tickets to just any old ...' She slammed the cupboard door shut, still talking.

But Stevie didn't hear any more. Because, after a moment of stunned hesitation, Tom was kissing her back with an intensity that said he'd been wanting to do so for a long time. His hands found her hips and pulled her closer. His mouth opened against hers. He tasted slightly spicy and smelled delicious. Stevie melted into his arms. Her fingers explored his curls, easing through the soft ringlets. She felt Tom's hand move up to her face, a thumb stroked her cheek, making her feel warm all over. She could be here like this, kissing him, forever. He pulled her even closer. She could feel his skin calling to hers through the layers of clothing. All other thoughts emptied from her mind. All she could think of was how much she wanted him.

Suddenly his phone rang. A second later, hers started vibrating madly at her feet, where her bag had ended up.

Tom pulled away with a sigh. 'I guess I should get that.'

Stevie bowed her head against his chest and sighed. 'Me too.'

He kissed the top of her head, removed her arms from round his neck and opened the door. Checking that there was no one outside, he stepped out, answering the phone as he did so. 'Mum. What's wrong?'

It took Stevie a second to recover her composure. Trying to push all thoughts of the curtailed kiss out of her mind, she rooted in her bag until she found the phone and answered it.

'Where are you?' Lady Beryl demanded.

'I hear you're looking for me, is something wrong?' Stevie pushed the door open and used the light to locate her shoes. They pinched when she put them back on.

'There are people fornicating in the coat cupboard.' Beryl shrieked down the phone.

Fornicating? If only ... 'Okay, I'll see what—'

'Never mind that,' Lady Beryl snapped. 'Come to the front room. This is more important. The disco is getting really out of hand.'

Oh dear. What could be more pressing than people fornicating in a cupboard? Saying she'd be right there, she shot out of the cupboard, startling a guest who was passing by.

Lady Beryl and Evelyn were standing outside the door to the disco. Lady Beryl stopped talking when she saw Stevie. 'What happened to you?'

Stevie realised her hair had come loose during Tom's embrace and was slipping down on one side. 'I wasn't looking where I was going ... in the garden.' She hastily retied it. 'What's the matter?'

Lady Beryl pointed dramatically at the door. 'Have a look in there.'

Stevie opened the door. The disco was going full swing. Dilan had his head down and was swaying with the music as he merged one track into another. The dance floor was a mêlée of coloured light. In the middle was Mr Farrier, dancing his heart out. His shirt was flapping open, revealing a hairy belly. A small crowd of people were fanned around him, clapping and cheering him on. His wife was dancing opposite him, just out of reach of his energetic limbs.

Stevie sidled up to Dilan, who removed one of his earphones so she could shout in his ear. 'How long has this been going on?'

'Isn't it great!' He shouted back. 'They're all loving it. I'm going to have to bring the cheesy tunes playlist full circle to keep him going.'

Stevie opened her mouth to protest, but shut it again. She looked at the people on the dance floor. Most people were watching Mr Farrier and laughing. The man himself was concentrating hard on his dancing and his wife seemed to be delighted with him. There didn't appear to be any immediate danger from anyone to anyone. And they all seemed to be having fun. The business-like side of Stevie pointed out that if Mr Farrier was having fun, he was less likely to think of suing them afterwards.

Mr Farrier made an expressive move with his hips, which would have been lewd if his belly weren't bouncing along with it. His wife clapped her hands. People cheered. Stevie sidled back out of the room.

Lady Beryl and Evelyn were waiting for her. 'Well?' said Lady Beryl.

Stevie stared at her irate face. The vision of Mr Farrier boogieing on down flashed through her mind. A giggle rose in her throat and burst out before she could stop it.

'Well, aren't you going to put a stop to it?'

Lady Beryl was so annoyed, it made Stevie laugh all the more. Evelyn's mouth began to twitch. She opened the door and peeked in. Then she too began to laugh. Soon the two of them were leaning against the wall, gasping for breath. Lady Beryl made huffing noises.

'I'm sorry Lady Beryl,' said Stevie wiping tears away from her eyes. 'But have you seen him? It's so *so* funny.'

Lady Beryl seemed to deflate a little. She peered into the room. 'Oh my goodness.' Her face was a picture of horror. 'He's taken his shirt off and is twirling it round his head!'

Stevie and Evelyn collapsed in more peals of laughter. After a moment, Lady Beryl smiled. 'I suppose it is rather funny,' she conceded.

'Funny, oh Beryl, it's hilarious,' said Evelyn. 'I think I shall have to go find a tissue.' She looked at Stevie and laughed again. 'Your make-up, dear.'

Stevie took gulps of air, trying to get a lid on her mirth. 'Right. I'd better go fix it.' She was breathing hard as giggles threatened to overwhelm her again. She set off to find a bathroom, wiping her eyes and occasionally giggling.

Chapter Eighteen

STEVIE HAD CLEANED off her smudged mascara and got the giggles under control by the time she ran into Tom again. He was frowning.

'What's up?' She thought of the last time she'd seen him and her arms itched to wrap themselves around him again. She was back in professional mode now, she told herself. Her hands curled into fists in order to resist the temptation to touch him.

'I seem to have lost Alice. Mum was looking for her. I've searched everywhere and I can't find her.'

'Have you checked the cupboards?' Stevie bit her lip. That had come out before she'd had time to censor it.

He gave her a sideways glance, his eyes twinkling. 'Even the cupboards.' His expression went serious again. 'The last time I saw her, she was heading off with those girls. I'm worried they're up to something.'

Now Stevie was worried too. Thinking back, she realised the girls had all disappeared as soon as Pete left, which was some time ago now. 'I'll help you look. Where have you checked?'

Tom ran through the list of places he'd been. 'That just leaves the family's rooms and the basement rooms.'

Stevie was likely to get lost if she tried to find Alice's room, so she suggested she took the basement while Tom ran up to the residential rooms.

The basement consisted of a number of small rooms that were used as storerooms, offices and one downstairs reading room. As Stevie descended the stairs, she heard voices. Oh good. They were here. She felt a wave of relief. If they'd left the house to go clubbing, finding them would have been next to impossible.

She followed the voices to one of the rooms and opened the door. The curtains had been drawn and the girls were sitting on the floor. The room was illuminated by candles, set in saucers and dangerously close to the shelves of paperbacks. All four girls looked up. Stevie flicked on the main light.

'What's going on?' Her eyes took in the girls' appearances. They seemed slightly glazed and were slow to react. They were drunk.

The open candle flames danced.

They were drunk and had put the house at risk.

Anger flared in Stevie. 'Well?'

'None of your business,' snapped Veronica.

Stevie ignored her. 'Alice, get those candles out. They could set fire to the books.' She strode in and began pinching the candles off, one by one.

'Hey!' Veronica stood up, unsteadily. 'Who are you to come in here—'

'I,' said Stevie, 'am a very angry adult.' As she neared the girl she smelled alcohol. She looked around until she saw a nearly empty bottle. She and Veronica both made a dive for it, but Stevie was faster. She sniffed. 'Vodka?'

So that was what had been in Veronica's big bag. She should have checked it. If these girls had drunk a full bottle of this stuff among them, they were likely to be very drunk indeed. It was a miracle that none of them had been sick already.

'Right. I'm confiscating this. Alice, is there a kitchen other than the big one upstairs where you can sit and have coffee?'

Alice shook her head.

'We don't want to have coffee,' Veronica said. The other two girls stood up and the three of them stood in front of her, their manner threatening. 'Why don't you bugger off and leave us to have fun.'

'Yeah,' Alice piped up. She was still on the floor.

'Because this house has an alcohol licence. If you are found here, drunk, we may lose that licence. *And*,' she added as one of them opened her mouth, 'you could have burned the whole place down with those damned candles.'

Veronica laughed. 'Nah. That only happens in the movies.'

'You know that for a fact do you? Or did you think you'd try it out in someone else's house?' Stevie pulled out her phone and called Tom, trying not to take her eyes off the girls the whole time.

'We're in the basement,' she said. 'They're drunk. Come down here. Don't tell Evelyn.'

Alice sniffed. 'Gran's going to kill me.'

'You should have thought of that beforehand.' Stevie held out a hand and hauled her to her feet. 'Right, you lot. I'm getting some coffee down you and sobering you up.'

'No you're not.'

'Yes. I am. Now come with me.'

The girls didn't move.

'Make me.' Veronica smirked.

Stevie was now so angry that she was starting to shake with it. She stepped up so that she was face to face with the teenager. She growled, 'Any more lip from you and I will take you down to the police station to be sobered up in their cells.'

'You don't know my real name,' Veronica sneered back, but there was a hint of uncertainty in her voice now.

'I don't need to,' said Stevie. 'That's for the police to find out.'

'You wouldn't *dare*.'

Stevie brought her face closer and looked into her eyes. 'Try me.' They glared at each other for a moment, each trying to call the other's bluff.

Veronica's gaze faltered and Stevie knew she'd won.

One of the other girls said, 'I feel sick.'

Stevie grabbed a nearby potpourri bowl, tipped its contents on the floor and shoved it under the girl's face, just as the vomit arced out of her mouth. All the others took a step back. The smell, interlaced with that of the displaced potpourri filled the room. The girls were all starting to look pale.

Tom appeared and took in the scene. 'Shit.'

'Tom, get some coffee into them. And some toast if they can take it. You,' she said to the girl who was retching over the now full bowl. 'Come with me.'

Stevie took her to the nearest bathroom and waited while she threw up some more. Afterward she helped her clean her face up, splashing it liberally with cold water, and took her, via the outdoor courtyard, to the kitchen.

Tom was giving the other girls coffee and water. Alice was huddled in a chair at the far end, sobbing. Veronica and the other girl were making cow eyes at Tom.

Stevie felt another wave of anger. She also felt curiously responsible for all of them. Especially Alice. She suddenly wondered if this was how Marsh felt when he'd found her stoned in Tom's room. No wonder he went mental.

'Feel better now?' she asked the girl who had been sick.

The girl nodded. She was staring blankly at the mug that Tom had placed in front of her.

There was a moment of silence as everyone avoided eye contact. Tom poured Stevie a coffee and placed it in front of her.

'Now then, Veronica, or whatever your name is,' said Stevie. 'Where were you planning to stay tonight?'

Veronica just sat there.

'Well?'

'We're taking the bus back to London,' Veronica muttered.

'And your parents are okay with you wandering around London at three in the morning?'

More silence. The other two girls stared at Veronica, who didn't flinch.

Stevie sighed. 'Let me guess. You two have told your parents that you're staying with her.' She pointed to Veronica. 'And her parents are either away, or don't care.'

Veronica said nothing, but the guilty looks from the other two confirmed she was right.

Stevie sent a silent question to Tom. He moved his head, indicating that they should go to the other end of the kitchen.

'What am I going to do?' she whispered.

'Put them on the bus,' said Tom. 'They look to be around sixteen. There are three of them. They'll be more or less sober by the time that coffee kicks in. Although I think you threatening to take them to the police sobered them up pretty well.'

'But they're just kids!'

'Not really. We can see them onto the bus. If you like, you can give them money for a taxi at the other end.'

'What if they get off at an earlier stop?'

'There isn't an earlier stop. It's a direct bus.'

Stevie considered the trio. Veronica seemed to be recovering her bravado, but the other two were well and truly subdued.

Tom's phone rang. 'What?' he said into it. 'What floorshow?' He grinned at Stevie. 'Apparently, there's a fat man dancing with his shirt off ...'

'Yeah. I know.'

Tom raised one eyebrow and returned to the phone. 'Actually Og, how're you getting home tonight?' He listened. 'I might call you back.'

He put his phone back in his pocket. 'Og's going back to London. She could watch them.'

'We can't ask her to do that. She's a guest.'

Tom shrugged. 'I doubt there's anything that those three can come up with to faze her.'

'Maybe.'

'I'll ask.' He pulled out his phone again.

Stevie returned to the girls and put her hand on Alice's shoulder. Alice was sobbing in earnest now. Stevie knelt beside her. 'Hey,' she said gently. 'It's okay.'

'It's not,' said Alice. 'Gran's going to murder me.'

Stevie looked at her with pity. Alice was only fourteen and right now she looked even younger. 'Well, hopefully we can sort something out.' She became aware of Veronica watching her with interest. Searching for a chink in her armour, no doubt. 'We'll talk about it later.' She patted Alice's shoulder.

'So,' said Veronica. 'Decided what you're going to do with us yet?'

'Technically, you're not my responsibility. You've told me you're over eighteen. I just need to get you off the premises.'

'Isn't *he* going to take us home?' Veronica looked at Tom and grinned. 'He can take me anywhere he likes. Any way he likes.'

Tom gave Stevie a horrified look that said he was not going to be left alone with these girls. Ever.

Stevie sighed again.

Stevie and Tom took everyone out of the side entrance and bundled them into a taxi, with Olivia sitting in front and the girls in the back. Once inside again, Stevie leaned against the side door while Tom locked it.

'I hope we did the right thing,' she said.

'You did,' he said. 'You couldn't let them stay here and risk Evelyn or Lady Beryl finding out.'

'I know.' Stevie closed her eyes. 'What's the time?'

'Just gone half one.' He leaned against the door next to her. 'Long night huh?'

'Tell me about it. I just hope nothing else goes wrong. I don't think I could handle any more.'

'You dealt with those girls really well,' he said.

She looked sideways at him to see if he was joking. He turned his head and smiled at her. 'I mean it. In fact, you're quite scary when you're being grown up.'

She stared, unsure how to take that. Was he trying to tell her that he no longer saw her as a child? How much of that was to do with how she handled the girls and how much was to do with the kiss?

He met her gaze, his eyes twinkling. Stevie felt her heart speed up. Footsteps approached and they both turned their heads to see who it was.

'Hello you two,' said Evelyn. She looked tired. 'What are you doing?'

'Just discussing how the ball went,' said Tom.

'It's not over yet,' Evelyn said. 'I think we might have to wind up the disco. Mr Farrier is getting a little less funny.'

Stevie nodded and peeled herself away from where she was leaning.

'Was Alice okay?' Evelyn asked Tom. Alice had been sent to her room to sleep off the alcohol.

'Oh yes. You know how it is. I think it was the excitement of seeing Pete in the flesh more than anything else. She wouldn't shut up about it.'

'I'm sure I'll hear all about it tomorrow,' said Evelyn. 'By the way, Stevie, Lady Beryl and Lord Grayingham left a few minutes ago. Important things to do tomorrow apparently.'

Meaning 'We won't come and help with the clean-up'. On the other hand, things were a lot easier without Lady Beryl around. 'I'll go have a word with Dilan,' she said, and trudged wearily towards the disco.

Dilan, was already winding down. A slow ballad was playing and a few couples, the Farriers included, were swaying in time to the music. Mr Farrier had, thankfully, recovered his shirt and jacket.

Dilan removed his headset. 'I thought Mr Disco over there was getting a little too manic, so I thought I'd take it down and finish. I know it's earlier than planned,' he said apologetically.

'No, that's fine. I was actually coming to ask you to do just that,' Stevie said.

When she cast an eye over the dance floor, Stevie couldn't help noticing at least one couple were lost to the rest of the world and engrossed in a kiss. She thought of her own kiss with Tom and allowed herself a moment of reflection before dragging herself back to the present.

'So, it was a good night, then?'

Dilan chuckled. 'More for some than others.'

Stevie thought of Tom again. 'Yes,' she agreed. 'Definitely.'

If the disco was closing down, she should really see if she could hint to the other guests that the evening was coming to an end. 'I'll be back in about ten minutes.'

'Cool. Should have this lot sorted and the lights turned on by then.' Dilan put his headset back on. 'Two more songs ladies and gentlemen,' he said into the sound system. 'Let's make them good ones.'

Stevie ended up by the door, handing out coats and accepting comments on how well things had gone. A few people asked for her card, which she gladly gave out.

'That were a cracking good laugh,' hollered Mr Farrier, as he staggered slightly. He was shouting, presumably because his ears were still ringing from the disco. His shirt was buttoned up but still untucked. 'I haven't had that much fun in years.'

'I'm glad to hear that,' said Stevie.

'And Cherry got to meet her pop star, so it's good all round.'

'That's fantastic.'

'Tell you what though,' he said, dropping his voice from bellow to merely loud. 'I thought it were a right rip off at the time, but I'm glad I paid up for it now.'

Stevie smiled and refrained from mentioning that they weren't going to see much of his two hundred and fifty pounds. That would go to the eBayer who sold the tickets on.

'And it's a bloody good cause, don't you think love?' he said to his wife. 'You got my cheque book handy?'

Cherry smiled and fished it out of her bag.

'You call us a taxi,' he said to Stevie. 'I'll make a little donation to your charity box.'

'Of course.' Stevie moved a discreet distance away and called a taxi. She could hear Cherry whispering to her husband.

'How much?' he said.

Whisper, whisper, whisper.

'For you my love, anything.' He wrote the cheque, folded it into four and dropped it in the collection box.

'The taxi should be here in about five minutes,' Stevie said.

The Farriers stood side by side, arms around each other's waist.

'So what do you do, Mr Farrier?' Stevie said, with what she hoped sounded like polite curiosity.

'Self-made man, me,' he said. 'Own a string of golf shops. Give the girl one of our cards, Cherry.'

Cherry produced a card from her bag and handed it over. Stevie gave one of her own ones back.

'If you ever need any golfing equipment, I'm your man.'

'I shall pass your card on to someone I know. I think he'll be very interested.'

'That's the idea. Word of mouth, that's what sells. Better than any of your posh adverts.' He grinned. 'We gave a bunch of cards to that fancy lawyer bird. I bet she's got golfing friends.'

Assuming he was talking about Vienna, Stevie nodded. 'I'm sure she has.'

After a few more minutes' chit-chat, the taxi arrived and the Farriers left. As they went out the door, Mr Farrier's hand was not too subtly fondling his wife's bottom.

Stevie shook her head and turned to say goodbye to another guest.

With everyone dispatched to their homes and the lights being turned off, Stevie took her shoes in one hand and headed up to her room. She finally allowed herself to think about her kiss with Tom. He had been so reluctant to kiss her before, yet once their lips had met, it was as though a dam of longing had been breached. Perhaps it was loyalty to Vienna that had prevented him from kissing her. After Vienna head-ed off with Pete, there was nothing to stop him from being with Stevie. Unless of course he still thought her too young. Or too needy.

As she entered an unfamiliar corridor, she realised she'd taken a wrong turn somewhere. This wasn't where her room was. It looked like a corridor of guest rooms. Stevie muttered a curse under her breath. She should have paid attention to where she was going, rather than daydreaming about Tom.

As if in response to her thoughts, a side door opened and Tom appeared. His hair was tousled. His bow tie and the top button of his shirt were undone. He looked unutterably gor-geous. Stevie felt like her blood had caught fire. He stopped and stared at her. 'What are you doing here?'

Stevie was so overcome with lust that it took a moment for her to squeak, 'I'm lost.' She realised it was true in more ways than one.

Tom's gaze moved from her face down to her bare feet and then back up again. His eyes met hers, smoky with want-ing. Without thinking Stevie moved towards him. She stopped in front of him, a mere heartbeat away.

He looked down at her and seemed to be fighting to find his voice. 'Stevie,' he began. 'I don't do commitment ...'

She didn't care about commitment. She didn't care about anything at that moment, except the need to touch him. If she didn't feel his lips on hers again soon she was going to explode. She recognised that tonight they were both giddy from the ball and that the chance to be with him would be gone by the morning. If one night was all she could have with him, then so be it.

'Did I mention commitment?' She reached up and slipped her hand against the side of his neck, just below his open collar.

Tom drew a deep breath, his eyes never leaving hers. He shook his head.

'Well shut up and kiss me then,' she said.

He made a sound that was part sigh, part groan and kissed her. They stood there, lips and bodies pressed together. His arms wrapped around her. She still had her shoes in one hand. Her free hand caressed his neck.

As their kiss intensified, Stevie felt herself almost boiling with the need for him. Tom's embrace tightened for a moment, then loosened. He stepped back, still kissing her. Then, after placing a final kiss on her lips, as though sealing a pact, he took her hand and led her to his room.

Once the door was shut behind him, Tom gathered her against him and kissed her again. Stevie let her shoes tumble to the floor.

Reaching behind her, Tom gently unzipped her dress. His finger trailed a burning line down the length of her spine. Stevie moaned and arched her back. Her dress whispered down to a puddle of blue silk at her feet. Still kissing her, Tom picked her out of her clothes and carried her to his bed.

Chapter Nineteen

STEVIE WOKE WITH TOM'S arm wrapped tightly around her waist, his body curled around hers. She stared into the room and let memories of the night before wash over her. A smile, entirely unbidden, stretched across her face. If she'd known what he was capable of, she would have jumped on him a long time ago, one night stand or not.

The curtains to the room were drawn, but light shone through the join. It was probably quite late. Her watch was still on her wrist. It was one of the few things she hadn't shed. She tried to angle her arm so that she could see the time without waking him up. The movement disturbed him. He opened his eyes and looked at her muzzily.

'Morning,' she said, smiling.

It took a moment for him to surface from sleep. In that few seconds Stevie had a mad moment of doubt. Had he forgotten who she was? Or was he regretting last night already?

'Morning.' He smiled back and Stevie's insides melted. He was just so gorgeous.

Tom rubbed his eyes. 'What time is it?'

Confused that Tom didn't seem to see anything unusual about her being in his bed, Stevie pulled the covers up to her chin, before checking her watch. 'Holy shit. It's nearly midday.' She sat straight up. Realising that her breasts were exposed, she grabbed at the duvet.

Tom's hand darted out and closed over hers.

She tensed.

Tom moved his hand up her arm and shoulder and cupped her cheek. He was frowning slightly. 'What's wrong?'

'Nothing.' She pulled the duvet up. 'I'm just a bit ...'

'Surprised? Confused? Regretting what happened?'

'No. Not that.' She looked at him. 'Not the last one.'

He grinned. 'That's good to hear.'

She smiled back, a little uncertain. 'So ... what happens now?'

'Well ...' His thumb stroked her cheek. 'We could get up and go help with the clearing up ...' He traced a line along her collarbone, making her whole body thrum with pleasure. 'Or I could distract you from your duties for a little longer.'

'That sounds like a lovely idea.'

He reached for her and her body responded immediately to his touch.

'Only for a little while, though,' she murmured as his lips followed where his fingers had just been.

'Absolutely.'

'I hope Evelyn didn't go looking for me.' Stevie pulled on her dress.

Tom was sitting naked in bed, watching her. 'I'm sure you're allowed to sleep in after all your hard work last night.'

'She might wonder why I wasn't in my room.' Stevie paused, suddenly realising she didn't actually know how to get to her room. 'Um ... Tom? Where is my room relative to here?' She reached behind her back and tried to do up her zip.

'Here, let me do that.' He slipped out of bed and stood behind her to do her zip up. Stevie felt a ripple of pleasure at his being so close.

'You are beautiful.' Tom kissed her shoulder. He picked up her hair grip, gently gathered her hair and pinned it up, finishing off with a kiss to the back of her neck. Stevie closed her eyes and wondered how it was possible to be this turned on by someone putting clothes onto her rather than taking them off.

'Just give me a minute and I'll walk you back part way,' said Tom. He pulled on a dressing gown and grabbed a towel. 'Ready?'

Stevie scanned the floor for anything else that belonged to her and picked up her shoes. 'Let's hope we don't run into anyone.'

HAVING SHOWERED AND changed into shorts and T-shirt, Stevie felt a lot more alert. Now all she had to do was try and concentrate on the rest of her job without letting anyone know about her and Tom. As she pulled her hair up into a ponytail, she wondered if there *was* a 'her and Tom'.

After all, he'd been pretty adamant that he didn't do commitment. As far as she knew, the night before had been a one off ... assuming the morning was part of the night before. She caught sight of her smiling face in the mirror and saw how happy she looked.

Would it be really obvious to Evelyn and Alice that something had happened? How bad would that be?

She had to pull herself together. This thing with Tom was probably going to last until it was time for her to leave the house. So a couple of days, if she was lucky. She should enjoy it for what it was and not get too attached. This was the way he did things. He'd told her so himself.

Giving her reflection a stern glare, she set off to face the debris from the ball.

As she approached the kitchen, she smelled bacon and suddenly realised she was famished. Tom was already there, frying things.

'Morning,' he said cheerily. 'Fried breakfast?'

'Good morning. And yes, please.' She tried not to look at him, in case her face gave too much away. 'Morning, Priya. Have you been here long?'

Priya and Evelyn were sitting at the end of the table, with mugs of coffee in front of them. Evelyn was opening the donations tin.

'We old people don't need as much sleep as you do,' said Evelyn. 'I've been up for hours.'

'I think yesterday went really well,' said Priya. 'People had a really good time.'

'That was the idea,' said Stevie. 'I'm glad it worked out. We all put a lot of work into it.'

'Especially you,' said Evelyn. 'I don't think I saw you stop for one moment.'

Stevie laughed. 'I did. But Lady Beryl found me and put me back to work.'

'She would.' Evelyn emptied a pile of notes and coins onto the table.

'She was most concerned that Amber hadn't taken a photo of her and Lord Grayingham.' There was coffee in the machine, Stevie poured herself a mug and sat down next to Evelyn.

'She can't help it,' said Priya. 'His position is pretty much all she's got. She was Jonathan Grayingham's PA before she married him. He didn't have a Peerage then, of course.'

'Still,' said Evelyn. 'It wouldn't have killed her to have helped a little with the ball.'

Stevie thought of all of Lady Beryl's friends who had taken her card. 'At least she came and supported us and did door duty. That was a great help.'

'Breakfast.' Tom slid a plate of fried food in front of Stevie.

'Thank you.' She looked up at him for the first time since coming in. He grinned at her and placed his own plate at the seat opposite.

'Was it just me, or did that Salzburg girl disappear with your pop star friend?' asked Evelyn.

Stevie assumed she was talking about Vienna.

For once, Tom didn't bother to correct her. He shrugged.

'Does that mean that you two aren't together anymore?' Evelyn lifted her mug towards Tom.

'We weren't together in the first place,' Tom said, with an exaggerated display of patience. 'She's a free agent. Always has been.'

'Well I'm glad you're really not together now,' said Evelyn. 'She wasn't good for you.'

Tom rolled his eyes.

Priya was sorting out the notes from the coins. 'There's a cheque in here.' She picked up a folded piece of paper.

'Oh, that's from Mr Farrier. He said he had such a wonderful time that he thought he'd make a small donation.'

'He's the dancing man,' said Evelyn.

'Oh yes. Dilan mentioned that last night. He said it reminded him of some of the Sri Lankan discos he's DJ'd for.' Priya unfolded the paper and gave a little shriek.

'What?' Evelyn grabbed the cheque out of Priya's fingers. 'Oh my.'

'What?' Tom and Stevie spoke at the same time.

'It's for five thousand pounds!'

'Let me see?' said Tom.

Evelyn laid the cheque in the middle of the table.

'Well, it looks genuine,' Tom said, after examining it. 'He hasn't signed it "Mickey Mouse" or anything.'

'He must have *really* enjoyed himself.' Priya sounded dazed. 'Goodness.'

'Fantastic.' Stevie grinned. Since the ball had more than broken even, all the proceeds from the charity box were pure profit. 'There's some writing on the back.' She turned it over. 'Please name a ward the Cherry Farrier Ward.' She raised her eyebrows. 'So they really were married. I wondered if she was just the other woman.'

'Wow,' said Priya. 'That's rather sweet that he wants to immortalise her in a hospital ward.'

'Depends on the ward, surely,' Tom said. 'She might be less than enthusiastic if it's the dysentery clinic.'

They spent the rest of the day cleaning up and putting things back in their original places. Stevie was pleasantly surprised to find that there wasn't any damage beyond a couple of red wine stains on the library carpet. She was on her hands and knees attacking one of these when Alice appeared. Stevie sat back and studied her.

The teenager looked awful. Her first real hangover, Stevie guessed. She remembered how that felt. Coupled with the guilt of what could have happened, Alice must be feeling like she wanted to die. Stevie felt a twinge of sympathy.

'How're you feeling?'

Alice winced. 'I've been better.'

'It's called a hangover,' said Stevie. She bit her lip. Oh no. She sounded just like Marsh. She'd have to put a stop to that.

Alice sank into a chair. After a moment she said, 'Uncle Tom keeps offering me fried things.'

Stevie grinned. 'And you don't want to eat anything?'

'No.'

'It might help. Try a slice of toast.'

'Maybe.' She sounded doubtful.

Stevie went back to tackling the wine stains.

'Stevie,' said Alice, after a while.

'Yes?'

'Thank you. For being so understanding last night.'

Stevie raised her eyebrows.

'I mean, you didn't tell Gran. That's ... well ... thank you.'

'I didn't tell Evelyn because I didn't want to upset her. She had a lot riding on this ball. I didn't do it for you, Alice.'

Alice nodded, clearly miserable. 'I can't believe I was so stupid.'

'It's called peer pressure. You need to learn to resist and stand up for yourself.'

'I know.'

She looked so sad sitting huddled in the chair that Stevie felt sorry for her. 'Hey, at least you got to meet Pete.'

A bit of life came back into Alice's features as she remembered that. 'I was so shy I couldn't think of anything to say. Jemmie did all the talking. Pete must have thought I was so lame.'

'Jemmie? Is that the girl who called herself Veronica?'

'Yes.'

Stevie had guessed as much from the list of email and postal addresses she'd compiled when selling the tickets. She also had a good idea about who had sold the tickets on eBay. She would pass the information on to Evelyn. Since the Farriers didn't appear to want to sue, there didn't seem to be any pressing need for further action. 'Are you going to stay in touch with them?'

'Well, they'll be on the forum,' said Alice. 'But no, I don't think I'll be friends with them or anything.' Alice stared into space.

Stevie watched her and felt as though she was witnessing an important turning point in Alice's life. She was glad she'd been on hand to help Alice make the correct choices.

Marsh must have felt like this all the time while she was growing up. And, being a man, he would've had no idea about how girls' minds worked. Poor Marsh. Stevie knew she hadn't made things easy for him. She gave the floor an extra scrub and moved on to find the next stain.

Alice hauled herself out of the chair. 'I'm going to the kitchen. For toast.'

Stevie smiled and returned to her work.

'Well,' said Evelyn. 'I thought you all did such a great job with the ball, that we should have a celebratory meal. I'll cook. And we can open one of Frank's special wines.'

'That *is* an honour,' Tom muttered to Stevie. 'Mum doesn't often bother cooking for just us.'

Did that mean Evelyn was a terrible cook?

He seemed to guess her concerns. 'Don't get me wrong. She's a wonderful cook. She just can't be bothered for just family.'

Just family. Did that mean she was part of the family now? 'If it's a family thing, do you want me to fend for myself?'

'Don't be ridiculous,' said Evelyn. 'You worked so hard on this ball we couldn't possibly leave you out. Besides, you're part of the family now, practically.'

'Oh.' Stevie cast a quick glance at Tom to see how he was taking that piece of information.

His face was thoughtful. He caught her watching him and looked away.

She felt a small stab of disappointment. So that was it. He still thought she was needy and looking for something permanent, while all he wanted was a fling.

'I'll go get the wine,' he said. 'Any particular type?'

While he and Evelyn discussed which bottles to open, Stevie examined her hands. Was she needy and looking for something permanent? She glanced up to see Evelyn, who was humming and flicking through pages of a cookbook. She thought about the house and its embracing feeling of warmth. She thought about the idea of being here as someone who genuinely belonged, rather than someone passing through. Part of a family. She would love that. In the short time that she'd been there, she'd come to view Evelyn and Alice as more than just clients, and now Evelyn had indicated she felt the same.

And then, there was Tom. When she'd first met him, she'd thought he was arrogant and annoying, but eminently fanciable. In the time they'd spent preparing for the ball, she'd seen him mellow and relax and turn into someone much more likeable. And she genuinely cared for him. But he clearly didn't want to be tied down. Perhaps they could be friends.

But did she really want to be one of his booty calls, like Vienna? An involuntary sigh escaped her.

Evelyn looked up from her book. 'Are you all right, Stevie?'

'Yes, I guess the long night is catching up with me.' Stevie forced a smile. 'I might go have a quick lie down.'

Stevie:

Ball went well. Lots to do today clearing up tho. Speak soon. Hope all well with Jane + baby. S

Marsh:

Glad to hear it. Jane and bump fine.

ONCE DINNER HAD BEEN cleared away and all the dishes put in the dishwasher, Alice and Evelyn disappeared up to their rooms, leaving Tom and Stevie free to take their glasses of wine to the gazebo. The fairy lights were still up and the place had a magical air about it.

Stevie leaned back and closed her eyes. The wine and good food were making her feel lovely and mellow. 'This is perfect,' she murmured.

Tom reached across and stroked her cheek. 'Isn't it?'

She looked over to see him smiling. 'You look different from how you were two weeks ago.'

As he caressed her cheek, he never looked away from her face. 'How do you mean?'

'Well, you were grumpy and had these frown lines from having a headache all the time.' She reached across and touched his forehead. 'Just there.'

He kissed her in reply. A long lingering kiss that made Stevie ache with pleasure.

'I've wanted to do this for a long time,' Tom said. He ran a playful finger down the curve of her neck.

'Why didn't you?'

His hand stopped moving. 'I wasn't sure it would be a good idea.'

'Why not?'

'I thought you wanted more than I could offer.' His gaze moved up to her face. 'I mean, this is lovely, but ...'

Suddenly, Stevie wished she hadn't asked. He already thought she was needy and now she'd just confirmed the impression. She shook her head and put a finger to his lips. 'This is enough,' she said, and leaned in to kiss him.

If a few days were all she had with him, she might as well make the most of it.

Chapter Twenty

Dear Thomas,

We are delighted to offer you the job as regional manager for the new Doha branch of the company. A formal letter containing details of the offer will follow.

We look forward to working with you.

The Directors.

TOM STARED AT THE MESSAGE. Wow. He'd done it. Despite everything that had happened, they were willing to take a chance on him. That was incredible. Clearly, his performance at the second meeting had undone the damage done by his outburst.

He should be over the moon. So, why didn't he feel anything? He sent a quick reply saying he would respond once he'd read the full offer, and put away his phone. He was supposed to be meeting Stevie in a few minutes.

What would he tell her? The past day or two had been fun. It was almost as though he had put down a load he hadn't even known he'd been carrying. It was a shame that it had to end.

Tom sighed and stood up. It didn't have to end just yet. The offer wasn't a real issue until he decided to accept it. He hadn't even seen the full details yet. He didn't need to tell Stevie about it. Not yet.

Once the aftermath of the ball had been cleared up, Stevie had very little reason to remain. She decided she would leave the next afternoon.

That morning she and Tom had breakfast together. Evelyn seemed to be leaving them alone and Alice hadn't rolled out of bed yet. They sat next to each other at the table in the kitchen, knees touching. The idea of not being able to do this every day hurt. Stevie told herself that she should enjoy what time she had left with him, but it didn't help.

'I can give you a lift, if you like,' he said.

'Don't worry about it. It'll be out of your way.'

'We could stop off for lunch somewhere en route. I know some nice places between here and London.'

Stevie considered. It certainly sounded more attractive than sitting in a bus full of tourists.

The doorbell rang.

Tom laid a hand on her knee. 'Evelyn will get it.' His touch burned, even though she should be used to it by now. He leaned closer.

She heard footsteps coming down the stairs and drew back, guiltily.

Tom removed his hand from high on her thigh, just as Vienna walked through the door.

She looked from Tom to Stevie and back again. 'Hello. Not interrupting anything, am I?'

'Just breakfast,' said Tom. 'What are you doing here? Shouldn't you be with a client?'

'Client postponed on me.' Vienna threw her bag onto an empty chair and sat in another. 'So I thought, rather than schlep back to London, I'd pop by here to remind you that the corporate event next week is black tie.'

Tom frowned. 'Corporate event?'

'Oh Tom! Don't tell me you've forgotten. You said you'd be my partner at the Finch annual dinner.'

'Sorry. So I did. I completely forgot.' Tom didn't look at either of them. He finished off his bacon and egg. 'Black tie. Okay.'

'Good job I reminded you.' Vienna eyed Stevie. 'How did the ball go? Make lots of money?'

'Not too bad, thanks.' Stevie could tell Vienna suspected something. 'How's Pete?'

'He's a lovely man. So very talented.' She sighed. 'And so very very busy. He's travelling all over the place, promoting his new album.'

Stevie stood and took her plate to clear it. Suddenly, she wasn't hungry any more. 'I've got a few things to sort out before I leave,' she said and glanced at Tom, who was wiping his plate with his toast. 'I'll see you in a bit.'

He smiled vaguely, still not making eye contact.

As Stevie left, she heard Vienna say in a theatrical whisper, 'I hope you know what you're doing.'

Instead of heading straight out of the back door as she'd intended, Stevie ducked into the little pantry beside the kitchen. From there she would be hidden from Tom, but would be able to hear what was being said.

'What are you talking about?' Tom said.

'That girl. You're sleeping with her.'

Tom must have made some sort of gesture of denial, because Vienna carried on, 'Oh come on, Tom, I've known you long enough and well enough to spot the signs. I just hope you understand what you're doing.'

Stevie was pressing against the side of the freezer, but that had nothing to do with the sudden chill that she felt.

'You've always been straight with your women,' said Vienna, no longer whispering. 'Sex is all there is. No commitments.'

'And?' Tom sounded annoyed.

'And, I don't think you've made that clear to her. She's young and naive. It will break her heart when she finds out she's just another notch on the bedpost. Poor little thing. She's clearly in love with you.'

Stevie nearly gasped. Was she in love with him? She couldn't be. Could she? She covered her mouth with her hands, in case any sound escaped.

'For your information,' said Tom. 'Stevie is more mature than you give her credit for. She knows I can't commit to a long-term relationship at the moment. I've told her and she understands. Besides which, it's none of your damned business anyway.'

'Have you told her about the job in Doha then?'

There was a moment of silence. It told Stevie all she needed to know.

Tom muttered something Stevie couldn't catch.

'Oh come on, we both know you're a shoo-in for that job. When were you planning to tell her? An hour before you left for the airport?'

Stevie didn't want to hear any more. She ran out of the back door, letting it slam behind her.

Back in her room she threw clothes into her suitcase, not really seeing or caring what was going in. She'd known that Tom wasn't going to make a commitment to her. He'd been completely upfront about that. But she hadn't known the reason. He was leaving the country. He had a new job somewhere exotic and he hadn't bothered to tell her about it.

What made things worse was that Vienna knew all about it. Of course he couldn't commit to a relationship. There wasn't the chance of one. Stevie had just been a small interlude in his arrangement with Vienna. A little side act to the main attraction. He'd used her.

She hurled her silk dress into the bag and stuffed the high heels savagely on top. She'd never be able to wear that dress again without crying, so who cared if it snagged.

It's not as though people hadn't warned her. She had just carried on building dreams out of thin air, like an idiot. *Stupid. Stupid. Stupid.*

A knock on the door made her pause.

Tom.

She wiped her face with her hands, hoping to take away the tear tracks. She had to be mature about this. Tom hadn't lied to her. He'd always told her he couldn't offer her anything serious. It was her fault that she'd gone and fallen in love with him.

'Stevie, can I come in?'

She had to pull herself together. Act like she could deal with this. Taking a deep breath, she opened the door. 'Tom.'

He stood, his hands in his pockets, shifty-eyed like a guilty child. 'Stevie. I ... I don't know what to say.'

Neither did she. Her eyes prickled. She had to clench her teeth to stop the tears. She turned away and returned to stuffing her bag. He stepped into the room. His presence was like electricity on her skin, only now it was tinged with pain rather than excitement.

'I'm sorry.'

'Is it true?' She pulled the bag closed and tried to do up the clasp. 'You're leaving?'

'Yes.'

The clasp was too blurred for her to close it properly. She clawed at it.

'Here. Let me.' Tom leaned across and secured it. The click sounded unnaturally loud.

'Stevie.' He reached for her hand.

She moved out of the way. Just being near him was hard enough. If he touched her now, she wouldn't be able to bear it. A tear escaped down her cheek. She brushed it away. 'You don't have to explain Tom. You were perfectly honest with me at the start. You don't do commitment. I understand that.'

Inside her chest, her heart tore. 'It's been fun. Really. But I guess all good things have to come to an end sometime.' She picked up the suitcase. 'Good luck with your job in Doha.'

She managed to look at him and the expression on his face made her feel even worse. Disappointed that he didn't say anything, she turned to leave. As she reached the door, he said, 'Stevie?'

'Yes?' She didn't turn around.

'I want you to know that I never thought of you as a notch on the bedpost. You were ... you are ... special.'

Special? She half turned. He was sitting on the bed, looking at his feet. A small flare of hope that she hadn't even noticed, guttered and died. 'But not special enough for you to stay?'

He avoided her eyes and shook his head.

Stevie nodded. So that was how it was. At least she knew now. Without another word, she hitched the bag onto her shoulder and left. She kept up a steady pace until she reached the end of the road, leaving Tom, leaving the house, far behind her. Tom didn't follow her. Part of her was relieved.

The rest of her was gutted.

THE FORMAL JOB OFFER letter arrived the next day. Since he was by himself in the study when he read the letter, Tom allowed himself a little victory dance. Yes! He was going to Doha. Head of operations, Middle East. Now that was a title to be proud of.

A giggle made him stop dancing and look round. Alice was leaning against a bookcase. She was holding up her phone, filming him.

'Nice old-man dancing Uncle Tom.'

He laughed. 'I got the job.'

She looked blank. He explained. 'So, you're looking at the Head of Operations for the Middle East,' he finished.

'Wow. Congratulations Uncle Tom. That sounds amazing,' said Alice. She threw her arms around him and gave him a hug.

Surprised, he hugged her back.

'So, are you moving to the Middle East then?' Alice said, when she'd released him. 'Can I come visit?'

'Of course you can come visit. You'll have to give me a few weeks to settle it, but after that. Sure.'

Alice squealed. 'That would be so awesome.'

Tom grinned. 'It would.'

Alice was bouncing on the balls of her feet. 'Is Stevie excited? Is she going to go across with you and be a party planner to Sheiks and things?'

His good mood ruptured. He'd been avoiding thinking about that. But now Alice had ... wait, how did Alice know about Stevie? They had tried so hard to be discreet. Tom tried to form the question, but Alice answered him before he even started.

'Oh come on. Did you think I didn't notice? I'm not blind.' She grinned. 'Gran doesn't mind. She likes Stevie.'

'Uh ... Stevie and I. That's not ... I mean, it's over.' This was unexpectedly difficult. Just saying it made his mood sink. Tom sighed. There was a headache lurking behind his eyes, he realised. He'd been headache free for days. Why had they come back?

'So that's why she left without saying goodbye.' Alice was no longer smiling. She put her hands on her hips and, for a moment, looked terrifyingly like her grandmother. 'Uncle Tom, what did you do? And don't say "nothing".'

He outlined what had happened, wondering how on earth he'd come to the point where he was explaining his life to a teenager ... and feeling sheepish about it.

Alice looked aghast. 'You can't let that happen, Uncle Tom. You guys were so good together. You have to go after her. I've got her number on my phone. You can call her now.' She waved her phone at him.

'And say what?' said Tom. The headache was crowding in now, making his temples throb.

'I don't know. Tell her you're not going. You can find another job in London. Or just stay where you are.'

Tom dug a knuckle into his forehead. There *had* been another job in London ... but Lambert Kassel hadn't got back to him and Doha had come through. 'Alice. I can't turn down this job. It's really, really important.'

'More important than the rest of your life?'

'It *is* the rest of my life. You'll understand when you're old—'

Alice put up a hand to stop him. 'That's just what Dad would say.' She shook her head. 'I love you Uncle Tom, but you're an idiot. Work isn't everything, you know.'

Tom sighed again. In the brief time he'd had with Stevie, he had been happy. A different kind of happy to normal. Calmer. More ... content. Since she'd left, he hadn't been able to concentrate. Or sleep. Everything in the house reminded him of her.

He stood up. He needed to think about this. And he needed a drink.

'Hey. Where are you going?' said Alice.

'Pub. Then maybe London,' he said. 'And more pubs.'

Chapter Twenty-One

THE FLAT WAS TOO QUIET for Stevie to relax in, so she put some music on and gave the place a good clean. It was in need of it anyway. She phoned the few of her friends who were still around, read the travel blogs of those who weren't and caught up with the gossip. She sent Louise an email outlining how the ball had gone, including how much money they'd raised.

Having caught up with all her social emails, she grabbed a Galaxy bar, poured herself a glass of wine and settled down to watch TV. But thoughts of Tom kept creeping in.

She mentally tracked the change in her feelings towards him. When had a mere crush tipped over into something that could make her feel so raw? They'd only really got to know each other over these last few weeks, yet she felt like she'd known him forever. How had she fallen so completely and blindly in love with him?

Perhaps that's what Marshall was trying to warn her about. Maybe that was just the effect Tom had on women.

Eventually, she fell asleep on the sofa and, for the first time in over a week, had her recurring nightmare. She woke up crying and cold with shock. For a moment, she was too disorientated to figure out where she was. Once the reality hit home, she started crying afresh. It was as though being with Tom had kept her fears at bay for a while, but now they were back, only worse. She now had an extra person she'd lost. Out of habit, she reached for her phone and got half way through Marsh's number when she stopped herself.

She was supposed to be an adult. She couldn't run to her big brother whenever she had a bad dream. He might be able to come round and see her now, but what would happen once the baby was born? He'd need to be with his new family, not to waste time babying his grown-up sister.

She huddled on the sofa in her living room, where every single light was on, and hugged her knees. Years ago a therapist had told her to write her feelings down. She found a piece of paper and a pen and started to write.

Eventually she felt a little better. Rather than read what she'd written and relive it all, she screwed up the paper and threw it in the bin. Going over to her notice board, she took Indiana Jones down and retrieved the photo of her family. When she finally went to bed, she fell asleep with it clutched against her lacerated heart.

The dawn chorus woke her at 5.00 a.m. She made herself breakfast, went for a run and managed to wait until a more reasonable six-thirty before phoning Marsh. He would be up. He always was.

'It's me,' she said, when he answered the phone.

'Stevie. How are you?' He sounded relieved to talk to her. She realised he must have been worrying about how she was, especially given his fears about how Tom might treat her.

'Um ...'

The pause was long enough for Marsh to tell what was wrong. 'You had the dream again, didn't you?'

'Yes.'

'Do you want me to come over?'

'Actually, I'm okay for the minute. If you could come over this evening though ...'

'Just a sec.' There was a muffled conversation at the other end of the line before Marsh came back. 'Sure. I can come round after work. Are you sure you don't want me to pop round now?'

'No, I'll be fine.' Stevie smiled at the phone, feeling a rush of affection for her brother. 'I'll cook dinner.'

'Is that a hint for me to bring pudding?'

'If you like.'

Tom:

It's official. I got the Doha job!

Just accepted it.

Olivia:

Congratulations!

That would explain why Dhidre looks like she's sucked a lemon. Love it.

I guess that's you off to sunnier climes in a few weeks then.

Tom: They want me to come over next week for a few days to discuss things and look at accommodation etc. So I guess I'll be leaving for good within a few weeks of getting back. Now that they've filled the position, they're keen for things to get started.

Olivia:

And what are you going to do about Stevie?

Tom:

I don't know. It's been a few days since I last saw her, but I really miss her. I keep thinking of things to tell her and she's not there. I miss her being there. It's like she grounded me somehow and now I can't take off properly again.

I thought about going to see her, but I'm worried it might make things worse. I've got a chance for a new beginning. It'll help me forget her and move on. Seeing her again will only make it harder when it's time to leave.

Olivia:

Just listen to you, gibbering like an idiot.

You fell in love with her, you fool. She didn't clip your wings or whatever else you think. She just let you be yourself, insecurities and all, and you let your guard down enough to fall in love.

If you run away from this now, you will regret it forever. Trust me on this one. We women know about this stuff. Even women like me.

Tom:

I didn't fall in love. I just let my guard down for too long. I should have stuck with Vienna. At least she didn't leave me feeling this terrible mixture of loneliness and guilt.

Olivia:

Vienna didn't leave you feeling anything, other than the need to get your end away. That's the difference between lust and love.

Tom:

Okay, you're starting to scare me now. Who are you and what have you done with Og?

Olivia:

Stop pissing around and go see her.

Tom:

Okay. Okay. I'll go see her.

Heaven knows what I'm going to say to her though. It'll never work out. My job is important to me. I can't give it all up for a girl I've known for two weeks.

Can I?

STEVIE HAD LUNCH WITH Louise and went over the details of the ball, a sort of post-mortem of what went well and how it could have been better. She came home, her head buzzing with ideas, to find the light flashing on her answer phone. Her first thought was that it was Tom.

She sat down next to the phone and stared at it. Did she really want to hear his voice again? What could he possibly have to say that would make things better? Her finger hovered over the delete button. Surely it was better to just let it go and try and get on with things. But she just couldn't bring herself to do it.

A stray hope that perhaps he was missing her as much as she was missing him made her press the play button. She sat there, hope rising, as it started to play.

It wasn't Tom. Disappointment seared her. She heard a woman's voice, but she wasn't listening. Tears prickled. She had been so convinced it was him. It took her a moment to pull herself together and replay the message.

'Hi Stevie, it's Lavinia Cosham. We met at Beryl Grayingham's charity ball.'

Stevie sat up. Lavinia Cosham? She frowned and tried to remember who that was. Could this be the start of another job?

'I think I mentioned that the Major and I were thinking of having a small celebration for our wedding anniversary soon. I was wondering if you could come up here and discuss a few details with us? Perhaps give us a quote.'

Stevie grabbed a notebook and pen to write down the number.

But Mrs Cosham didn't leave one. 'I'll speak to you soon,' the message concluded.

Stevie lowered her notebook and stared at the phone. She punched out 1471 to see if she could find the number that way, but the number had been withheld. Damn. Damn. Damn. Her next potential commission and she didn't have the number.

'Don't panic, Stevie,' she said out loud. 'Don't panic.'

Evelyn would probably have the Major's contact details. If not, there was always directory enquiries services. There couldn't be that many Major Coshams in Oxford.

Of course, speaking to Evelyn would mean she would have to talk about Tom. Or worse, he could answer the phone. Stevie drummed her fingers on the arm of the sofa. What should she do?

Deciding that the commission was more important than protecting her fragile feelings, she called Evelyn.

'Stevie. I'm so glad you called. Tom said you left in a hurry. Is everything okay?'

'Oh yes, I just ... had some things I needed to get on with in London.'

'Well, I'm glad you called. We need to sort out your payment.'

'I'm preparing an invoice for expenses ...'

'And then there's the percentage of the profits,' said Evelyn. 'You'll be pleased to hear that it comes to a tidy sum.' She named the amount.

'Goodness.' Stevie mentally calculated how much original profit that would have been. 'How did we make that much?'

Evelyn chuckled. 'I told Lady Beryl about that little man buying a ward name for his wife and Lady Beryl decided that was just what she needed. So she and Lord Grayingham are paying for a ward and some equipment.'

Stevie laughed. The sum was more than she'd hoped to make. She'd feel bad taking that away from the kids who needed it. 'Tell you what, Evelyn,' she said. 'Why don't I invoice you for half of that amount, plus expenses and you can donate the rest to the charity.'

'Are you sure? You earned that money, fair and square. Until you came up with your marketing scheme we thought we would barely break even.'

'I'm sure.' If this one event led to more jobs, then it would more than compensate.

'Oh, and I've had several queries from people about using the house as a venue for graduation parties and things. Of course, if they need an organiser, I shan't hesitate to recommend you. After all, you know the house so well now.'

Not so well that she didn't get lost and wander into Tom in the middle of the night ...

Stevie squashed that thought. 'Actually, Evelyn, that's the main reason I'm phoning. I had a call from Major Cosham's wife about a possible event, but she didn't leave her phone number. I was wondering if you have it?'

'Lavinia Cosham? Oh, I'm sure I do have her number. Just a minute.' There was a rustling sound.

Stevie pictured Evelyn sitting in her office rifling through her Rolodex, under the proud gaze of her late husband.

'Ah yes, here it is.' Evelyn read out the number. 'I hope that works out for you. I might see you there, you never know.'

'That would be lovely,' Stevie said.

'Oh, by the way, did you hear Tom's news?'

At the sound of his name, her heart lurched. 'No.'

'He's been offered this super job in the Middle East. He's very excited about it.'

So he would be leaving. Soon. 'That's great.' Stevie tried to sound enthusiastic, but failed. She concentrated on keeping her voice steady. 'Tell him I said congratulations.'

'I'm thinking of cooking dinner again,' said Evelyn happily. 'Maybe even opening one of those special bottles of wine that Frank laid down when Tom was born. I was saving it for when he got married or something, but I think this is almost as good.'

'I'm sure he'd like that.' Stevie breathed in slowly. 'Evelyn, I have to go. I'll email you soon. Thank you for Mrs Cosham's phone number. Bye.' She hung up a little too quickly, hoping Evelyn wouldn't notice.

Clutching the notebook, she stared at the window of the flat, not really seeing it. So that was it. Tom was going to Doha.

If she had ever needed confirmation that he didn't feel the same way she did, this was it. She had been stupid to fall for him. Marsh had tried to warn her, but she had been too pig-headed to listen. She was so busy trying to prove she could make her own decisions that she'd let her heart rule her head and now she was paying the price.

She looked down at the phone number Evelyn had given her. It represented a whole new start for her. If this business took off, she could do what she loved. No more opening envelopes and waiting tables for minimum wage. She would be busy and fulfilled. And alone.

The photo of her family was lying on the coffee table. She picked it up and studied the faces of her parents. In all her memories, they had the faces from this photo. The same fixed smiles. Her mother squinting against the sunlight. Her father with a crease on his forehead as he worried about the traffic getting home. She could barely remember them now.

But she remembered the pain. The terrible emptiness they'd left behind. She was starting to feel it again. It was as though realising that Marsh now had a family of his own to care for had opened up the wounds she had learned to live with. And then falling for Tom and losing him had made things worse.

By the time Marsh arrived, it was far too late for dinner. He'd texted her to say he was running late, so she'd ended up having a sandwich and feeling even worse about her life. She was in tears again when he rang the bell. She opened the door to find her brother standing there with two shopping bags, his suit crumpled from being on the tube and his hair windswept.

There was the briefest pause as he took in her puffy eyes and tear-smudged make-up. In that pause Stevie had a sudden image of her father, tired and dishevelled marching into her room saying 'For heaven's sake Stevie, it's past ten o'clock. Go to sleep!' It wasn't the face from the photo, but a real living memory of his beloved face, grumpy but alive. The strength of it made her catch her breath.

'What's wrong?' Marsh stepped in. He dropped his bags on the floor and gave her a hug.

She buried her face in his shoulder and squeezed him back. Her ear pressed against his chest, she could hear his heartbeat, telling her that he, at least, was still alive. Still there for her when she needed him. She released him and took a step back. 'You know.' She managed a watery smile. 'The older you get, the more you look like Dad.'

Marsh frowned, confused. 'I guess there's worse people to look like. Now, do you want to tell me what's bothering you?'

'It's a long story. Best sit down.'

'In which case ...' Marsh reached into one of his bags. 'It's a good job I picked up this.' He pulled out a tub of ice cream. 'I wasn't sure how big the crisis was, so I got the biggest tub of Ben and Jerry's I could find.'

She kissed his cheek. 'You're the best brother in the world.' She plucked the tub out of his hand. 'I'll get a spoon.'

She got a bowl and a spoon for him too, but he shook his head. 'Jane keeps buying cold things. She's hot all the time.

Our freezer is full of ice lollies. I don't think I could stomach more ice cream right now.'

'You don't have to eat Jane's ice cream.'

He gave her a look that told her she had no idea how his marriage worked.

'Right.' She sank into the sofa next to him and dug the spoon straight into the tub.

'Before you start,' said Marsh. 'Does this involve Tom Blackwood?'

Stevie grimaced.

Marsh sighed. 'Go on.'

It all came out in a jumbled, emotional rush. She gave him a fairly garbled account of the ball, how she had fallen for Tom without ever intending to, how she'd left. How she still felt. When she finished, there was silence. She sniffed, wiped her eyes and ate another spoonful of ice cream.

'Well,' he said, 'are you sure about ... being in love?'

Stevie shrugged. Having told someone all about it, she was starting to feel a little better about the whole fiasco. 'I didn't think I was. But when Evelyn said he was going, it was like losing people all over again. It's like there was this place inside that I never knew existed and now it's crumbling. It hurts. Like, physically.'

Marsh nodded. 'Sounds like love, all right.' For a moment he stared into space. 'I felt like that when I thought I'd lost Jane.'

Stevie remembered that time all too well. 'The worst of it,' she said, as she levered out another hefty scoop of ice cream, 'is that everyone told me this would happen. Everyone. And I thought I was grown up enough to handle it.'

He gave her a long sideways look. 'What have you done to handle it?'

'Well, I've called you. Like I always do.'

He laughed gently and laid a hand on her arm. 'No, you waited until the morning to call me. You normally just phone at whatever time at night. And from what you've just said, you've been trying to get on with your life. You've accepted it hurts. But you're doing your best to carry on. Sounds to me like you're being pretty grown-up about it.'

She stared, ice cream spoon in her mouth. Marsh, her big brother who always treated her like a baby, thought she was handling this well. Perhaps she was. Marsh didn't give praise lightly. She swallowed too much ice cream too quickly and winced at the resulting stab of pain. 'Really?'

'Yes. Really. It wasn't so long ago you'd have just sat in here with the curtains drawn and cried for three days.'

She thought about it. That was true. She had done that in the past.

'So, I think you're doing pretty well. I'm just sorry that it had to happen at all.' He scowled. 'If I ever see Tom, I really will hit him.'

Stevie smiled. 'Marsh, you'd never hit anyone. Besides, it's not Tom's fault. He told me he didn't do commitment and I convinced myself that was okay. He didn't lie to me.'

'Still. He should have known better. You're young ...'

'I thought you just said I was quite mature.'

'You're still young.'

Stevie threw up her free hand. 'I can't win.'

Marsh smiled at her. 'I'm afraid you'll always be thirteen to me.'

'Well, I just hope Jane's having a boy. Because a girl wouldn't stand a chance with you for a dad.'

The smile dropped from his face and she immediately regretted what she'd said. 'Sorry. Did I say something wrong?'

'No, no. It's just ...' He shrugged, and spread his hands out. 'You know. It's a big thing.'

'Is everything going okay? Is Jane okay?'

'Oh yeah. After the initial terrible time, she seems to be blooming now and there haven't been any problems.'

'So, what's bothering you?'

He didn't reply, just stared at the floor, his brow furrowed.

'Are you worried about becoming a dad?' she said softly.

'Well, it is a scary thought.' He gave her a half smile. 'It's a huge responsibility.'

Stevie didn't know what to say. She was used to him stressing and obsessing about exams and work. Those were easy to deal with. Marsh was clever and good at what he did. Although he sometimes doubted himself, he knew deep inside that he would pass whatever test he faced. But this was different. No one could predict how good a parent he would be.

Stevie looked at the tub of ice cream in her hand. When in doubt, ice cream was always a good standby.

She offered the tub to Marsh. He smiled and picked up the empty bowl and spoon from the table in front of him.

'Thanks.' He helped himself to a large dollop.

Stevie nodded in acknowledgement. She watched fondly as her brother ate the melting ice cream carefully so as not to get any on his shirt. Since she was thirteen, he had been her father, mother and best friend as well as her big brother. If anyone could take credit for how she had turned out, it would be him. At the time she'd thought he was bossy and overbearing, but the last few weeks had taught her just how difficult teenage girls could be. Poor Marsh had had no choice but to throw himself into the role and hope for the best.

'For what it's worth,' she said. 'I think you'll be a great dad.'

He gave her a sceptical glance. 'Yeah?'

'You brought me up, pretty much.'

He shook his head. 'You brought yourself up. I just made sure you had food and clothes and a house to live in.'

'Uh-huh. Not to mention lecturing me on the dangers of drugs. Making sure I did my homework. Picking me up when I missed the last train home. Scaring away boyfriends you didn't like. Grounding me for nicking money out of your wallet …'

'I never scared away any of your boyfriends.'

'Derek Williamson?'

'Okay. One. He really wasn't right for you though.'

Stevie rolled her eyes.

'Anyway,' she said, firmly returning to the subject. 'Since Mum and Dad died, you've been the closest thing I've had to a parent. So if I turned out even remotely normal, it's all thanks to you.'

'And Aunty Caroline. And all those social services people.'

Stevie waved the suggestion away. 'They just popped in now and again.'

They sat together and ate ice cream in silence for a few minutes.

Finally Marsh said, 'Do you really think that?'

'Don't milk it. I'm not saying it again.'

While Marsh was still there, Stevie got another phone call from someone who'd taken her card at the ball. This time it was about a graduation party. She made notes and asked a few questions to get a general idea, then agreed to call back with a quote. She hung up and found Marsh watching her, a curious expression on his face.

'What?' she said over her shoulder, while making a few last notes.

'I've never seen you in action before. It's an eye opener to see the all-new, professional side of you.'

'It's not that new,' said Stevie, even though it was.

'I'm impressed.'

Stevie stared. Had Marsh actually said he was impressed? 'Wow. That's high praise coming from you.'

He grinned. 'Must be the ice cream, gone to my head.' He looked at his watch. 'Listen, I'd better go. I want to get home before Jane goes to bed.' He gathered his things. 'Are you going to be okay?'

Stevie nodded. She was feeling much better for having poured out all her feelings. Being independent was all well and good, but it was comforting to have her big brother around to talk to sometimes. 'I'm all grown up now, see?'

Marsh laughed. 'If you say so.' He pulled on his coat.

'Thanks for the ice cream. And the chat.'

Marsh inclined his head in acknowledgement. He picked up his briefcase and was about to say something when there was a knock on the door. He gave Stevie a puzzled glance.

It was nearly 10 p.m. Who could it be at this hour? Feeling glad that Marsh was here, in case it was some weirdo, she opened the door.

Tom was standing outside. His suit collar was open at the neck and his curls were tumbling onto his forehead. He looked a little unsteady, like he'd just come from the pub. 'Hi.' His smile bypassed her brain and registered straight in her stomach. 'Can I come in?'

Stevie's thoughts skittered around. Tom. He was here. He was gorgeous. 'Um ...' Did she really want to talk to him? What was there to say?

Marsh came and stood behind her. Tom's eyes flicked over her shoulder to look at her brother and his eyes widened slightly. Stevie remembered that the last time they'd met, Marsh had been in a high temper.

'Marsh,' said Tom, recovering his composure.

'Tom.' There was ice in Marsh's voice.

'I've come to see Stevie.' He looked back to Stevie. 'Can I come in?'

Stevie glanced at Marsh, who said nothing. His expression told her that he would gladly kick Tom's arse down the stairs, but he was waiting to see what she wanted. She understood that he was giving her room to be the adult she claimed to be.

She sighed and opened the door. 'Come in. Marsh was just leaving.'

Marsh gave her a nod. 'I'll call you tomorrow.' He left, not bothering to say goodbye to Tom.

Tom watched him go. 'He's not changed much.'

'Did you just come here to be rude about my brother?'

'No. No.' Tom entered, a little sheepishly. 'I came to see you.'

She didn't invite him to sit down. The mere sight of him, standing close enough to touch, was clawing at her heart. She wanted to throw herself into his arms and kiss him. She was pretty sure he'd kiss her back. But that would achieve nothing. It would merely hurt more when he told her he was leaving. She folded her arms across her chest. 'Evelyn told me you got the job in Doha. Congratulations.'

'Thanks. Actually, that's what I came to talk to you about.'

Was he going to say he'd turned down the job so that he could be with her? Hope fluttered in her chest. Did he care about her as much as she cared about him?

He ran a hand through his hair. 'The thing is, Stevie,' he said. 'I really like you. I've been with women before and none of them have had the impact you've had on me. None of them.' He took a step towards her. 'I think we had something ... have something ... special. And it would be such a shame for it to end before it's even started.'

Her heart almost stopped beating in anticipation of what he was going to say. Not trusting herself to speak, she nodded.

'So, I want you to come to Doha with me.'

The crash of her dreams was almost audible. She gasped. 'What?'

'Come with me. I can say you're my partner, we could get a big double flat together. It's a senior position, I'll make more than enough money for both of us. You could—'

Stevie was no longer listening. Anger exploded through her. How dare he? Did he think he could just click his fingers and she would drop everything and run off with him? 'I could what, Tom? Keep house for you? Be there at the ready whenever you fancy a shag?'

Tom took a step back, as though singed by her anger. 'No, I didn't mean that at all. I meant, come with me. Be my girlfriend. You can find a job over there, if that's what you want.'

Stevie thought of the two potential events she had lined up. Her career as an event organiser was only just beginning. She had her dream job within her sights, and he was asking her to just chuck it. Clearly, he felt that her career was less important than his own. What happened when things went wrong? She'd be stuck in the Middle East, reliant on him, and her fledgling career would be dead. 'I already have a job here. I've had loads of offers since the ball. Things are going well, thank you.'

'Of course they are. You're good.'

'And you want me to leave everything and come and be your plaything?'

'That is not what I'm saying!' His voice rose.

She glared. 'What are you saying then?'

'I'm saying that I want to be with you! Although God knows why I bothered.' He put his hands on his hips and glared back.

Stevie's arms tightened against her chest. Suddenly, a stab of something else was thrown into the mix of emotions. He'd just said he wanted to be with her. She was more than a two-night stand. She knew Tom well enough to know that it was not an admission he would make lightly. But he wanted her on his terms. Just like when she'd first slept with him, it was on his terms.

But she'd learned her lesson. It took a moment for her to find her voice. 'I'm sorry, Tom,' she said, knowing this to be true. 'But I can't do what you're asking.'

'Why not? If I want you and you want me ...'

Stevie sighed. 'When we met, you told me you were married to your job. And you are. If I leave everything I have behind and come with you, what happens when your job takes over? Because it will. It'll start with working one weekend, just to get something finished, and then before you know it, you'll be busy and I'll hardly see you. I won't be able to find work there as easily as you think. What am I supposed to do then?'

Tom looked deflated. 'But we'll be together.'

'I know. But it's not as simple as that.' She pressed her jaws together in an effort to stop herself from crying. She knew he meant well, but he really hadn't thought it through. This job was important to him and she knew that the old workaholic Tom was there, just below the surface, and would reappear within weeks. 'I want to be with you too, but you're asking too much. I can't just leave everything to become your live-in woman.'

Tom sighed, all the fight gone out of him. 'Where does that leave us, then?'

'Pretty much where we were when I left Oxford, I guess.'

His expression was so sad that it was all she could do not to reach for him. 'You're a very special person, Stevie,' he said finally.

Her vision swam with tears, but she tried to smile. 'So are you.'

He stepped towards her and placed a gentle kiss on her cheek.

She closed her eyes.

'Bye, Stevie.'

'Bye, Tom.' She opened her eyes and a tear rolled down her face. She would have wiped it away, but she was afraid that if she moved her arms, her chest would shatter.

At the door he paused. 'If you change your mind ...'

She shook her head. 'I won't.'

He pulled the door gently shut behind him.

Stevie sank to the floor and unlocked her arms. A huge sob erupted from somewhere deep inside. She put her face in her hands and gave herself up to the pain.

Tom:

Well, that wasn't such a great idea. I feel like a total shit now.

I asked her to come with me. She said no.

The worst of it is, she's right. If she comes with me, I will have to work silly hours to make it in this job and I won't be able to spend as much time with her as I'd like to and she won't have anything to do. We might be phenomenally lucky and find her a job, but the chances aren't huge.

I feel worse now than I did before. Somehow, seeing her again just reinforced how much I miss her. I know it's only been a few days since she was in Oxford, but time seems to go slower without her around. It's like TV– once you've seen things in HD, normal TV suddenly seems really crap. That's what it's like. She made me see life in sharp focus. Now everything looks dull.

Oh, and I told her I wanted a longer term relationship. I didn't mean to, it just came out. Now that it's out there, I know it's true. Which makes everything suck all the more.

I'm off to get another drink.

Olivia: Oh Tom. I don't know what to say. If you ever want to talk about it some more, you know where to come.

Tom: Thanks Og.

Chapter Twenty-Two

From: Olivia Gornall:

To: Tom Blackwood

Hey. Long silence from you. I take it to mean that you're busy. So, what's it like over there? I've never been to that part of the world.

Is the dream job as good as expected?

Og

From: Tom Blackwood

To: Olivia Gornall

It is all good here, at least it would be if the insomnia and headaches weren't back. It's a pain because I'm so busy that when I do get to bed I'm exhausted. Then I can't sleep.

From: Olivia Gornall

To: Tom Blackwood

I'm sure it'll get better. It's all worth it to be living the dream.

From: Tom Blackwood

To: Olivia Gornall

The thing about living the dream is that it doesn't feel like I expected it to. I mean, it all sounds great. The job's interesting, the salary package is great, the flat is amazing etc, etc, but it all feels a little ... hollow. I just can't get worked up about it anymore. It's like I'm living someone else's life for a while and I'll have to give it back. It doesn't feel REAL.

I'm not sure what I thought would happen, but I was expecting to feel happier than this.

I miss Stevie. I think about her all the time. When I'm not busy thinking about work, she's in my head. Actually, I catch myself thinking about her even when I *am* supposed to be thinking about work. It's like she's waiting there all the time, at the back of my mind. I keep seeing things and wishing I could share it with her. It's crazy. I only knew her properly for a few weeks and I feel like I've lost something that was always there.

I hate to admit it, but I've rather lost interest in women too. I've been introduced to some stunning girls over here. Stunning and ... er ... willing. But I can't bring myself to care.

From: Olivia Gornall

To: Tom Blackwood

Oh dear. You do have it bad.

Have you been in touch with her?

From: Tom Blackwood

To: Olivia Gornall

I emailed her once. She didn't reply. I think it's probably best if we didn't start talking. It'd only make things worse. Like picking a scab.

God, I knew this love stuff was a bad idea. I wish I'd just stuck to lust. Things were okay then.

From: Olivia Gornall

To: Tom Blackwood

'Tis better to have loved and lost than to never have loved at all' – apparently.

From: Tom Blackwood

To: Olivia Gornall

That's just bollocks.

STEVIE POURED HERSELF a glass of wine and put her feet up. Evelyn's party had turned out to be a goldmine of new contacts. Someone had even told her she'd been recommended by Lady Beryl!

Things were looking good. By the end of the year she had set herself, she was likely to have a viable business. The only problem was that all the work was in or around Oxford. Which always made her think of Tom. Not that it took a lot to do that. All sorts of stuff made him pop into her head. She had been dreading going to Oxford to talk to the Major and his wife, but it turned out they lived in a village just beyond the city, so she hadn't passed any familiar landmarks. Nevertheless, she'd felt the house and memories of Tom calling to her all the time she'd been there.

At least she had work to take her mind off things. She sighed and looked at her computer. Tom's email to her had been difficult enough to read the first time, but she found herself pulling it up and reading it over and over. Each time, she told herself she should just delete it, but she couldn't bring herself to do it.

Reaching over, she opened it once more.

From: Tom Blackwood

To: Stevie Winfield

Hi

Just a quick line to say that I've arrived in Doha safely and have plunged straight into work. It's all very hectic.

I went to see the desert today (it was part of my induction tour). It was ... well, it was hot. Like stepping into a sandy blast furnace. But it was also mind-blowing and majestic.

I wish I could have shown it to you. There are a hundred and one little things I want to share with you. I miss you.

Tom

Just reading the email made her throat constrict. If she'd gone with him, she would have been able to share all of that. But she knew that it wouldn't last. He was busy. She would feel neglected and become needy and whingy. To split up had been the sensible option, but God, it hurt.

So far, she hadn't replied. There was nothing to say. Re-opening communications would only cause more pain. She had tried seeing other people. She'd gone out one evening with Dilan, the DJ from the party. All night she'd caught herself comparing her dinner companion to Tom. Even though Tom was thousands of miles away, he hadn't left her thoughts for a moment. Poor Dilan never stood a chance. He seemed to realise it too. He'd walked her home, but hadn't hung around at the doorstep waiting to be invited in. She almost felt sorry for him.

Was it going to be like that on every date from now on?

Sighing she clicked reply. She had done this before and deleted the email without sending it. Previous emails had included chatty paragraphs about her day, as though she were using it like a diary. She couldn't possibly send that sort of drivel to Tom, but knowing she wasn't going to send it liberated her, so she chatted to him, as though he were there.

This time however, she was feeling so down, she simply wrote, 'I miss you too. I don't think life is ever going to be the same without you.'

She stared at the message. So short, but it covered just how she was feeling at the moment. Sighing again, she drained her glass and leaned across to click delete.

Her hand slipped and she hit send instead.

Stevie stared at the screen. 'Oh shit!' She scrabbled around trying to cancel it before it went, but there it was – in her sent folder. She swore some more and sank back into her chair.

'Great. Just great.' She rubbed a hand over her eyes. 'And now I'm talking to myself. Ugh.'

From: Tom Blackwood

To: Olivia Gornall

My office is now fully kitted out. It looks great. The desk is about the size of my bed!

In other news – Lambert Kassel just offered me that job I interviewed for a couple of months ago. It was so long ago that I had totally forgotten about it.

Typical. You wait for ages, then two job offers come at once.

From: Olivia Gornall

To: Tom Blackwood

Congratulations. I guess you'll be turning it down. You've already accepted this one.

From: Tom Blackwood

To: Olivia Gornall

Yes. I'll turn it down.

I'm on probationary period with this job until the end of the month – it's company policy with jobs that require relocation. So, I could leave at quite short notice if I wanted to take the L&K job, but this is a better job.

I'll send L&K an email in the morning. I might have an evening to have a glass of wine and feel smug about being offered not one, but two good jobs within the space of six weeks.

Tom

From: Olivia Gornall

To: Tom Blackwood

Sounds like you're returning to your old form. Good. I was starting to worry.

From: Tom Blackwood

To: Olivia Gornall

So was I. I still haven't slept properly though, but I think I'm getting used to it.

I've got to go to a work do tomorrow night and it made me think of Vienna. I wonder ...

Oh. There's an email from Stevie. Back in a minute.

From: Olivia Gornall

To: Tom Blackwood

You can't just say that - give me details.

What did she say???

From: Olivia Gornall

To: Tom Blackwood

Tom? Are you still there? What did Stevie's email say?

To: Tom Blackwood

Helloooooooo?

STEVIE KICKED OFF HER shoes as soon as she entered the flat. She'd been up to Oxford for the day to talk about the graduation party. She had a good gut feeling about the job. The people were nice and the event was straightforward to organise. It would be a good start.

But walking around the city had made her feel tired and reminded her too much of Tom. She popped her laptop on the coffee table and set it up to charge. She hadn't had a reply to the email she'd mistakenly sent to Tom. She was torn between relief and misery that he'd not taken it seriously enough to respond.

'At least the work is going well,' she said out loud, and then shook her head. This talking to herself thing was getting worse. 'I'm going to have to get a cat or something.' She poured herself some wine. 'But then I'll end up a barmy old cat lady.'

Walking past the shops in Oxford, she'd seen the cutest cuddly toy bunny and felt suddenly compelled to buy it for her unborn niece or nephew. She took the floppy little thing in her hands and stared at it. It looked plaintively back at her. Over the last few weeks, her ambivalence towards Marsh and Jane's baby had begun to fade, not least because they'd shown her ultrasound pictures of the tiny human being that was growing inside Jane's now rounded tummy.

She was going to be an aunty. The idea rather appealed, now that she'd had time to process it. She could be the cool aunt who appeared at weekends and played and took the child to interesting and fun places that its parents would never dream of going to. She didn't know where yet, but she was sure she could be more creative in her outings and games than her brother. Perhaps having a tiny person to pour all her love into was the perfect antidote to her broken heart.

She went over to the noticeboard where the photo of her family and the postcard of Indiana Jones were now happily side by side. 'I'm going to be an aunty.' She waved the bunny at them.

For a moment she wondered if she still wanted a family of her own. That normal family with the house, the pet, the white picket fence that she'd unwittingly revealed to Tom all those weeks ago. The dream of it was still there, but now instead of a nameless figure, the man who would have all that with her was Tom. Somewhere along the line, she'd absorbed him into her dreams.

'It's not to be,' she said to the bunny, with a sigh. 'I'll just have to wait until someone else comes along and pops himself into my perfect future.' She took a sip of wine. 'I just hope I don't have to wait too long.'

She was about to put the bunny safely back in its bag when the doorbell rang. She wasn't expecting anyone.

'Perhaps it's Mr Right?' She put her wine glass down and went to open the door, bunny still in hand.

Tom was standing at the door, looking tanned and heart-stoppingly handsome. He had one hand tucked behind his back. When he saw her, a huge grin spread across his face.

Stevie was so surprised she shut the door again. She looked at the bunny, then threw it in the direction of the sofa and quickly ran her fingers through her hair. She opened the door again, half expecting to find she'd imagined him.

He was still there. No longer grinning. 'Hi.'

'Hi.'

They stared at each other for a moment. Tom looked good. The desert sun had turned him a lovely golden shade of brown. His hair was shorter, making him look less mussed up, but still fabulous. His eyes shone deep blue against his tan.

Stevie remembered her manners. 'Come in.' She opened the door wider. 'What are you doing here?'

He followed her in. 'I had to come and talk to some people at work.'

His reply deflated her spirits. So he was back on business. That figured. But what was he doing here, in her flat?

He brought out his hidden hand and presented her with a bunch of red roses. 'For you.' The grin returned.

'They're lovely.' Stevie took them, a little hesitantly. The smell reminded her of the night in the gazebo.

He looked too pleased with himself. It was almost as though he thought that a bunch of flowers would make everything okay. A sudden thought popped into her mind. Perhaps that was what he did with Vienna. A curl of anger added to the mix of feelings churning inside her.

Tom was shifting his weight from one foot to another. 'I got your email.'

So that was it. Her email, sent by mistake. He'd read it and thought that she was pining after him. So he'd come over to try and seduce her. If he thought he could get round her that easily with his roses and his tan and his lovely, muscly arms ... Well he had another think coming.

'I'm not Vienna,' she blurted.

Tom stopped fidgeting. 'What?'

'I'm not Vienna.' She thrust the flowers back at him. 'You can't just come round here and give me flowers and expect me to just roll over and pick up where we left off.'

Tom seemed surprised to find himself holding the flowers again. 'What are you talking about?'

'You're here for work and you just thought you'd pop in and see if you could get a nice night out and a shag while you were in town. Well, I'm not your little slapper on call. If that's what you want, you may as well just leave now.' She opened the door.

'Stevie ...' He moved fast, putting himself between her and the door and pushing it shut.

'I mean it.' Her eyes were full of tears. Something primal inside of her was screaming that if another one night stand was what he wanted, then dammit that was what he could have. It took all her willpower not to give in. She had to remain strong. She wasn't going to be some businessman's mistress. That was a sure way to end up as a mad cat lady.

He dropped the roses and put his hands on her upper arms. His touch reminded her of so many nice things those hands could do. She wriggled and started to protest.

He pulled her to him and kissed her. Not hard, just enough to stop her talking.

Her mind emptied of all the arguments that had been queuing to get out. She found herself melting and kissing him back. This wasn't getting her anywhere. She couldn't just give in at the first delicious kiss. Calling up all her reserve willpower, she pushed him away. 'I won't end up a mad cat lady.'

He gaped. 'What on earth ...?'

'Just go, Tom. Please.'

'Not until I've said what I came to say.'

'But—'

He put a finger to her lips. 'Will you just shut up and let me finish.'

Caught between his firm hold on her arm and the disturbingly pleasant sensation of his finger brushing her lips, she nodded.

'I didn't come to London on a business trip. I came to London to tell my employers I was resigning. I'm leaving Doha and coming back to London.'

Stevie stared, unable to comprehend what he was telling her. 'But the dream job—'

'Wasn't such a dream job without you there with me.'

'But your job is so important to you.'

'It is. And that's why I've accepted another one, with a smaller firm. It's not as high-flying, but it's doing what I love doing and I'll be able to spend time with you.' He looked into her eyes. 'I love you.'

For the first time in a long time, Stevie was speechless. A bubble of something she hadn't been aware of carrying burst in her chest.

He had given up his dream job for her. He was coming back. For her. Tears filled her eyes.

'Tom.'

'See,' he said. 'I came to tell you I love you. Not to seduce you.' He glanced at the flowers lying on the floor. 'Well, maybe to seduce you eventually.' He looked back to her. 'Okay?'

She nodded.

'Is there anything more you want to ask?'

She shook her head.

'Any more objections?'

She shook her head again and rested her hands against his chest.

He grinned. 'Well shut up and kiss me then.' He pulled her close and kissed her. Properly. Stevie slid her arms around his neck and kissed him back. With his arms around her again, it seemed like all was right with the world. How could she ever have thought she could live a life without him?

Eventually she led him away to her room, leaving the roses, forgotten, on the floor.

From: Tom Blackwood

To: Dr Evelyn Blackwood

Dear Mum

Stevie and I would like to book the house next June. For a whole weekend. As the venue for our wedding reception. ;-)

Love

Tom

From: Dr Evelyn Blackwood

To: Tom Blackwood

Tom darling, that is fantastic news! I am so very proud of you. Of course you can have the house next June.

Stevie – welcome to the family.

I shall have to buy a new hat.

Evelyn

The End

WHAT NEXT? OLIVIA (Og) gets her own story in *Girl In Trouble* – and she goes to Stevie and Tom's wedding.

The first chapter is included here - after the bit where I entice you to sign up to my newsletter by offering you a free book.

Want a free book?

Join my mailing list to be the first to hear about my new books and to get exclusive behind the scenes information that other people don't get to see. You also get:

- A FREE copy of *Girl At Christmas* – a Smart Girls novella.
- An exclusive short story that you can't get anywhere else.

GET THE FREE BOOK

If you don't have a QR code scanner, just type this link into your browser: https://www.subscribepage.com/ghab

Chapter 1 of Girl In Trouble

OLIVIA FOLLOWED HER best friend Tom into the bar. She stepped out of the way to allow the wave of backslapping and hand-shaking as the guys swarmed around him, to congratulate him or tease him, sometimes both at the same time. Apart from the bride-to-be's brother, Marshall, and a few guys from school, Olivia didn't really know any of the men there. It didn't bother her. She was there to make sure Tom had a great stag do.

It was a few moments before Tom turned around. Someone had already given him a set of comedy plastic boobs to go over his 'STAG' T-shirt. "What's the plan, Og?"

"Pub crawl," said Olivia. She pulled a list out of her jeans pocket. "Twenty-six letters of the alphabet, twenty-six pubs. A drink in each." She waved the paper under his nose. "So, best make a start, eh?" She moved towards the bar.

"Wait a minute, she can't be part of the stag party," said a voice.

Olivia stopped and turned slowly. She knew better than to spin around too fast in these heels. When dealing with loud, plummy voices, it didn't do to fall over. The owner of the voice was a stocky bloke who had the particular clean-cut look of a public school educated man. That figured. It went with the accent.

"This is Og," said Tom, putting an arm around her shoulders. "She's my best man. Og, this is Ralph."

Ah. Ralph. From Tom's work. The chap standing next to him, looking amused was probably the other one from work then. Tom had mentioned them both.

"She can't be your best man," Ralph pointed out, with exaggerated patience. "She's a girl."

Olivia glanced at Tom and gave a minute shake of her head. Having Tom jump in and defend her wasn't a great start to a stag night.

"Yes, I'm a girl," she said, giving Ralph a quick grin. "And I am also doing best man duty at his wedding. So I get to both arrange and go on the stag night. Tom's okay with that, so I hope you can deal with it too."

Ralph didn't look like he could deal with it. The man who had been standing next to him stepped forward and shook Olivia's hand. "I'm Will," he said. "You have to excuse Ralph. He's had a couple already." His eyes sparkled at her. "I'm sure he didn't mean any offence."

Now this was more like it. "None taken." A quick glance told her that Will looked promising. She was the only girl on a stag night. She was in for a ton of fun. She turned to Tom. "Okay, let's get this party started."

By the time they got as far as K (*The King's Arms*), Ralph was getting really irritating.

"So, you and Tom," he said, gesturing drunkenly at them. "You're best mates?"

"Yes. Known her since I was ... sho big?" Tom held his hand down to around knee height. He grabbed a table to steady himself.

"You must have had a thing at some point, eh?"

Tom shook his head. "Nope."

"What never?"

Olivia stepped in. "Never."

"Seriously?" God, this guy didn't give up.

Olivia looked at Tom. She was fond of him, but no matter how old they got, she always thought of him as the kid with the scratty knees that she'd played with. Objectively, Tom was hot. But … well, he was Tom.

"I suppose there was that time at Liam Dennison's sixteenth …" she said, grinning. "Remember, Tom?"

Tom crossed his legs. "Oh yeah."

Everyone leaned forward. Ralph actually licked his lips. "What happened?"

Olivia leaned forward too. "Tom got very drunk and he made a pass at me."

"See. I knew it!" Ralph's eyes gleamed with triumph.

"And she kneed me in the balls," said Tom. "So, if Stevie and I can't have kids, it'll all be your fault."

"Kids? Stevie isn't getting broody already?" Olivia elbowed him in the ribs. Tom's fiancée Stevie was only twenty-three and was pretty much a baby herself, as far as Olivia was concerned. "Fast work."

"Sod off," said Tom, good-naturedly.

"I think," said Will-the-fit-one-from-Tom's-work, "it's time to move to the next pub."

Marshall, Tom's brother-in-law to be stood up. "Speaking of babies, I'd better head back." He checked his watch. "There's a train in ten minutes."

"Oh, okay, sure," said Olivia. Marshall's wife had just had a baby. The poor man looked exhausted. "Thanks for coming." She nudged Tom in ribs.

"Yesh," said Tom. "Babies eh? Hard task masters."

Marshall smiled. "Wouldn't have it any other way." He shook hands with Tom. "I'll see you at the wedding, Tom. Have a great evening."

As she watched Marshall duck of the pub, Olivia tried to imagine Tom leaving a pub crawl early to go change nappies. Nope. Couldn't see it. Not at all.

"BUT, OLD CHAP, YOU can't have a best man who's a woman." They were now in The Mitre and Ralph was leaning on his elbows, across the table from Tom. His face was blotchy red and his eyes were unnaturally wide.

Olivia watched from the bar. "Is he always this irritating?" she said to Will, who was standing next to her. He had been spending longer and longer with her at each pub. She knew, without a doubt, that she could take him home with her if she'd wanted to. They were both staying at Tom's mum's B&B, so it would be easy enough.

Will nodded. "Sometimes worse."

"Ugh."

Ralph was still talking, his plummy voice seemed to get louder the more he had to drink. "But she's a girl. Best man is a man's job. Sez in the title. A girl can't do a man's job." He waved an arm in Olivia's general direction. "Look at her. She's got tits and everything."

"Right," said Olivia. "I've had enough of this." She turned to the barman. "Can I have two pints and two whiskey chasers, please?"

"What are you doing?" said Will. Like Olivia, he had been pacing himself. They were probably the only two more or less sober people in the group.

"He's so adamant that I'm inferior because I'm a girl," said Olivia. "We'll see about that."

Will eyed her doubtfully. "Are you sure about this? He's pretty big and you're ..."

"What? Just a girl?"

"I was going to say, svelte," he protested.

"Svelte?" She smiled.

"See, not just a girl." His eyes met hers. "Never that."

Yep. He was definitely up for it. Olivia paid the barman for the drinks. "Help me carry them over, Will, please."

"Right, Mr Big Mouth." Olivia plonked the pint glass and chaser in front of Ralph. "I challenge you to a downing competition. If you win, I will go home and leave you lads to your willy-waggling."

Ralph grinned. "Easy."

"If I win," Olivia leaned closer, her eyes narrowed, "you shut up for the rest of the night and have to wear your trousers tied around your shoulders like a sweater." She straightened back up and nodded to Will as he put her pint and chaser down on the table in front of her. "You okay with that?"

Ralph shrugged. "Whatever, little lady."

Olivia glanced at Tom, whose shoulders were already starting to shake. She hoped he would contain the fit of giggles until after she'd beaten Ralph.

"We need a better forfeit if you lose," said Ralph. "You have to take your trousers off and walk around in your panties."

All eyes went to Olivia. "Whatever," she said.

Ralph hesitated. Alarm bells must have started to ring in that pathetic excuse for a brain. "I mean, you don't have to—"

Olivia picked up her pint. "Look, sister. Are we talking? Or drinking?"

They had attracted the attention of the rest of the pub now. A chant of "Down it, down it" rose around them. Ralph stood up and glared at Olivia. She stood her ground and smiled at him. They picked up their pints, clinked them together and started to drink.

Olivia downed her pint and as soon as she'd put it down, someone handed her the shot glass. She screwed her eyes shut and gulped it down. It flamed down her tired throat and sent a shudder through the length of her body. When the pain subsided, she opened her eyes to see Ralph gaping at her. The pint glass in his hand had about half an inch of beer left in it. The shot glass was still on the table in front of him.

A cheer burst through the pub. The alcohol hit her blood stream and made her sway. Someone put their hands on her waist to steady her. A glance over her shoulder showed her it was Will-the-fit-one. Oh good.

Tom gave a whoop of laughter. "You've been trousered!" He pointed at Ralph, who had now turned bright red. "Off."

The rest of the pub took up the chant. Olivia smiled. She wasn't interested in Ralph any more. She was having far too much fun leaning backwards and enjoying the sensation of Will's arms around her.

This is the end of the sample chapter. To keep reading, buy *Girl In Trouble* now!

Other Books by Rhoda Baxter

SMART GIRLS SERIES: All books can be read as stand-alone stories

Girl On The Run

Girl In Trouble

Girl At Christmas - FREE when you subscribe to my newsletter

Trewton Royd small town romances – all books can be read as standalone stories

Pat's Pantry - short story (FREE on most platforms)

Snowed In

Belonging

Christmas For Commitmentphobes

That Holiday In France

BOOKS WRITTEN AS JEEVANI Charika

Christmas At The Palace – shortlisted for Emma awards 2019, Pink Heart Society Reader award 2019

This Stolen Life

A Convenient Marriage – shortlisted for RoNA award 2020

If you enjoyed this book (or even if you didn't), please could you leave a review at your book retailer of choice. Your reviews help other people decide if the book is right for them or not. It doesn't have to be very long. Just a line or two about what you enjoyed (or hated) would be great. Reviews, even bad ones, help sell books, so I'd be really grateful.

Thanks in advance. ☺

Acknowledgements

THE SETTING IN THIS book is based on a real house in Norham Gardens in Oxford. Back in the day, it was owned by the Convent of the Sacred Heart and housed a multi-faith, multi-national community of students and Sisters. I learned so much about the world and the true meaning of community in the years that I lived there. One year, we hosted a ball there to raise money for charity. We really did use the old blackout boards to cover the windows and turn the front room into a disco. Incidentally, the charity that Priya is raising money for, Project PEDS, was real at the time I wrote the book (it was originally published in 2013), but has now been absorbed into the World Children's Initiative. The children's hospital they were equipping is now up and running and saving lives.

On a personal note, I'd like to thank Jen Hicks, as always, for nagging me to write; Uncial Press for editing edition 1 and Choc Lit for editing edition 2. This book was nominated for a RoNA award (Romantic Comedy) award. I didn't win, but I had a fun time in London. That was the year that I met the ladies of the Naughty Kitchen – without whom I'd have gone mad a long time ago. Thanks also to Romantic Novelists Association, for general all round awesomeness.

Thanks as always to my family for encouraging me –especially to my husband and children for putting up with me when I'm only half in the real world. I couldn't do this without you.

Last of all, a huge thanks to YOU for buying this book and giving me an excuse to spend time with imaginary people without needing to seek medical attention.

About the Author

RHODA BAXTER WRITES contemporary romances with a dash of fun. She also writes multicultural women's fiction as Jeevani Charika. Her books have been shortlisted for awards such as the RoNA Romantic Fiction awards (twice – once per pen name!), Love Stories Award and the Emma Award.

Rhoda started off as a microbiologist and then drifted out of research and into technology transfer. She is a qualified IP administrator and still works as a freelance IP consultant.

When choosing a pen name, she was hit by a fit of nostalgia and named herself after the bacterium she studied during her PhD.

She has lived in a variety of places including Sri Lanka, Yap (it's a real place), Halifax, Oxford and Didcot (also a real place). She now lives with her young family in East Yorkshire, where there are enough tea shops to keep her happy.

You can find her wittering on about cake and science and other random things on her website (http://www.rhodabaxter.com), onFacebook[1], or on Twitter (@rhodabaxter). Please do say hello if you're passing.

You can alsofollow her on Bookbub[2].

---

1. https://en-gb.facebook.com/RhodaBaxterAuthor/

2. https://www.bookbub.com/authors/rhoda-baxter

Don't forget, you can get a free copy of one of her books byjoining her reader newsletter.